peter corradi

Copyright © 2010 Peter Corradi

All rights reserved.

ISBN: 1442112433

ISBN-13: 9781442112438

Library of Congress Control Number: 2010904769

For my loving wife, Claire, my inspiration and advocate. This dream of mine would not have been realized without her strength and resolve.

CHAPTER ONE
The Witness

Craig awoke, startled and shaken. His pajamas stuck to his clammy body as he sat up, wiping the perspiration from his forehead. Above his octagonal mirror, just below his speaker, his school banner from Centerville Junior High School met his sleep-swollen eyes. A drop of sweat formed above his eyelid, and he was reminded of the source of his anxiety.

The words "We'll getcha, kid … you're dead" came to mind.

Craig swallowed the thick saliva that secreted in his mouth. The booming voice of Mr. Juncosa broke the morning silence.

"Craig, up and at 'em. It's seven o'clock!"

Mr. Juncosa, Craig's father, was a morning person. He was always jovial and talkative, and Craig realized how difficult it was going to be to respond to his exuberance.

"Okay, Dad. I'm up," Craig feebly responded.

He deliberately slowed down his morning ritual in an attempt to stall the inevitable breakfast conversation with his father.

"Craig! Your eggs are getting cold. Get a move on!"

His father's voice startled him again and he realized the futility of his stalling tactics.

"Be right there!"

Craig's voice cracked, and he quickly slipped on his new Nike sneakers and hurriedly straightened his bed. When he entered the kitchen area, his father greeted him with a paternal pat on his backside. Craig offered a half-hearted smile and sat down opposite his father. The moisture in his scrambled eggs had long since evaporated into the sunlit kitchen. The tightness in his stomach turned to nausea as the odor of the eggs reached his nose.

"What's on the agenda today, Craig?" came the ritual question from Mr. J.

"Nothing much, Dad," answered Craig as he slowly sipped his orange juice in an attempt to avoid confronting those cold, dried-out eggs.

His father ravenously devoured his four eggs, bacon, and toast, washing each forkful down with black coffee. Craig was grateful that his father's normal upbeat mood seemed relatively mild as he sipped the last drop of orange juice from his glass. When Mr. J got up to refill his coffee cup, Craig stealthily scraped his eggs into the dog's dish and quickly placed the empty plate into the sink. Mr. J didn't sit down again but carried his refilled coffee cup into the utility room, where he opened his toolbox and carefully surveyed its contents.

"Lost another tape measure yesterday, that's the third time this week. Something must be eating them up."

Fortunately, Mr. J's conversation didn't require answers because Craig was lost in deep, anxious thought. His mind raced as he scurried into his room and retrieved his loose-leaf notebook from under his fish tank.

Since his mother had left home, Craig had been forced to organize himself and had become quite adept at locating whatever he needed at any given moment from his cluttered room. His sister, Melissa, had also left home to live in an apartment with her girlfriend, and Craig had, through necessity, become quite domesticated. He shared the household chores with his father. The first thing he had learned was that the closet could hide a lot and give his room some semblance of order and neatness.

Since the *incident*, a month ago, Craig had been truant from school for a total of eight days. So far, his forged notes had gone undetected by the school attendance monitor. The first quarter was rapidly approaching its end and, unless he was able to doctor up his report card, his father would soon discover the truancies. If nothing else, Mr. J always scrutinized Craig's report card and instinctively knew when it was due. No chance of avoiding the confrontation that would occur when his report card arrived home.

He would deal with that when he had to, but for the time being, his ninth truancy was being carefully planned.

He would disappear into the woods bordering the school property after the bus ride to school.

Gabor's Horse Farm provided a safe refuge from school authorities and gave Craig an opportunity to talk things out with Jerry. Jerry was the twenty-seven-year-old stable hand who worked for Mr. Gabor and who had become Craig's close friend and confidant.

"See ya, Dad. My bus is coming. Gotta run …"

"Do well today, son," said Mr. J, momentarily stopping his tool organization to provide a bit of fatherly encouragement.

Since school was not on his agenda for the day, Craig's anxiety disappeared. He eagerly boarded the bus in anticipation of his meeting with Jerry. His attempt to go unnoticed by the other kids was short-lived as Vinny beckoned him to an empty seat in the back of the bus.

"Ya goin' to Alyssa's party Saturday night, Craig?" queried Vinny as Craig took a seat beside him.

"I don't know," shrugged Craig, as he attempted to keep all attention off himself.

"Listen Vin, I'm not going to school today, so keep it down, huh? I don't want every kid on the bus to know I'm here."

"Okay! Okay! Don't get uptight about it," Vinny replied. "What happened now?"

"Do me a favor Vin, make believe I'm not here". Vinny got the message and turned to another kid.

Craig cringed as the bus entered the school gate and laboriously rattled up the hill to the circle drive where the students were dropped off.

How am I going to get off the bus unnoticed by Mr. Bacardi? thought Craig.

Mr. Bacardi, the assistant principal, was standing in his customary place, greeting the disembarking students. Craig's bus was the fourth in line of yellow school buses. As each bus emptied its passengers and drove off, the next bus would creep up to the wide orange line, stop, and empty out.

Vinny's pudgy face came into focus, and Craig's plan took immediate shape.

"Vinny," whispered Craig, "do me a favor. Get in front of me, and when you step down off the bus, call Mr. Bacardi."

"What will I say?" asked Vinny nervously.

"Anything, think of something; I just don't want to be noticed."

As Craig's bus approached the orange line, forty-five students simultaneously stood up and moved to the aisles. Craig took his place behind Vinny's large frame and nearly knocked Vinny over in his attempt to remain close to him.

"Take it easy," Vinny muttered nervously.

"Sorry," Craig whispered as he continued to lean forward.

It worked like a charm as Vinny's abrasive voice got Mr. Bacardi's attention. The distraction allowed Craig to scurry behind the bus. Now out of Mr. Bacardi's sight, Craig leaped the low bushes bordering the circle drive and raced to the edge of the woods. Once there, he stopped momentarily to look back. Satisfied that he had gone completely unnoticed, he sat on a protruding rock and allowed his pounding heart to rest and return to normal.

The distant bell, signaling the beginning of the school day, snapped Craig out of his anxious trance, and he ran the one-quarter mile trudge through the woods to the Gabor Horse Farm. He passed the Pit, the student-made clearing, littered with beer cans and cigarette butts. The area was off-limits to students, but because of its secluded location, school officials found it extremely difficult to enforce. Truants and cutters met there to plan their day's activities and share a cigarette or joint. Craig did not frequent the Pit, but lately he saw a lot of it on his way to the horse farm.

It was a windless day, and only the sound of dead leaves crunching under his feet could be heard. He could still faintly feel his heart rhythmically pumping as he skipped over fallen trees and skillfully avoided thorn bushes on his trek toward Gabor's. The days were turning colder, and Craig felt a chill creep up his backbone. Suddenly, a strange panicky feeling made him shudder, and he stepped up his pace, longing to greet Jerry's cheery face.

The split rail fence came into view, and a warm, pleasant feeling crept into Craig's chilled body. Soon he would be chatting with Jerry and getting what he hoped would be some good advice. He jumped the fence with three feet to spare and sped off in the direction of the north barn.

Once inside the barn, Craig stopped, turned around, and looked to see if anyone had spotted him. Mr. Gabor wasn't the friendliest man around. He had developed an aversion to the 'young punks' who used his farm as a short cut to school.

"Jerry? Jerry?" beckoned Craig as he walked toward the center of the barn.

Jerry was usually in one of the stalls, tending to a horse's needs. When no answer came, Craig felt the chill return, and he clutched his left arm in an attempt to rub it away. He nearly jumped out of his skin as Jerry's large, stubby fingers grabbed and twisted his left ear lobe.

"You playing hooky again, Junky?" snapped Jerry as Craig caught his breath and sighed heavily.

"You scared the hell out of me, Jerry," cracked Craig, "and stop calling me Junky."

Jerry's six-foot-three, two-hundred-pound frame loomed over Craig and gave him a feeling of well-being. The big redhead with the pug nose and freckled arms reminded Craig of his Uncle Jim. In his muscle shirt and Levi's, Jerry looked the part of a lumberjack. His missing front tooth and scarred cheek added to his ominous look.

"You're gonna get in a lot of trouble when you're caught, Junky," drawled Jerry.

"I gotta tell you something, Jerry. I need some advice."

The urgency in Craig's voice was immediately detected by Jerry, and he gently sat Craig down on a nearby stool.

"What's the matter, kid? You sound like you're in a lot of trouble."

"I didn't have the guts to tell you until now, but I can't hold it in anymore. I'm scared silly, Jerry. I witnessed a murder, the murder of that kid in Centerville a few weeks ago! You remember the one, in the paper?"

Jerry was not well-read and was semi-literate, and he seldom picked up a newspaper. His preoccupation with horses afforded him little opportunity to keep abreast of any news. With the exception of Mr. Gabor and his wife, he seldom socialized with others and led a rather isolated life.

"Really," Jerry answered with a note of uncertainty and disbelief in his voice.

Little beads of perspiration began to form on Craig's forehead as he began to recount the series of events that he had witnessed on that fateful night in October. His mind had been through the nightmare so many times, and he described the events lucidly and with grave detail.

Jerry's round, green eyes gradually enlarged with shock as he listened attentively. Craig told about fixing the chain on his bike that night and how he wanted to test ride it to see if he had repaired it correctly. He went on to name the streets he pedaled down, the turns he made, and the people he passed on his journey. Then he described the macabre scene he accidentally witnessed as he was returning to his home via the path behind Nick's Pizza Parlor and the nearby elementary school.

Jerry almost fell to the barn floor as he sat heavily on another stool next to Craig. Silence reigned for a few minutes as Jerry attempted to digest the bizarre events Craig had witnessed.

Craig had a look of relief on his handsome, sharply defined face. His blue eyes seemed to smile from within. He contented himself in the thought that he finally was able to verbalize to someone those grim facts he had kept pent up inside for so many weeks. His long blond hair, disheveled from his journey through the woods, lay flat against his forehead, glued there by small beads of perspiration.

In his own inimitable style, Jerry made a feeble but heartfelt attempt to console Craig and alleviate some of the tension and anxiety that had built up over the weeks.

"Take it easy, Craig. We'll work it out somehow. Have you told your father yet?"

"No! No! I can't, Jerry," Craig blurted out. "He'll force me to report the incident to the police, and then I'm dead!"

"What d'ya mean, you're dead?" queried Jerry.

Suddenly, the voice of Mr. Gabor beckoning Jerry to the south barn felt like an electric shock to Craig, and he scurried inside a stall and hid crouched in a corner.

"Come to my house tonight, Craig, and we'll talk more about it," whispered Jerry as he responded to Mr. Gabor's call.

"Be right there, sir!"

"Get out of here now and get back to school," directed Jerry.

Craig remained crouched in the stall for what seemed like an hour, though it was no more than five minutes. He finally got up, crept toward the open barn door, and ran on tiptoes until he reached the split rail fence. He hurdled it and continued running through the heavily under brushed woods toward the Pit. The sound of voices coming from the Pit made Craig freeze in his tracks. He remained still for a few minutes, listening to the muffled voices of the Pit's occupants.

He thought he detected a familiar voice, but he couldn't quite make it out. He began to edge toward it, trying his darndest to evade the dead, crispy leaves that crackled under his feet. The voices stopped momentarily, and Craig froze again. When they started up again, he finally recognized the familiar voice. It was Vinny's, but who was with him? His curiosity was short lived and he quickly distanced himself from the Pit area.

He had no intention of returning to school that day. He had been lucky so far going undetected, and he wasn't about to get caught.

Craig had a three-and-a-half-mile walk home, and as he walked along the broken sidewalk, he felt strange. An eerie feeling swept through him as he passed Calderwood Elementary School. Once again, a vivid picture of the crime he had witnessed there developed in his mind.

The pungent smell of pizza emanating from Nick's Pizza Parlor around the corner stimulated his suppressed hunger. Craig gambled with the risk of being seen to enjoy a slice of Nick's pizza. Nick was a middle-aged Italian man who liked Craig because, as Nick put it, he was a "nisa polita boy."

Nick's deep, booming voice welcomed Craig as he entered the small, converted shack.

"You gotta no school today?" asked Nick with a knowing smile on his face.

Nick was a very perceptive man in spite of his third grade education, and Craig knew he couldn't fabricate a believable story.

"Ah, I just needed a day off, Nick," said Craig sheepishly.

"You wanna slisa, Craig?"

"Make it two, Nick, and a large Coke."

Craig remembered he had not touched his eggs that morning and realized why he was so hungry. Lately, his appetite had diminished, and he had actually lost a few pounds. His growing body, however, demanded nourishment and, from time to time, he would gorge himself when the hunger pang struck. Before he left Nick's, Craig had devoured five pieces of pizza.

He could feel the heaviness in his stomach as he got up and bade his farewell to Nick. It then struck him that Nick and his father met frequently at the Knights of Columbus. He turned to make an urgent appeal to Nick.

"Do me a favor, huh, Nick?"

Before he could blurt out his appeal, Nick gave him his answer.

"Donna worry, Craig, I dona tella you fader, but donna do dis no more. You needa you education or you finish uppa lika me—makin'a pizza."

Craig thanked Nick with a smile and left. As Craig approached his block, an uneasy feeling once again crept into his body.

What if his father was home? What would he do if he caught him?

The green pickup truck was nowhere to be seen, and Craig made a beeline for the side door of his house. Once inside, he sat for a few minutes and began belching as the pizza digested rather reluctantly.

Craig began to relax on the comfortable reclining chair and dozed off. His nights had been, to a large extent, sleepless for the past few weeks, and his young body began to crave rest. His sleep was short-lived as the screeching sound of an automobile startled him out of his light repose.

The afternoon sun was shining through the French doors behind Craig's chair. The warmth of the sun, combined with the stillness and quiet of the house, caused sleep to come again. With slumber came the recurring horrible dream that had become so familiar and much too persistent.

CHAPTER TWO
A Family in Crisis

Craig's parents had been separated for over a year, and he was far from recovered from the trauma of losing the maternal influence in his life. Caustic words, hostile looks, and long periods of silence between his father and mother had created an unbearable environment for both Melissa and Craig. Melissa was much more outspoken than Craig, and she made many feeble attempts to reconcile them.

As well-intentioned as she was, Melissa was not a professional marriage counselor and was too emotionally involved to help mend a shattered relationship. The separation came a few weeks into Craig's eighth-grade year, and it came as both a welcome relief and an overwhelming loss to an adolescent subjected to the tensions and anxieties of marital disharmony. Needless to say, his grades for the first term were extremely low.

Mr. J. was summoned by Mr. Meyer, Craig's guidance counselor, to discuss his poor academic showing. Mr. Bacardi, the assistant principal, was also invited to the meeting, since along with his poor grades, Craig had also been referred to Mr. Bacardi's office a number of times for disruptive and insubordinate behavior.

The meeting was embarrassing to his father. When he confronted Craig at home that night, he grounded Craig for one month.

"No son of mine is going to disgrace the Juncosa name," he said angrily.

Mr. J was a first-generation son of an immigrant stone mason, and the values he learned from his old country parents were deeply embedded in his mind. Honesty, hard work, and a strong sense of integrity defined him.

"Failing is bad enough, but to be a wise guy too is a little too much for me to take!"

Craig desperately wanted to please his father, who was also attempting to recover from a broken marriage. Money and the children had been the overt reasons for their marital discord, but Craig had a strange intuitive feeling that it was more than that. Whenever they argued, it was usually over family finances or Craig and Melissa, but the real reasons seemed to be submerged and circumvented.

Melissa, who had graduated from high school in June of that year, had decided to leave home after her futile attempts at reconciling her parents. Mr. J was furious when Melissa gave him the news of her decision to leave and take an apartment with her girlfriend.

"What's the matter? Isn't this house good enough for you?" he said, half in anger and half pleadingly.

His daughter was the apple of his eye, and the thought of her leaving shattered him.

"Dad, it has nothing to do with you or this house," consoled Melissa. "I want to be out on my own and be independent. I have a job now and it will be good for me to learn how to be self-sufficient."

Craig listened from his bedroom to the conversation taking place in the kitchen. He was confused and distraught over the entire family mess that he was embroiled in, but had mixed emotions about Melissa's impending departure from home. She was constantly harping about how messy he left everything, and Craig was almost inured to her constant preaching. It would be a relief to get her off his back, even though there were times when Melissa would lend him a sympathetic ear when he was in trouble or needed someone to talk to. She would be missed, but it was not a tragedy.

Before the final separation, Craig's mother stayed away for weeks at a time and returned from time to time to pick up a suitcase or chitchat with Craig and Melissa. Her marriage was so utterly damaged that she even found it difficult to be warm and motherly with her children.

Melissa said, "Mom is on the verge of a nervous breakdown, and that's why she seems so distant and apathetic."

Craig pleaded with his mother to stay and try to mend the relationship, but she only offered a maternal smile and ran her fingers through his soft blond hair. She never answered Craig, and this added anger to his confusion.

When she finally left and the separation was finalized, she did have a few words to say.

"Craig, I love you so very much; I only wish it could be easier. I don't mean to hurt you or want to hurt you. It's just that your father and I could not continue to live as husband and wife. There were too many differences that we couldn't resolve. It's better this way for all us."

Craig would be troubled and never forgive her for abdicating her parental responsibilities and leaving him. He came to resent his female teachers, and he was disruptive in their classes. This point was brought out at the meeting in school, and Mr. Meyer had recommended to Mr. J that Craig should take advantage of the school's psychological services.

"I'm not going to no shrink; there's nothing wrong with me," Craig lashed out angrily when his father advised him that he had signed a consent waiver agreeing to allow the school psychologist to test him.

Somehow, Mr. Meyer convinced Craig to keep the appointment with Dr. Scott. The meeting was destined for failure right from the beginning. It was short-lived when Dr. Scott began to probe into Craig's family situation.

"It's none of her damned business, and I'm not going to tell her anything!" Craig angrily vented his frustration to Mr. Meyer after running from the psychologist's office to the guidance office.

Dr. Scott seemed extremely calm and far removed from the whole episode as she opened Mr. Meyer's door and delicately motioned to Mr. Meyer. Mr. Meyer excused himself, and Craig was left sitting in the tiny office, rubbing the ache out of the back of his neck. When Mr. Meyer returned, he consoled the noticeably upset youngster and sent him back to class.

Craig's anger turned to embarrassment by the end of the school day, and he dropped into Mr. Meyer's office before leaving school to apologize to him and to extend his apology to the well-intentioned Dr. Scott. Craig was a very sensitive person and possessed the important qualities of remorse and repentance. He realized he needed help but was not ready to accept it, especially from a woman.

The second quarter was a little better than the first as Craig began to adjust to a motherless home. He decided he didn't want to repeat the eighth grade. When his midterm report card arrived home, his father, in a reluctant manner, praised Craig for his improvement over the first quarter.

His father's muscular and hairy arms glistened with sweat as he spoke to Craig while he was doing some carpentry work in the utility room. The veins in his wrists protruded as he hammered a two-by-four in place, and he stopped momentarily to provide some encouragement to Craig.

Mr. J had a ruddy, outdoor complexion. For the last few years, he wore a mustache and goatee that was getting progressively whiter in contrast to his dark brown hair. From time to time, he would threaten to shave it off, but eventually succumbed to his children's pleading to leave it on. They said it made him look distinguished, and his father's vanity and need for praise provided the incentive to continue wearing it. There wasn't an ounce of fat on his father's six-foot-one-inch, large-framed body. Hard work and a relatively light appetite kept him trim and muscular.

Once, a few years ago, his father had struck him for disobeying his mother, and Craig never forgot the mighty impact of his large, calloused hand on his backside. That was the first and last time he had administered physical punishment to Craig.

From time to time, Craig would hear his parents argue over the psychological pros and cons of corporal punishment and was glad to hear his mother's anti-physical-punishment position win out over his father's insistence on trusting the paddle method.

His mother was a beautiful, blond, blue-eyed woman who had succumbed slightly to bulges here and there from an insatiable sweet tooth. She still had a voluptuous figure, and her smooth, delicate, white skin belied her forty-one years. She was on a perpetual diet and would forego any kind of pasta and starchy food of any species if an appealing dessert was on the menu for dinner. Once a week, she would attend the exercise classes at the nearby racquetball club and rode her bicycle a good five miles a day to help keep her thighs and calves leaner. She looked much younger than her husband and secretly enjoyed the moment's flattery whenever someone mistakenly took her for Mr. J's daughter.

Pride and a rigid, uncompromising nature were qualities she possessed and which would, unfortunately, eventually destroy her marriage. She had a strong personality and always made her presence known and deeply felt when family matters were discussed. Somehow, things always went her way whenever a decision had to be made. Mr. J resented the fact that he always ended up conceding to her, but, for the sake of harmony and peace, lived with her decisions.

Her only real resistance came from Melissa, who had inherited some of her mother's traits. Craig remembered the confrontation that occurred between mother and daughter after Melissa's sweet sixteen birthday party: two uncompromising, stubborn females insisting that their point of view was the correct one. Before it turned into a melee, Mr. J interceded and called it a draw. The little humor he injected into the volatile situation provided just the ingredient to cool things down. However, Melissa's determination to get in the last word fanned the fire enough to keep Mom steaming.

"I'll bet you were no angel when you were my age. The parents who are the strictest are the same ones who were wild when they were kids. You experienced it, so now you would deny your children the same experiences."

"Enough!" screamed her mother as she pointed in the direction of Melissa's room. Melissa was already heading toward it, and the argument came to an abrupt end with the slam of her bedroom door. A strange, hostile silence permeated the entire house until it was broken by Mr. J's directive to both of them to calm down.

Craig secretly sided with his sister but outwardly supported his mother's argument. Melissa had already reached womanhood, and the mother-daughter conflicts were increasing in number and intensity. This wasn't his problem and he wisely refrained from getting involved. He had other and much more pleasant things to deal with.

Craig had discovered girls, and all of a sudden his pre-puberty aversion to them began to change. His father picked up the sign immediately when Craig began to be extremely concerned about his physical appearance. The pleading and constant urging for him to take his daily shower or wash his matted-down hair ended. Craig's showers became more and more frequent, and he took them without being told.

He saved his allowance and bought his own blow drier and insisted that specific items of clothing be available for school each day.

Her name was Laura Donohue, and she made the first advance toward Craig. At first, he attempted to brush off her cajoling, but gradually succumbed to her female mystique. She was a cute little brunette who was not only good-looking but also had brains and would loan her completed homework assignment to Craig from time to time. She realized Craig was not achieving up to his capabilities in school and tried her best to encourage him.

"With just a little effort, Craig, you could really do much better in school."

Craig was satisfied with being a C student and had all but convinced his parents that he was working up to his potential. Laura knew better and refused to accept his just average description of himself. Craig looked forward to meeting her at her locker between classes. They shared a common lunch period and, after eating with the boys, he would meet her near the exit door. They would hold hands, whisper sweet nothings to each other, and occasionally chance an embrace or two. Mrs. Healey, the teacher's aide assigned to that area of the cafeteria, liked Craig and Laura and would rarely enforce the no-embracing rule unless Mr. Bacardi was in the area.

"Come on, kids, break it up. The assistant principal is here, and he'll fire me if I don't do my job."

Holding hands was permissible, and they would walk away, hand in hand, toward the school quadrangle. Laura bitterly complained about how strict her parents were.

"I can't stay out after dark on school nights, and I have to be in before ten on Friday and Saturday nights. They treat me like a baby, and I hate it! I had such an argument with my mother last night, I almost ran out of the house! Parents just don't understand that a person has to have some rights and privileges."

"Their argument is always the same. 'I don't care what other parents allow their kids to do; you'll do it our way.'

I guess they really love me, but how I wish they would ease up a little."

Craig was secretly glad her parents were strict. This way, any competition for Laura's attentions would be limited and he sort of liked having someone he could call his own.

Once a week, the Donohue parents would allow Craig to come over to the house and visit Laura. They would watch TV, listen to music, and steal a kiss whenever possible. Craig enjoyed the relationship but was not yet willing to share the identity of his new friend with his parents.

When school ended in June, Craig had a strange feeling in his stomach when Laura gave him the news that she would be gone for the summer. He had grown accustomed to Laura's gentle smile and loving concern for him. The thought of her absence for two whole months left him with a forlorn and empty feeling. She reassured him over and over that she would write every day, and it would almost be like being together. This consoling promise, along with Craig's new mini-bike, dulled the pain of departure when Laura finally left for summer music camp on a hot, sticky July night.

"See you in September. Be good and don't forget that letter a day!"

"You, too!" sobbed Laura as she boarded the bus at the Centerville depot.

Displays of affection were severely limited since both Mr. and Mrs. Donohue were there to send Laura off to camp. Craig waited until the bus disappeared over the hill and felt a swelling dampness that began to blur his vision. He quickly wiped his eyes, refused a ride, bade his farewell to the Donohues, and began the mile trek back to his home.

It was a long, hot, lonely summer for Craig, and when Laura's letters began to taper off in August, he actually looked forward to school.

He had worked with his father from time to time and was paid the minimum wage. He was saving up to purchase a dirt bike. The two hundred dollars looked mighty good to Craig, and he celebrated by treating himself to the biggest ice cream sundae they were able to make at the local ice cream parlor.

He had already taken two spills on his new bike, the second one resulting in a pulled groin muscle and a badly scraped arm.

"Get rid of that darn thing before you kill yourself!" warned his father. He had reluctantly succumbed to Craig's constant pleas for the bike. After each accident, his father would annoyingly remind him of his opposition to the purchase of it.

"I told you so, didn't' I? The damn things are dangerous, but you didn't believe me."

Craig listened respectfully to his father's reprimands but nonetheless ignored him.

September didn't come a day too early for Craig as he began to feel pleasingly anxious about his return to school. Laura's absence for the entire summer combined with her failure to write one letter during the last two weeks in August dampened Craig's interest in her. From time to time he thought of her, but not with the same lovesick feeling he had had in June. The thought of seeing her again did quicken his pulse, however, and when she called that last Saturday night of the summer, her soft voice once again melted Craig's heart.

He had a very romantic nature, and when he heard, "Hi, Craig, how are you?" he fell in love again.

"Fine, Laura. How was camp? I missed your letters in August. What's the matter? Were you too busy?"

He barely heard her answers as the sound of her voice seemed to have an hypnotic effect on him.

"Are you still there, Craig?"

"Yeah, yeah, uh huh," Craig sheepishly replied.

"I gotta run now and unpack. We just got back last night. See you in school Monday, okay?"

Laura ended the conversation abruptly and hung up without waiting for an answer from Craig.

Craig had grown an inch or two over the summer but nowhere near the growth Laura had undergone. Laura had grown some four inches, and her straight, girlish figure had blossomed into soft and budding curves. When he first set eyes on her in the corridor that first day, he hardly recognized her. When she approached him and kissed him gently on the cheek, he felt flushed and a little boyish.

"Gee, Laura, have you changed! You look so … so … you look so fantastic!" Craig couldn't find the words to describe what he saw in front of him.

Laura smiled maturely and returned the compliment. For some strange reason that he couldn't explain, Laura seemed so much more dominating, almost to the point of overwhelming him. Their relationship changed, and when she refused a date to the school dance with him, he knew it was coming to an end. Craig was much too proud, and after the refusal, he went out of his way to avoid meeting her in school. When she finally forced a confrontation with him, he was cool and abrupt.

"What's the matter with you, Craig?" queried Laura. "Why are you avoiding me like the plague?"

Craig shrugged his shoulders and muttered some inaudible words of denial. Laura got the message, and they agreed to remain good friends as they parted. Craig felt relieved after the meeting and was now able to meet and politely greet her without his pride getting in the way. He swore off girls after their breakup and decided to concentrate all his efforts on his studies.

"This school year is very important, everything counts now!"

These familiar cautionary words of forewarning, to apply yourself now and don't tempt your fate, were repeated by his teachers, Mr. Meyer, and even his father. He decided to take their advice and set to the task of becoming scholarly. His new commitment to school and studies was to come to a sudden, bizarre, and frightful end some three weeks into the school year.

CHAPTER THREE
The Dilemma

The piercing ring of the phone jarred Craig out of his dream-filled sleep, and he literally jumped up and out of the reclining chair. He instinctively checked the kitchen clock for the time: 4:15 p.m. It was safe to answer it since the school day had long since ended. He cleared his throat and delicately picked up the receiver.

"Hello?" answered Craig nervously.

"Juncosa, listen carefully. You'd better forget what you saw or you're a dead kid. Make believe it never happened, ya understand? We'll know where it came from if it ever gets out, and it's your funeral."

Click. The phone went dead. Craig held it to his ear until the buzzing tone signaling a clear line began. He sat heavily on the couch and held his aching stomach. Tears began to swell in his soft blue eyes as he incoherently muttered an unheard answer to the unknown caller. He sat for a long time as fragmented thoughts raced through his mind.

You never snitch on another kid, no matter what. The peer code was strong and enforced. For the most part,

Craig agreed with the code, but this was different. It wasn't like some stupid little incident in school.

He remembered the time Mr. Bacardi had questioned him about the firecracker that had been set off in the cafeteria. He knew Tommy Albrecht had set it off, but he denied it, telling Mr. Bacardi he wasn't anywhere near the area when it went off. Mr. Bacardi was also aware of the peer code and knew he wasn't going to get very far in his investigation of the incident. After preaching to Craig about the serious danger firecrackers posed to people in crowded school buildings, he released Craig from his office and sent him back to class. Tommy Albrecht got away with it and the peer code once again won out over the school authorities. Tommy thanked Craig for his silence and he gained another friend.

"This is none of my business and I'm not getting involved," Craig rationalized as he got up from the chair and went into his room.

This was a matter for the police, and he was going to stay out of it. Resolved that he was making the right decision, Craig grabbed his iPod and turned the volume up to drown out all distracting thoughts.

He couldn't suppress his thoughts and was once again drawn to his closet. He began pulling out the neatly folded newspaper articles he had strategically placed under his guitar case. He had stapled the four articles together. The one on top had appeared on page two of the *Sunday Daily Journal*. The small school photo of Peter Stohler and the headline, *Boy 14 Found Slain in Woods*, jumped out at Craig as he once again read the account of the bizarre incident that had shook the small community of Centerville.

CENTERVILLE – The body of a 14-year-old boy was found yesterday morning at 3:45 a.m. covered with leaves in a lonely patch of woods seven blocks from his home. The victim was identified as Peter Stohler, son of William and Sarah Stohler of 17 Ashland Road Centerville. He had been missing after he left his home about 9:30 p.m. on Friday, with his father, to patrol the vandal-ridden neighborhood. The body, which was discovered by neighbors, was found in a wooded area behind the Calderwood Elementary School playground.

"It is a homicide, no doubt about that," Dr. Irwin Mossler, deputy Norfolk County medical examiner, who was on the scene, said last night.

Mossler, who completed the autopsy, said that the cause of death was strangulation. He would not elaborate. He said Peter had apparently been killed in another location and that his body had been dragged to the spot where it was found.

Craig's hand shook uncontrollably as he began to fill in all of the missing facts that he had witnessed. The assumptions made by the medical examiner were quite accurate, and Craig was amazed at their investigative ability. He, however, knew all the details, which caused him to cringe.

The growing mystery and impending investigation created a restless, frightened, and angry community. Apparently, the police had unlawfully questioned some local youths in connection with the killing, and this had brought the investigation to an untimely halt.

"The entire procedure violated due process," said an attorney for one of the youths who was illegally detained and questioned.

Craig remembered Mr. Kubek's legal explanation of the police methods used in the investigation. The social studies teacher had explained to his students that any admission or confession obtained from a young person following an extensive period of interrogation without parental contact is highly suspect and inadmissible in a court of law. Craig wasn't sure of the meanings of some of the legal terms used by Mr. Kubek but suppressed any inclination to raise his hand to ask. Instead, he went to a dictionary after class and looked up the words. After discovering the meanings of the words, he still wasn't sure he was able to understand Mr. Kubek's statement. What he did realize was that the culprits might go free.

The police had unlawfully questioned some youths, and whatever they told the police could not be used as evidence in court. The police had allegedly violated their rights, and the law protected them from any further questioning.

Craig continued to probe into the investigating techniques the police had used. Whenever the case was discussed, he would listen attentively and digest all of the facts. He heard a prominent defense attorney say on the six o'clock news that it would be almost impossible to get a legal indictment if what the police allegedly did was true.

The more Craig heard about the case and the mishandling of suspects by the police, the more he realized the possible consequences. The thought horrified Craig as he concluded that he could turn out to be the only key witness to the crime and that his testimony alone stood between convicting the murderers and watching them go totally unpunished.

To a young boy who was already experiencing all of the emotional and physical changes and problems of adolescence, this was too much to take. His dilemma was compounded by the fact that he had to face one of the murderers in school every day. This accounted for his heavy truancy record in the last few weeks. He couldn't take the anxiety and tension much longer. What should he do?

The heavy slam of the front door broke the silence of the late afternoon, as Mr. J returned from his day's work. Craig quickly replaced the articles under his guitar case and scurried to his desk, where he opened a book and simulated reading.

"You home, Craig?"

His father's footsteps got louder as he approached Craig's bedroom and peered in.

"Hi Dad!" his voice crackled with guilt and almost betrayed his truancy.

His father was always pleased when Craig took it upon himself to study without prompting.

"Hittin' the books, huh, son? Good boy! You need a good education to survive in today's world."

Without turning around, Craig acknowledged his father's words of wisdom with the nod of his head. The last thing he had on his mind was school and his studies. The urge to tell all to his father was extremely strong, but he suppressed it, knowing full well what his father would force him to do.

The two steaks his father had pulled out of the freezer that morning were thoroughly defrosted, and Mr. J began the task of preparing dinner for the two of them. Craig stayed in his room awhile, trying to compose himself before going into the kitchen to attend to his chore of setting the table. His father was adding the dressing to the dinner salad when Craig finally entered the kitchen.

"How was work today, Dad?" asked Craig in an attempt to avoid any questioning about school.

Mr. J began a long narrative on how the new, young carpenters on the job shirked their responsibilities and how things weren't like they used to be in the business. Craig had heard these complaints many times before and barely listened as he began to set the table. To encourage his father to continue talking, Craig would occasionally ask another innocuous question he knew his father loved to talk about. He succeeded in avoiding any discussion about school, and when they sat down to eat, Mr. J was all but talked out and both quietly consumed their dinner.

Mr. J was perusing the newspaper when a knock on the front door caused Craig to drop a glass he was drying at the kitchen sink. He realized at that point that he was totally unnerved and could not continue to function in this state of mind. Every unexpected noise, interruption, or ring of the phone jolted his frayed nerves, and it began to show in his face.

Melissa opened the door and cheerily greeted her brother and father.

"Hi, Dad, hey Craig, what's you up to? Just how are my two favorite men in the whole wide world?"

Melissa had changed since she had left home, and Craig liked her a lot better. As a guest in the house, she was much more congenial than as a live-in. Craig found her conversation almost bearable now as she discussed her job and apartment with her father. Mr. J had finally accepted Melissa's decision to leave home and go it alone, and Melissa detected it in her conversation with him. As a result, her visits became more frequent and she stayed longer.

Craig had lost track of the conversation and was about to switch on the TV when he heard Melissa mention the name Peter Stohler. His body became rigid and he tuned into the conversation wide-eyed and attentively.

"Did you know that kid?" asked Melissa innocently.

Craig gulped, took a deep breath, and replied, "I used to see him in the cafeteria, but I didn't know him personally."

The answer evidently satisfied her because she didn't pursue any further questioning. She instead turned to her father to continue her conversation about the murder.

Craig decided to disappear from the scene before the conversation reverted back to him again, and quietly made his exit through the French doors and out to the patio. He headed for the large weeping willow tree on the far corner of his backyard and climbed to his favorite branch. Craig loved the solitude and privacy the tree afforded him, and from time to time when problems became too burdensome, he would seek refuge in the tree.

It was dark and he couldn't see very far, but he could see the glare of oncoming headlights on Route 52A. The stretch of road was a straightaway behind his development, and dragsters found it difficult to resist the urge to floor it at this point. Consequently, the screech of brakes and the sickening noise of steel striking steel were much too familiar sounds to Craig. Just as Craig's legs began to tire, Melissa's high-pitched voice carried crisply through the cool night air.

"Craig, I'm leaving. Aren't you going to bid your sister farewell?" Melissa asked sarcastically as Craig was swinging from the last branch onto the hard ground around the base of the large tree.

Craig ran up to his big sister and planted a large, wet kiss on her cheek. Melissa was taken aback as she wiped the dampness away.

"Whatever has gotten into you?" she asked.

Craig didn't know himself but suddenly felt a sibling need and strong attachment to her.

"Can I go back to your apartment with you, Liss?" Craig asked almost pleadingly. "I haven't seen it since you fixed it up, and you promised me an invite."

Before Melissa could answer, Craig had his school jacket on and was out the front door, heading for her car.

"Is it okay, Dad? I know it's a school night, but I'll get him home early. I did promise him an invite," Melissa called to her dad,. Mr. J reluctantly consented.

The urge to confide in Melissa was strong. On many occasions, Craig had spilled out his problems and frustrations to his older sister, and she was a good listener. From time to time she even offered good solid advice that worked for Craig if he decided to take it.

The drive to Melissa's apartment was a sobering as well as an enlightening experience for both of them. For the first time, his sister spoke to him not as a small brother but rather as an equal member of the family.

"You know, I was completely shattered when Mom and Dad separated. It really hit me hard, and for a long time afterward I resented both of them for the emotional turmoil it caused in me. I hated both of them, especially

Mom, who I felt abandoned both of us. I couldn't imagine a mother being so insensitive and indifferent. I had a long talk with Mom last month when I visited her at Grandma's house, and she made me realize the futility of continuing the relationship that existed between her and Dad. I think they still love each other very much—at least Mom still loves Dad. There were many problems that were never resolved between them that went back to before we were born. They stuck it out for our benefit until it got unbearable for both of them. Did you know that they are still communicating and have agreed to see a marriage counselor together?"

Craig was so wrapped up in what Melissa was saying that he failed to realize an answer was expected.

"Did you?" she repeated.

"No, I didn't know it," answered Craig, amazed.

For the moment, Craig had completely forgotten about the problem that had obsessed him for weeks. No one had ever offered any reasonable explanation as to why his parents had separated. He had accepted the reality of the separation, but never had any understanding of the reasons. He still did not understand, but Melissa had shed new light on it, and, for the first time, he felt a little empathy. Melissa refused to go into detail when Craig asked her to give a more explicit explanation of the unresolved problems they had.

"Just believe me that they were real problems," she said condescendingly.

Craig once again felt like a little brother but chose not to pursue the matter. His sister's frankness and candid discussion with him pleased him. The last thing he wanted to do at this time was to ruin this new relationship that seemed to be developing between them.

As Melissa pulled up in front of the brick garden apartment complex, a feeling of anxiety began to swell up inside him. Craig desperately wanted to share his frightening experience with his sister, especially now that she had opened up to him.

"Liss," he said, "I got something to tell you."

"Wait till we get into the apartment," she interrupted.

Melissa always had difficulty parking the car, and she needed total concentration to do it correctly. Even then, it looked like someone had haphazardly parked or was in a mad rush to get somewhere. The car was a good three feet from the curb, and the front end nosed out into the street. Melissa was satisfied with her parking job, so Craig suppressed an urge to criticize.

As they boarded the elevator together, another tenant got in with them, and Melissa struck up a polite conversation with him. As the door opened on the third and last floor, she bid her farewell to her fellow tenant and motioned Craig to follow her.

Apartment 3D was a cheery, art-filled dwelling. His sister's roommate was a commercial artist, and many of her most prized works adorned the apartment.

"Neat, Liss, real neat," commented Craig.

"Hi guys!"

The deep female voice of Melissa's roommate greeted them and Melissa formally introduced her kid brother. Craig was impressed. Janet was a buxom blond with large, green eyes and full lips. Craig deliberately lowered his voice in a futile attempt to add a few years to his age. His ego was severely deflated when she offered what was meant to be a compliment.

"Boy is he going to be good-looking when he grows up!"

Craig felt like crawling into the nearest hole as the crimson heat of blush crept across his boyish face. Melissa graciously accepted the compliment and jokingly cautioned Craig to be wary of blond artists.

"How about some milk and a piece of homemade cake?" asked Melissa, adding insult to injury.

"No thanks, but I'll have a cup of coffee," answered Craig, still trying to impress her roommate with his maturity.

"Coffee?" asked Melissa, surprised. "Since when do you drink coffee?"

At this point, Craig decided it was a losing battle, and in an attempt to avoid any further embarrassment, asked to use the bathroom. He stood in front of the bathroom mirror, turning his face and body from side to side and testing various facial expressions. He could hear muffled conversation coming from the living room as he gave one last comb to his soft, blond hair. When he entered the living room, he became the center of attention again as the two girls dropped their conversation to focus in on him.

"How's school, Craig?" asked Janet.

"Lousy. Let's talk about something pleasant."

He hated that damn question, that same one he had heard almost every day for the past nine years. Janet detected the annoyed look on Craig's face and immediately changed the subject. The conversation was light thereafter as everything from the weather to the Yankees and Mets seemed to get equal time.

Craig's original intention to confide in Melissa and share his nightmarish experience with her never materialized. By the time he was ready to leave, the desperate urge to share with his sister had subsided and the drive home consisted of some more banal conversation.

"Thanks, Liss. See ya again soon."

"Be good, Craig. Take care of Dad."

As the car drove off, that strange, empty feeling crept back into his stomach when he realized that, with the exception of Jerry, he still bore this terrible burden alone. Mr. J was asleep on the sofa as Craig tiptoed up to the TV and gently switched it off. He knew it was next to impossible to get his father up and into bed once he fell asleep. He made him as comfortable as possible, covered him with an afghan his grandmother had made, and quietly stole off to bed.

The solitude and silence always increased his anxiety level, and the thought of school tomorrow didn't help.

He couldn't forge any more notes and miss any more school. He had to face the inevitable confrontation with the Graham kid.

What about Graham's older friends? Who had made the threatening phone call? Were there more kids involved than he saw? Would they get him even if he didn't reveal them? A thousand unanswered questions raced through his mind.

Craig grabbed his pillow with two hands and placed it tightly over his head along with the sheet and double blanket. Peaceful, heavenly sleep finally came as the tired body of a troubled boy, contorted into a tight fetal position, endured the night.

CHAPTER FOUR
Uptight

It was a gray morning with an October chill in the air as Bus X transported its group of sleepy students to school. It was a comparatively quiet ride with the exception of a few girls huddled in the back of the bus murmuring plans for their lunchtime rendezvous. Craig had elected to sit alone, and his anxiety increased as the bus drew closer to Centerville Junior High School. His plans for the day did not include skipping school and he had a neatly folded forged note in his shirt pocket that would hopefully allow him reentry to school. Craig had excellent handwriting and was able to sign his father's name with a real look of authenticity. The attendance monitor seldom scrutinized notes from home, and his truancy would surely go undetected.

Mr. Bacardi was standing in his usual place as Craig's bus pulled up to the orange line and discharged its young passengers. He greeted the students as they stepped off the bus, and Craig got a special greeting as Mr. Bacardi called him by name. He could almost feel his face turn ashen as he approached Mr. Bacardi, expecting to be interrogated about the previous days absence.

"Are you feeling okay?" questioned the assistant principal as he surveyed the sallow complexion of a frightened young man.

"I'm fine, Mr. Bacardi," stammered Craig.

"Listen, Craig, will you let me know tomorrow if your bus is picking you up on time? We've had many parental complaints about late busses and we're trying to spot check."

Craig felt the color return to his face as he sighed heavily and gulped his reply, "Sure thing, Mr. Bacardi. I'll keep track of the time and let you know."

"Thanks, Craig. I'd appreciate it. You'd better get going now or you'll be late for homeroom."

Craig walked briskly away from Mr. Bacardi until he was out of his line of vision and then made a beeline for the attendance office. After submitting his absence note and getting a pass from the monitor, Craig headed for homeroom, contented that he was safely readmitted to school.

The pledge to the flag started the traditional school day, followed by the announcements. Most of the kids didn't hear them as they chatted with friends and exchanged homework assignments. Craig was in no mood to make idle talk and half listened as a student read the morning announcements. The name Peter Stohler made him quiver as he shushed the kids next to him and leaned forward to hear.

"A Peter Stohler Memorial Fund has been started by a group of Centerville students. Anyone interested in joining the group and helping to raise money should contact their Student Council Representative."

Craig's blood seemed to run cold, and once again the eerie scene was recreated in his mind. *No kid has ever had a problem as serious and as unsolvable as mine*, he thought as he left homeroom and headed for his first-period math class.

As he walked briskly down the main corridor, a startling sight appeared before him. Standing just outside the corridor exit door, holding hands in a near embrace, stood Laura Donohue and Travis Graham. Craig positioned himself behind a large column and watched the newly blossomed romance progress.

Travis Graham was the youngest of the group of villains who had been present on that awful night. He was the only one from Centerville Junior High who Craig had recognized in the scene that developed before him behind Calderwood Elementary School.

How could Laura Donohue get involved with such a creepy character? thought Craig.

The sensitive, kind, and compassionate Laura holding hands with a murderer, or at least an accessory to a murder!

Craig waited for a group of students that was passing by and stealthily slipped behind and stayed close to them until he was safely out of the couple's sight. He was so deep in thought that when the bell signaling the end of his math class rang, Craig couldn't remember a single thing that had happened in class.

The trancelike trek to his social studies class was violently interrupted by Vinny and Roland as they mischievously came up behind Craig and dumped his books. Vinny wasn't very coordinated, and, in the process of dumping his books, he also caused Craig to stumble over a little seventh grade girl who unfortunately was in his path at the time.

Craig was in no mood for horseplay and practical jokes, and he saw red. He jumped up, spun Vinny around, and landed a solid right to Vinny's nose. Blood spurted from his friend's nose and, before Craig knew what had happened, a teacher who had witnessed the vicious attack was escorting him to Mr. Bacardi's office.

The written discipline referral stated: "This young man maliciously assaulted and caused bodily harm to another student."

Mr. Bacardi shook his head in disbelief as Craig sat in the hot seat in the assistant principal's office. Craig was so frustrated and in such as state of shock that he offered no explanation for his bizarre behavior when Mr. Bacardi questioned him about it. Instead, he simply admitted the assault and sat passively and unemotionally as Mr. Bacardi wrote up his suspension notice. The series of events that had occurred since school started had numbed Craig.

As the school nurse tended to Vinny's battered nose, Craig sat outside the main office, holding his head in both hands. In spite of his mischievous and sometimes malicious nature, Vinny did have some good qualities, as Craig was to discover.

Vinny had asked to see Mr. Bacardi. Holding an ice pack on his nose and tilting his pudgy head upward, he described to Mr. Bacardi how he had initiated the incident and why Craig had every right to be angry with him.

Fortunately, Vinny's intercedence on his behalf worked. Mr. Bacardi, who Craig thought was always fair, reinstated Craig. He did give him a lecture on the dangers of losing one's temper and warned him about using his hands on anyone.

On their way back to class, Craig apologized to Vinny and thanked him for saving him from suspension and the inevitable wrath of his father.

"Hey, I was only kidding around, man. Boy, are you uptight! We only dumped your books—you didn't have to attack me."

Craig apologized again for overreacting to the practical joke as they parted ways.

Word had spread fast, and when Craig entered Mr. Kubek's social studies class with a pass from the main office, a hush came over the entire class as he took his seat in the back of the room. Mr. Kubek, unaware of the incident, immediately got back to the subject matter.

A juvenile law unit was an integral part of Mr. Kubek's curriculum and, incidentally, his favorite unit. The industrial arts class had built a judge and juror's bench for Mr. Kubek, and the classroom was transformed into a student courtroom. The students would simulate actual trials, and each student had an opportunity to act as judge, juror, attorney, and defendant during the course of the law unit.

It was quite a good learning experience for students, and Mr. Kubek's law unit was a very popular one. He received praise from the community for his efforts to teach kids about the law. The course of study was being adopted by school systems throughout the state, and Mr. Kubek was becoming somewhat of a local celebrity as he was called on from time to time to speak in other school systems about his model program. Many articles had been written about the program. His proudest moment came when an extensive article appeared in the *Times* education section. He framed the clipping, and it hung over the judge's bench in the classroom. He was truly a dedicated teacher who loved the classroom and gave his all to teaching kids. Young people, being very perceptive, realized and appreciated his dedication.

Rights of the accused and due process were being discussed, and Craig had recently taken a keen interest in the law as he followed the progress of the Stohler murder investigation in the newspaper. The recent events surrounding the murder provided a built-in relevance to the course of study, and Mr. Kubek capitalized on it.

At first, Craig was reluctant to get involved in the class discussion. His keen interest combined with the rest of the class's exuberance and active participation prompted Craig to also participate. Craig wasn't the extroverted type and usually didn't voluntarily contribute to class discussion, so when Mr. Kubek saw Craig's hand up, he seized the opportunity to get him involved.

"Is it true that if the police violated the rights of those kids who were questioned, they could go free?" asked Craig.

Mr. Kubek hesitated for a moment, and utilizing his teaching expertise, asked if anyone knew the answer to that question. A petite girl in the back of the room raised her hand and began to answer.

"Due process calls for the right of the accused to have an attorney present and a fair hearing. According to the newspaper articles, the kids who were picked up by the police weren't given this right."

Mr. Kubek praised the student for her factual answer and began to expand on it.

"Another factor enters this case," said Mr. Kubek. "The four suspects were all young people and their parents are alleging that they were questioned illegally by police and some were not even notified by the police that they were in custody. According to state law, police must notify the parent of any juvenile under the age of sixteen as soon as he or she is taken into custody so that a parent may be present for the interrogation."

Craig knew that some of the boys were over the age and wondered about them. Mr. Kubek answered his question in his next statement.

"Attorneys for the older suspects claim their clients were held for questioning for many hours and police did not afford them the opportunity to make phone calls."

"Why do criminals get so much protection?" interrupted another student somewhat angrily.

"In our country, you are innocent until proven guilty in a court of law," answered Mr. Kubek. "This is the basis of our judicial system."

"Yeah, but they're almost sure these were the kids," answered the boy.

Mr. Kubek tried to draw an analogy for the student by asking him if he ever got in trouble for something he didn't do. When he answered in the affirmative, Mr. Kubek asked him how he felt being accused of something he didn't do. The analogy worked as Craig saw the rest of the kids nod in agreement. The bell aborted the discussion for the day, and Mr. Kubek hurriedly assigned some reading on the judicial process as the students started exiting his room.

Craig attempted to digest what had been said in class and quivered at the thought that the law might end up protecting those kids. Boy, what a predicament he was in!

When the bell ending the fourth period sounded, Craig's stomach was beckoning for food.

Vinny and Roland met him at his locker, and they all broke into hysterical laughter as Vinny reenacted the dumping-of-books scene and the subsequent meeting with Mr. Bacardi in a nasal voice. Fortunately, there was nothing broken, and the only reminder Vinny had was an extreme soreness around the bridge of his nose.

Craig grabbed his brown lunch bag from his locker, and the three of them headed toward the cafeteria, Vinny still speaking with a nasal tone.

The cafeteria was chaotic as usual as four hundred hungry teenagers scurried here and there, gulping down peanut butter and jelly sandwiches, milk, and assorted junk food. Everyone kidded Vinny about his appetite, and when he started on the first of his three sandwiches, a couple of kids pushed a large garbage can over to his seat. Inscribed in black magic marker on the can were the words "Vinny Robinsky's Lunch Box."

Vinny was used to getting ribbed about his unusual appetite. He good-humoredly smiled at his agitators. Down deep, it hurt a little, though, and for the hundredth time, he swore to go on a diet to shed some of that excess weight.

Roland was the gopher kid at the table. The rest of the kids used him to fetch various items of food during the lunch period. Craig didn't like the way the other kids used him and, on many occasions, advised them to stop doing it.

Roland would always give him the same answer: "I don't mind doing it; they're my friends."

Craig finally gave up, and Roland continued to bounce back and forth between the table and the serving line with goodies for the rest of the kids. Roland was an insecure person and felt that the only way he could remain part of the group was to continue in the role the kids had assigned to him.

The last fifteen minutes of the lunch period, after everyone's hunger had been satisfied, were devoted to social games. As chairs became vacant, a few girls would wander over to different tables and sit next to their favorite boys. It was during this idle period of time that plans were made for after school and weekend activities.

Craig was just draining the last drop of milk through his straw when two delicate hands were placed over his eyes from behind. A very familiar scent of hand lotion immediately gave away the female trickster. Craig gently removed the hands and, without looking around, casually greeted the Donohue girl.

"Hi, Laura, what's new?"

Craig's greeting was abrupt and rather cold as he attempted to remain as unemotional as possible with her. Inside, he could feel his heart pounding. His ear lobes became reddened and warm.

"How'd you know it was me?" asked Laura jokingly.

"My secret," Craig replied smugly.

"Listen, Craig, I was thinking. We had a lot in common, and just because we're not dating anymore is a pretty silly reason not to continue the good friendship we had. We're being so stupid avoiding each other in the corridors and making believe we don't see each other when we pass. Craig's first reaction was to blame the broken relationship on her, but good reason and sense prevailed for once and he shrugged his shoulders in agreement and said, "Okay with me."

"Don't be so enthusiastic about it," said Laura sarcastically.

Craig noticed that good feeling he enjoyed when Laura and he were dating. Since their breakup, he had lost interest in girls and, combined with his other problems, had all but abandoned his social life. Laura rekindled a somewhat dormant vitality and lust for life that Craig naturally possessed. They conversed about school and did a lot of reminiscing as they laughed and joked about all of the funny things that had happened to them when they were going together.

Craig began to feel very comfortable with Laura again and was thoroughly enjoying their conciliatory meeting when a familiar voice rudely interrupted them.

"Hey, Laura, what ya doin' hanging around with this creep?"

"He's a friend of mine, Travis, and he's no creep," replied Laura defensively.

Craig's first impulse was to get up and deck Travis Graham, but he suppressed the urge. Laura detected the anger in his eyes and tried to cool things off by redirecting their attention to a food fight in progress across the cafeteria. Craig seized the opportunity to avoid a confrontation with Graham. Instead he headed toward the crowd that was gathering around the two teacher aides who had responded to the crisis. He was seething inside as he stood to the side and watched Mr. Bacardi expertly settle the dispute and put the culprits to work cleaning the rest of the cafeteria.

Craig glanced over to where Laura and Travis had been standing and saw them walk away arm in arm. Travis was an amicable, fun-loving person who excelled in sports. He was a good six inches taller than him and was a basketball star. He had a ruggedly handsome face and was very popular with the girls. Many of his friends were in the high school, and that made him even more impressive to a lot of the kids. He hadn't even looked at Laura last year, but her blossoming womanhood had attracted Travis when she returned in September. Laura seized the opportunity to be part of his entourage.

Travis's mother had divorced and remarried three times, and her reputation in the community was tarnished. She feigned an interest in Travis by frequently asking for conferences with the school authorities to discuss his progress in school. At many of the conferences, she would berate Travis by insisting that he was responsible for her failures in marriages and life in general.

"He makes my life so miserable," she would lament. "He disobeys me and has absolutely no respect for me or any of my husbands. He's defiant and extremely rude towards me. My present husband has tried so desperately to take Travis under his wing. He's taken him fishing and camping and even took him to Puerto Rico for a week. Travis is an ingrate and nothing satisfies him. I don't know what to do with him anymore."

She steadfastly refused to see a family counselor and resented anyone who recommended social or psychological help for one or both of them. After each conference, she would leave in a huff, muttering incoherent charges of school incompetence and indifference.

The rest of the school day was uneventful as Craig prepared for physical education, the last period of the day. He was interested in sports but did not look forward to his phys-ed class. Most gym periods were spent playing murder, a modified version of dodge ball. It consisted of two sides throwing a large, inflated ball at each other across the gym floor. If nothing else, the game provided an outlet for adolescents to release some of their pent-up frustrations by throwing a ball as hard as they could at each other. Craig didn't try very hard to avoid thrown balls and usually ended up sitting out most of the game. He was content sitting on the sidelines, watching the battle.

The showers didn't work properly, and most kids left the gym period perspiring and rather unpleasant smelling. Craig consoled himself in the thought that he did not have to return to class smelling like the boys locker room but instead prepared to leave school for the day.

It was a pleasant October day, and he decided to walk the three miles home rather than ride the bus. As he left the school gate, the lady crossing guard amicably greeted him and halted the oncoming traffic so Craig could cross the street safely. He thanked her with a smile and a nod, and began a slow jog down River Street. The October sun combined with a pleasant coolness in the air, exhilarated Craig, and he felt a spurt of energy as he increased the pace of his jog. River Street was a relatively secluded street with only a few old Cape Cod houses nestled far into wooded areas. Most of the land was owned by the nearby veterans' hospital. People were reluctant to build a home so close to a VA hospital and a junior high school. Weathered "For Sale" signs dotted selected vacant lots along the left side of the road, and occasionally a small house would spring up here and there.

Craig felt his shoelace come undone, and he jogged up a steep incline and decided to stop for a breather and retie it. The screeching sound of brakes shattered the early afternoon silence, and Craig instinctively jumped away from the street and into a clump of privet hedges. Three older boys jumped out of the car, violently slamming the doors, and began menacingly walking toward him.

"Hey, creep, what the hell ya doing sleeping in the bushes?" a deep, sarcastic voice inquired.

A round of menacing laughter from the other two boys sent a chill up Craig's spine as he attempted to untangle himself from the hedgerow. Just as he was about to get up, a large boot caught him across his chest and he tumbled back into the bushes, clutching his chest in pain. He lay there for a moment, grimacing. He tried to catch his breath as the three assailants stood over him, waiting for his next move. Craig decided to remain perfectly still as the pain began to subside. His heart was pounding, and he could feel their cold eyes leering at him even though he was face down in the bushes.

"Just a little reminder, creep, that if you open your mouth to the cops, you'll end up permanently on your back, six feet under."

Craig remained silent and still as a foot was jammed under his stomach.

"Turn your ass over and listen carefully. If you mention one word about what you saw we will know where it came from and you are one dead snitch." Craig complied with a little urging from the foot under his stomach. They were all about the same height but varied significantly in weight and muscular development. The blond-haired boy was lean and sinewy looking and carried a large scar under his left eye. The other two were darker-complexioned, and both were heavyset and muscular. One in particular, the taller one, looked to be well over two hundred pounds and had a red sweatband around his forehead that kept his dark, shoulder-length hair behind his head and out of his eyes.

Fear gripped Craig as he looked dolefully at them, hoping for mercy.

"Please don't hurt me, I … I won't say a word to anybody. I … I promise," Craig pleaded.

He recognized two of them as the culprits involved in the Stohler murder but didn't recall if the blond boy was with them on that grim October eve. Craig fought off the tears that began to swell up in his eyes and lifted his back to remove a branch that he was almost impaled on. He felt a trickle of blood on his lower back as he tucked his tattered shirt back into his pants.

"If you want to stay healthy, kid, then you would be very wise to completely forget what you saw."

The voice of the blond boy was a little more civil, and he almost detected a bit of humanness in it.

"Let's get out of here," he said anxiously as they jumped into the red sports car and screeched away.

Small pebbles and dust showered Craig as he protected his head from the flying debris left in the wake of the speeding car. As feeling began to come back to his numbed body, the sensation of pain came upon him. His initial fall into the bushes and the subsequent kick he received took a toll on his body. Craig began to notice some bleeding scratches and bruises caused primarily by the fall into the thorny hedges. There was a dull ache in his chest accompanied by a severe soreness that became more intense each time he inhaled. All of the wounds were superficial. He was happy that he survived the ordeal still physically intact and able to walk away.

Craig decided to head back to school, where he could use the bathroom to clean up and wash away the blood that dotted his face and arms. What if Mr. Bacardi or one of the teachers spotted him? He would have to answer questions, and that was the last thing he wanted to do.

His mind was still in a confused state as he walked slowly toward the school entrance.

With the exception of a few kids waiting for the late bus, the school grounds and building were empty. Occasionally a teacher would walk out of the red brick building, briefcase in hand, and head toward the parking lot. Craig waited behind a clump of evergreens, rubbing his sore chest and reexamining his scratches and bruises. Off to his left, a bridle trail stretched into the wooded area surrounding the gateway to the school. Riders from the Gabor Stables frequently used the trail. When Craig noticed it, he was reminded of a possibly safer and friendlier sanctuary where he could clean up, nurse his wounds, and recuperate from his ordeal. He began to follow the trail on his way to another meeting with Jerry.

CHAPTER FIVE
The Gentle Giant

"Craig! What in the world happened to you? You're bleeding all over. You better come with me," as Jerry clasped his broad hand solicitously on Craig's forearm.

"I'll be okay, I just gotta talk to you, Jerry. I'm really scared to death."

"Listen, kid, it's just about quitting time for me and I've got a few things to tend to before I leave. Wait here, catch your breath and relax for a few minutes. Then we'll go to my place, clean up and we'll talk."

The sense of urgency and fear in Craig's voice had a sobering effect on Jerry's usual jovial mood. As Jerry completed the last of his daily chores, Craig sat on a stool in the corner of the stable, holding his head in his hands and anxiously rocking back and forth. Jerry quickened his pace, realizing Craig's desperate state.

"Be right with you, Junky—just a few more minutes," Jerry said consolingly.

Jerry was the only one who knew anything about Craig's dilemma, and he guessed that Craig's condition was probably related to it.

"Meet me at my car, kid. I've got to see Mr. Gabor before I leave," said Jerry. "I'll be there in a minute."

Craig headed for the blue Jeep parked behind the main house. As he walked, he noticed a quiver in his right hand and felt a distinct weakness in his legs. He opened the car door and slipped into the back seat, taking the opportunity to lie down and rest for a few minutes. He closed his eyes and took a deep breath, remembering what his health teacher said about relaxing his body. Scenes began to flash though his mind as the experiences he had recently endured were recreated.

Craig instinctively jumped when he heard the car door open but was immediately relieved when he saw the big redhead slide in behind the wheel. Jerry started the car and began to slowly leave the farm via the long dirt road leading out to Route 52A. He didn't say much during the short trip to the little Cape Cod he rented a mile or so from the horse farm. It was a small house nestled into the woods on the outskirts of town. The landlord did very little to enhance the appearance of the house, and it was unkempt and looked almost abandoned. Jerry was not one to be overly concerned with neatness and looks and did a minimum of maintenance on the small cottage. Weeds and overgrown, untrimmed bushes hid the house from the road. There was a little screened porch that you first entered before going into the main part of the house, and here Jerry stored a lot of junk he rarely used or was going to discard.

Once inside the house, Jerry helped Craig nurse his superficial wounds. Jerry's enormous yet gentle hands comforted Craig who welcomed the nurturing touch. Jerry was a simple soul who took life casually and non-competitively. His only love in life was horses, and he did not have a vested interest in life outside the horse farm. He was content to live alone and tend to his simple needs and the needs of the horses he worked with each day. He was not threatened by anyone and, for the most part, minded his own business. He lived a relatively secluded and uneventful life.

Mr. Gabor was very pleased with Jerry, who was a hard worker, a non-drinker, and very reliable when it came to taking care of horses. His background was obscure and very vague. He was not native to the area and had arrived quite mysteriously from somewhere in the Midwest, looking for work. He volunteered very little information about himself and kept his distance with people. With the exception of Mr. Gabor's son, whom he socialized with from time to time, he was pretty much a loner.

Jerry was a good listener and very seldom passed judgment on what Craig had to say. He had taken a liking to Craig, who occasionally helped him with his work after school. Most of their conversations consisted of small talk and horses. Craig enjoyed his company because he could be himself and didn't feel a need to impress Jerry.

Craig heard the toilet flush and tried to compose himself before Jerry came out of the bathroom.

"Wanna soda, kid?"

"Okay, thanks," answered Craig.

"Now, what the hell happened to you?" questioned Jerry as he poured two tall glasses of root beer.

Craig described in detail the event that had taken place that afternoon, and Jerry listened very passively, nodding his head at appropriate times. When Craig finished, there was a strange silence that permeated the tiny, cluttered living room where they sat. Jerry got up and refilled his glass with root beer as Craig wondered why there was such a delay in Jerry's response.

"Listen, kid, I'm not much for advice." Jerry broke the silence with an unusually serious tone of voice as he returned to his chair.

"I never told anyone this before, but I left my hometown many years ago because I was in trouble. I thought I could run away from it—get away, far away where I would not be bothered and where I could forget. I got a girl pregnant and she wanted me to marry her. The last thing I wanted was to be married and tied down with a wife and kid, so I split and never returned."

Craig had never heard Jerry speak so seriously and personally, and he listened attentively.

"For years it preyed on my mind, and I wonder to this day what has happened to that child that came into the world without a father. I will carry that guilt and responsibility for the rest of my life, and it ain't fun, believe me! So kid, I ain't gonna tell you what to do, but remember, you can't run forever and you won't forget so easily."

Craig was speechless as he stared open-mouthed and wide-eyed at the big redheaded stable hand who had just opened up his life to a young kid. He just couldn't believe that Jerry was capable of enduring all of that worry and turmoil in his life. He was such a simple human being who just did not seem to fit the character in the story he had just heard.

Jerry gave a long, relieved sigh as if he had just unloaded a terrible burden, got up, and disappeared into the bedroom. Craig heard the rustling of hangers and clothes from a closet and looked toward the bedroom door for Jerry's reentry into the living room. When he finally came out of the bedroom, he was dressed in a clean pair of jeans and a red, long-sleeved woolen shirt.

"Come on, Junky. I'll take you down to Super Burger for some dinner," said Jerry in his usual jolly way. "Life is too short to get caught up with all of its problems. We'll fill our bellies and feel better. Let's go!"

Craig wasn't hungry and still had not fully recuperated from his ordeal, but he desperately needed someone to be with and agreed to go along.

On the way to the fast food restaurant, Jerry began to ask a few questions about the incident—some things that Craig had not told him.

"Do you know the kids involved in the murder?" asked Jerry.

"I'm not sure of all of them, but I can positively identify three of them," said Craig.

Jerry was smart enough not to ask for names or descriptions and avoided any further questioning regarding identifications. Instead, he pursued another line of questioning related to what Craig had actually observed.

As Craig recounted the events of that night, Jerry began to frown, and deep ridges formed on his freckled forehead. When he finished the account, Jerry shook his head slowly and tightened his lips in a show of concern as he pulled into the restaurant's parking lot. He deliberately and abruptly changed the subject to food, rubbing his belly and praising the meaty hamburgers they were about to consume. Craig was still not hungry, and retelling the events he witnessed didn't help to stimulate his appetite.

"Let's eat in the car," Craig pleaded. "I just don't feel like going into a crowded restaurant and seeing people right now."

Jerry was very obliging and drove around to the take-out window. He parked the car in a far corner of the lot and opened the glove compartment, placing the soft drinks and orders of French fries on its door.

He handed Craig one of the four large burgers he had ordered and directed him to eat in a commanding voice. "Come on; get something in your stomach, kid. You'll feel better."

Craig unenthusiastically bit into the burger, chewing very slowly, finding it difficult to swallow. Occasionally, he would sip his soft drink primarily to wash down the food that was stubbornly refusing to go down. Jerry, meanwhile, devoured two of the burgers and began on a third when Craig refused to accept it. Craig forced the remaining half of the burger down and handed Jerry his portion of French fries.

"Boy, you eat like a bird, Junky. How the hell are you going to grow if you eat so little?"

Craig smiled politely and assured Jerry that he usually ate much more but just wasn't hungry at the moment. Jerry understood and gently patted Craig on his back.

"Come on, kid. Something will break soon and they'll probably arrest those kids without your getting involved."

Jerry's reassuring words helped him to relax a bit, and he gulped down the remaining soda, chewing on a few small pieces of ice that had settled to the bottom of the cup.

"You think they'll catch them, Jerry? Do you really think so?"

The urgency and fear in Craig's voice gripped the gentle redhead, and he answered reassuringly, "Sure, kid, of course they will. You just wait and see."

As darkness began to set in, Craig suddenly realized that he had not notified his father that he would not be home for dinner. Mr. J insisted on knowing Craig's whereabouts at all times. On those rare occasions when he did not, his father became extremely angry. Craig spotted the public phone booth across the parking lot and excused himself to make the call.

"Hi, Dad, sorry I didn't call sooner, but …"

"Where the hell have you been?" Mr. J abruptly interrupted. "You had me worried stiff. Where are you?"

Craig unsuccessfully attempted to calm his father down before explaining, and when he realized the futility of his attempts, simply said he would be home as soon as possible.

He shot across the parking lot and breathlessly pleaded with Jerry to get him home immediately. Jerry obliged, and his car raced out of the parking lot as if a chase were in progress. The ride home was a silent one, and both Jerry and Craig were now preoccupied with a very immediate concern, that of getting Craig home as soon as possible.

As the Jeep pulled up in front of the Juncosa home, Jerry immediately volunteered to explain Craig's lateness to his father.

"Come on, kid. I'll go in with you and take the blame."

"That's all right," said Craig. "He won't buy it anyway. He'll say it was my responsibility to call him."

Jerry insisted and followed Craig to the front door. Mr. J was waiting at the door and opened it before Craig could grab the doorknob. The look on his face reminded Craig of the time he lied to his father and was severely punished. Jerry's presence evidently caused his father to suppress the built-up anger and, instead of exploding, he sternly invited both of them in.

"Dad, this is Jerry, a friend of mine who works at the Gabor Farms," said Craig meekly.

Mr. J offered an abrupt "Pleased to meet you" and turned to walk into the family room.

"Why the heck didn't you call, son?" asked Mr. J in a civil by but noticeably irked tone of voice.

"I forgot all about—"

Jerry interrupted at this point, placing his large hand gently over Craig's mouth.

"Mr. J, it was my entire fault, sir. I invited Craig out for a burger and I didn't give him the opportunity to call. We didn't realize how late it was, and Craig called as soon as he discovered the hour."

His father, still with his back to the two of them, reluctantly accepted Jerry's explanation and walked into the kitchen. Jerry decided that he could no longer offer any further assistance. He bade him a polite farewell, gave Craig a reassuring pat on his head, and left.

A long period of silence followed the kind of ominous silence that was very uncomfortable and made Craig squirm.

Craig attempted to quietly steal into his bedroom until his father bellowed, "Don't ever pull this stunt again!"

All of the built-up frustration was released at once, and Craig realized just how angry his father was. He gently closed his bedroom door and could still hear the muffled voice of his father continuing the severe reprimand. Craig sat on his bed and patiently waited for his father's temper to cool down. Finally, the chastising seemed to subside, and Craig remained perfectly still on his bed waiting to see if the silence would last.

He stayed in his room for the remainder of the evening, rubbing his sore chest and scrutinizing the wounds inflicted by the thorn bushes. In Mr. J's fit of temper, he had not noticed the cuts and bruises, and Craig was thankful for that bit of luck. With the exception of a scratch on his face and one on the back of his hand, the rest of his cuts were well hidden by his clothing.

The eleven o'clock news brought Mr. J from out of the utility room where he was organizing his toolbox and into family room. Mr. J never missed the news, and Craig knew he would have to face his father soon to bid him good night. He decided to strategically amble out of his room and into the family room during the news report, hoping his father's attention would be directed to the TV. It worked. Mr. J just barely looked up as Craig entered, and he immediately returned his attention to the newscaster. Craig took a seat on the couch and pretended to become quite involved in the news report. A commercial broke his father's attention, and Craig's body stiffened in preparation for continued reprimands. Instead, his father quietly asked him what he had been doing all that time in his bedroom.

"Nothing much, Dad—reading a little, and I did some math homework."

Craig hoped this would ease the tension and help his father to forget the source of his anger. Craig was pleasantly surprised when his father answered.

"Listen, son, I'm sorry for getting so damn angry, but you had me worried. You have to realize that when you're expected and you don't show up, it worries the hell out of a parent. I realize now that you didn't do it on purpose, but make sure you think of it next time, okay?"

His father's voice was back to normal, and Craig once again apologized for his forgetfulness.

"Who's the man who brought you home, Craig?" queried his father.

"Jerry. I don't know his last name, but he's a real nice man who I talk to a lot, and I help him out with the horses occasionally."

"He seems like a nice person, and he was considerate enough to come into the house with you to try to help you explain."

"He is very nice," answered Craig, "and he likes me a lot."

"Listen, son, I've got something I want to talk to you about. Sit down for a minute and hear me out."

Craig was expecting to hear more about his negligence, but was pleasantly surprised as his father began to speak.

"I don't know whether you're aware of it or not, but your mother and I have been seeing a marriage counselor together for the past few weeks."

There was a deliberate pause as his father looked for Craig's reaction to the statement. Craig, instead, suppressed any emotion even though a warm, pleasant feeling began to envelop his body.

"You know, son, your mother and I still care for each other very much," Mr. J continued. "When we separated, we both thought our differences were irreconcilable, but we've since learned that we can possibly work them out."

Craig wasn't sure of the meaning or the word *irreconcilable*, but it didn't matter. What he did understand and was elated about was that his parents might once again be reunited. His father paused again to allow Craig to digest everything he had heard, and then continued.

"I don't want you to get your hopes too high, though, son. As I said, we are trying to work out our differences, and the first step is that we've agreed to see a marriage counselor together. It takes a good deal of time to repair a severely damaged relationship. Our marriage had been going bad for many years, and there are a lot of problems and emotions to deal with."

Craig could no longer hide his emotions, and he ran to his father and enthusiastically embraced him. His father smiled knowingly and patted him tenderly on his back. As Craig pulled back, his father noticed the mist that had gathered in Craig's eyes and knew then how important their reconciliation would be to their son. Craig was a little embarrassed as a tear rolled down his face. He scurried into the kitchen to wipe away the evidence of his emotions.

His father understood and remained seated, allowing Craig to be alone for a while.

Craig didn't know how to verbally express his happiness. Instead, he asked his father if he could get him anything from the kitchen. This was his way of showing his approval and happiness about the news he had just heard. Mr. J politely refused and thanked him for his thoughtfulness. He knew Craig was at a loss for words and was very pleased that he was so obviously elated and excited about the thought of all of them once again being together.

Craig found he was extremely vulnerable and he suddenly had an irrepressible urge to tell his father about his dilemma.

"Dad, I've got something to tell you," Craig murmured.

"What's that?" asked Mr. J.

"I … I … I'm doing much better in school this year."

Craig just couldn't reveal his horrible secret to his father. As much as he wanted to share his problem with him, the words just wouldn't come out. The frustration of the moment combined with the ordeal he had experienced brought Craig to tears.

"What is it, Craig? What's the matter?" asked his father.

"Nothing, Dad, I'm just so happy to hear about you and Mom." Craig's response was perfect, and his father smiled paternally and encouraged him to get it all out of his system.

"It's good to cry, son. We men have been taught that to cry is shameful and feminine, but it's a release for men as well as for women. If men cried more often, they would have fewer emotional problems."

Craig didn't hear a word his father said as he sauntered out of the family room and into his bedroom.

"Night, Dad."

"Night, Craig."

Those were the last words they exchanged that day as Craig closed and locked his bedroom door. The tears flowed as Craig tried desperately to muffle the crying sounds that accompanied the tears. It was a good release for him as he continued to sob for a good half-hour. He could still hear his father puttering around the house and was waiting for him to retire so he could sneak into the bathroom and wash his tear-lined face.

He never got to the bathroom, and woke up at 7:30 a.m. fully clothed. Another day he had to face! Craig knew he couldn't tolerate any more confrontations. He had reached a breaking point.

CHAPTER SIX
Escape From Reality

When the bell ending the fourth period rang, Craig was relieved. The brief respite provided by his lunch hour would give him time to collect his thoughts and relax. Craig felt no hunger as he opened his locker and removed the brown bag containing a peanut butter sandwich and an apple.

"Hi, Craig," said Vinny as he sped by on his way to the cafeteria.

Vinny usually bought the hot lunch provided by the school, and raced to get a decent place in line. As Craig was about to close his locker, he saw the top of a green bottle wedged between two library books. He recalled the incident that landed the bottle in his locker. A few weeks earlier, a student whom he barely knew, and in somewhat of a frenzy, asked him to hold the bottle in his locker for him that day. He reluctantly agreed, and the student never returned to claim it. He had forgotten all about it after the bottle had slipped in between two books in his cluttered locker.

Craig occasionally experimented with alcohol and on a few occasions, succumbing to peer pressure, shared a joint with his friends. But for the most part, he was not drawn to mind-altering drugs. On those occasions when he did partake, he didn't find it as pleasant an experience as it was made out to be. He did recall that it made him very relaxed and uninhibited.

Suddenly, he had an uncontrollable urge to take a few swigs from the bottle of alcohol in his locker. The short bottle contained Southern Comfort a sweet, strong liquor.

Craig checked the corridors for any lurking school authorities, grabbed the bottle, and surreptitiously slipped it into the brown lunch bag. He nervously exited the building from the side corridor door, quickened his pace, and headed for the woods bordering the school property. He looked back once to see if anyone was observing his exodus and then began a slow jog until he reached the edge of the woods. Safely inside the woods, he headed for the Pit.

He didn't expect to find it occupied during the lunch hour. Craig was not aware of the fact that a few students used the Pit on a daily basis to smoke their joints or down a few bottles of warm beer for lunch. He hesitated at first, straining to hear the voices coming from the area, but decided he would be immediately accepted because of the merchandise he carried. As he walked into the open area, six or seven students were sitting on a fallen tree that provided a relatively comfortable spot.

"Juncosa, what the hell are you doing here?"

A familiar voice from the far end of the tree momentarily startled him. Bobby Vager occasionally sat at Craig's lunch table when he wasn't "eating lunch" at the Pit.

"I got a bottle of Southern Comfort and decided to have it for lunch," Craig said in a macho tone of voice.

"Good thinking—good thinking, Juncosa," said Bobby Vager. "Join the fun."

Anyone was accepted in the Pit area, providing he or she came to take a hit in one form or another. Craig's ticket to the Pit was the bottle of Southern Comfort he pulled out of the brown lunch bag.

"Look at this, guys, Juncosa's got Comfort!"

"Okay, man, I love Comfort."

Craig took a large swig and offered it around to the others. The intense burning sensation almost choked Craig but he suppressed the coughing sensation that overtook him. When it was returned to him, half the bottle had been consumed. The burning feeling had disappeared by then, and a pleasant, warm sensation began to swell in his stomach. The second, third, and fourth gulps went down much easier, and Craig began to enjoy the warm, mellow feeling that now permeated his entire body.

"This is a helluva lot better than that freakin' cafeteria, eh, Juncosa?" questioned Vager.

"Sure as hell is," answered Craig in a semi-stupor.

He wasn't used to drinking, and the mind-altering qualities of alcohol began to take effect almost immediately.

"This is fantastic shit, man. I never knew how great it was. I gotta getta hold of more of this shit."

Craig began to drunkenly laugh and giggle infectiously, and each of the other kids followed suit. The bottle of Southern Comfort was soon depleted, and Craig eagerly accepted a half-smoked joint from a pretty girl whom he found at his side after the laughter subsided.

"Thanks, baby. I needed that," said Craig as he voraciously sucked on the joint.

Once again, laughter broke out, and Craig decided then and there that this was the only way to spend a lunch hour. No one heard the distant peal of the school bell ending the fourth period, Craig's lunch period. The raucous laughter began to get louder and louder. A few of the boys broke into song, taking turns rapping. For the first time in many weeks, Craig completely forgot about the dilemma gnawing away at him.

"Hey, guys," called a relatively sober voice. "We're going to miss fifth period. We better start back."

"What the hell for?" said another more drunken voice.

Craig barely heard the two comments as he had struck up a delightful but rather inane conversation with Sue Vager. Sue was Bobby's sister and the girl who had slipped him the joint. She was a pretty girl, but hard-looking and not as well spoken as Craig would have liked her to be. She was extremely attractive to Craig at this point, though, and he was fast becoming an ardent admirer of Sue Ann Vager. They talked about teachers, other kids, and school in general. Most of their conversation was of a negative nature, as Sue seemed to be very critical of everything they discussed. Craig didn't care and found himself agreeing with almost everything she had to say.

A few of the kids began to filter out of the clearing and into the woods, presumably returning to school. Bobby Vager interrupted their conversation.

"Hey, sis, we better get the hell back to school. You, too, Juncosa!"

Craig turned to Bobby, who had grabbed his sister's arm and began pulling her away from him.

"Hold your horses," Craig said defiantly. "Maybe she doesn't want to go just yet."

Bobby looked puzzled as he retorted, "Listen, Juncosa, this is my kid sister and I don't want to see her get into any trouble. She's got a study hall now and …"

Craig rudely interrupted Bobby. "She's old enough to make her own decisions, so butt out!"

In Craig's drunkenness, he had become very belligerent and nasty. Vager was a good three inches taller and thirty pounds heavier than Craig, but Craig didn't give a damn.

"I said I want her to come back with me, Juncosa—got the message?"

Bobby's tone of voice had changed to a very threatening one, and Craig wisely backed off.

"I'll see you later about this, Juncosa," said Bobby in a voice full of challenge.

Throughout this entire scene, Sue Ann remained silent, observing Craig's behavior. Bobby grabbed his sister's arm again and began walking her toward the wooded area. He pushed her in front of him, turned toward Craig, and shook a raised fist at a very drunk Craig Juncosa.

Craig found himself alone in the Pit and suddenly became aware of the silence around him. His head began to throb slightly as he heavily sat on the fallen tree trunk and put his head between his knees. The throbbing became more intense, and Craig decided to try to walk it off. He headed in the direction of the school without thinking about the consequences of getting caught under the influence of alcohol. He heard the bell ending the fifth or sixth period. He wasn't sure which one and didn't really care as he swayed from side to side unsteadily and walked toward the red brick building. Once inside the school, he got lost in the hustle and bustle of the between-period corridors. He didn't know where he was and stopped for a minute to get his bearings.

"Hi, Craig." The sexy voice of Laura Donohue momentarily perked him up.

"Hey, Laura, how the hell are you?" He turned away quickly to avoid a meeting and staggered in the direction of his locker. The last thing he felt was a dull blow to the back of his neck.

When he awoke in the nurse's office, the first thing he heard was the voice of his father talking to the school nurse. Craig didn't budge as he attempted to listen to the muted conversation.

"He must have consumed an awful lot of liquor, Mr. Juncosa," said the nurse in an almost apologetic manner.

"When he was first carried into the office, the strong odor of alcohol almost knocked me over. He's been asleep for a good hour and a half. We tried getting a hold of you immediately, but we couldn't track you down until we called a neighbor."

The gruff voice of Mr. J reached Craig's ears. "What the hell did he drink, where did he get it, and when did he drink it?"

His father just couldn't believe what he was witnessing and hearing, and was firing irrational questions at the nurse.

"You're going to have to discuss that with Mr. Bacardi, sir," answered the nurse. "I'm just the nurse and my authority doesn't exceed the administration of first aid to students in need."

Mr. J calmed down for a minute and apologized for his abruptness.

"Where do I get a hold of a Mr. Ba .....?"

"Bacardi, sir," said the nurse. "He's across the hall in the main office."

Mr. J quickly exited the nurse's office and walked into the main office. The school secretary was on the phone, and he nervously tapped his finger on the long counter separating the office area from the visitor's section. The secretary gracefully placed the receiver down and looked up at his angry face.

"Can I help you, sir?" questioned the secretary softly.

"Yes, ma'am, I'd like to speak with Mr. Bacardo."

"That's Mr. Bacardi, sir," corrected the secretary. "Have a seat and I'll buzz him."

Mr. J was in no mood to take a seat and stood ominously overlooking the secretary dialing the assistant principal's interoffice code.

"Mr. Bacardi, there is a gentleman here who would like to speak with you," the secretary said in a calm, cool tone of voice.

She hung the phone up once again and looked up at the angry parent nervously waiting to lash into the school disciplinarian.

"Have a seat, Mr. Juncosa. Mr. Bacardi is busy right now in conference. He'll be with you as soon as possible.

She waited a good ten minutes before dialing Mr. Bacardi again. Then she invited him to follow her into Mr. Bacardi's office.

The throbbing in Craig's head was so intense; it forced him to sit up. He began rocking back and forth in a futile attempt to ease it. The nurse noticed him but deliberately ignored his attempts to alleviate the pain and discomfort. Suddenly, he made a dash for the washroom, slamming the door behind him. He hadn't eaten anything since the early morning and, after some of the residual alcohol emptied out, he had a severe attack of the dry heaves.

If he ever wanted to lie down and die, it was now. As he leaned over the commode, retching miserably, his legs became extremely weak and he fell to his knees, striking his head on the side of the commode. A large lump grew just above his temple, and he began to sob.

Craig didn't know it then, but the worst was yet to come. After a short and relatively mild conference with Mr. Bacardi, Mr. J returned to the nurse's office to pick up his suspended and deathly ill son. There was absolutely no compassion in his father's voice as he commanded Craig to get his things and meet him in the pickup truck parked outside the school entrance. He dragged himself to his locker, holding an ice pack to his head and reeking with the acid odor of vomit. His eyes were puffy and reddened from the liquor and crying.

Fortunately, it was during the eighth period and the corridors were empty. He grabbed his jacket and his notebook and randomly selected a few books to make it look good to his father, and began the long trudge down the corridor and out to the school parking lot. He felt like walking death as he opened the door of the pickup truck and slowly slid into the seat next to his infuriated father.

The uneasy silence that followed completely unnerved Craig as his father drove toward their home much faster than usual. Craig didn't know what to do or say, and wisely decided to maintain the silence. Mr. J stopped so suddenly in front of the Juncosa house that Craig almost slammed his still throbbing head into the windshield.

"Get the hell into that house and don't leave it until I get back."

Craig had barely stepped down off the truck when his father floored the pickup and sped off squealing the tires. Mr. J was usually a very conservative driver, and Craig knew his anger was uncontrollable and extremely intense. He began to sweat profusely as he entered his house and rushed to the bathroom, where another round of dry retching began. Craig now knew what it meant to be sick. His whole body seemed to be wracked with pain, and he literally fell into his bed, burying his head under his pillow, trying to block out the entire world around him. He fell into a deep, dream-filled sleep, occasionally twisting and turning his aching body. The grimace etched into his sleeping face revealed the anguish and fear that so filled his young heart.

The headache was unbearable as Craig was startled out of his drunken spell by the unusually hard slam of the front door. The entire house seemed to shake from its foundation as he grabbed his forehead with both hands and grimaced.

"Get your tail in here, Craig," the booming anger-filled voice of his father shouted.

Craig decided then and there that this was an extremely inopportune time to confront his father. The drop from his bedroom window was no more than eight feet. Once before when his parents were in the heat of an extremely bitter argument, he had exited from his bedroom window and found refuge on his favorite branch on the weeping willow. Craig raised the window, removed the storm screen, and lowered himself feet first into the soft bushes below the window. He could hear the hard knock on his door as he scampered across the empty lot next to his house and out to Route 52A.

He ran for two or three minutes along the gravel shoulder until his breath came in short, hard pants. Craig was perspiring profusely and his head felt as if it would explode. He stopped for a minute under a streetlight to wipe away the perspiration with his shirt. He felt a dull ache in the back of his neck that he hadn't noticed before and wondered why that would accompany a hangover. What he didn't know at the time was that Bobby Vager was responsible for that ache.

He had rabbit-punched Craig in the corridor as he was wandering aimlessly in a drunken stupor.

Craig decided to head for Melissa's apartment. She would be compassionate and understanding and he would be safe for the night.

When Craig arrived at Melissa's apartment, he paused outside the building to comb his hair. His head still throbbed, and he rotated it to try to work out the dull ache that continued to numb the back of his neck. As he walked toward the apartment door, he heard the sound of laughter coming from the living room. *Damn it! She has company*, thought Craig. *I can't go in there and face her friends.*

He hesitated a moment and then turned around and headed back toward Route 52A. Instinctively, he turned facing traffic and stuck his thumb out. He had decided to run away rather than confront his father, the school authorities, and ultimately Travis Graham and his cohorts. As Craig jumped into a large panel truck, he suddenly felt free, and a feeling of relief swept his entire body. Even his headache and dull neck pain seemed to disappear. He was on his way to anywhere.

"Where to, son?" said the middle-aged driver of the truck.

"How far you going, sir?" answered Craig.

"I'm going to Baltimore," said the driver.

As if he had rehearsed it, Craig began to fabricate a story that the driver found to be extremely credible. Craig knew Washington was just south of Baltimore and had convinced the man that he was going there to meet his older sister. When the man questioned him about a suitcase, he told him he had sent it ahead a few days earlier. Convinced that Craig was telling the truth, he ceased his questioning and told him to relax and enjoy the trip. Craig breathed a sigh of relief and settled back for the five-hour trip to Baltimore.

CHAPTER SEVEN
The Runaway

"Wake up, son. Come on, boy, wake up!"

Craig felt his upper body shaking as he came out of his deep sleep.

"You want something to eat, son? We're in Delaware."

Craig's eyes were small slits as he tried to focus in on the unfamiliar surroundings. The first thing he saw was a small neon diner sign with the R missing.

"Come on, boy. Let's get something to eat," urged the driver again.

"Okay. Sounds like a good idea," answered Craig.

His headache was gone, but he still felt that dull neck ache. The driver jumped out of the truck first and beckoned to Craig. Craig laboriously turned the door handle and stepped down off the truck.

"This is a good eating place even though it looks like a greasy spoon," said the driver.

"Whenever you see the other trucks parked by a diner, you know the food is decent. Truck drivers get to know all the good eating places."

Craig barely heard him as he followed the driver into the dimly lit diner. A pungent, meaty smell greeted his nostrils as they took seats at the counter and waited for service. A pudgy, middle-aged woman sauntered over to them and placed menus in front of them.

"Coffee, boys?" asked the waitress.

"Sounds good," said the driver.

"I'll have a cup, too," said Craig.

He wasn't a coffee drinker, but he thought he would act the part.

"You really went out like a light," said the driver inquisitively.

"Yeah," answered Craig. "I was really excited about making this trip and I hadn't slept too well the past few nights."

"Why are you hitchhiking, son?" asked the driver somewhat suspiciously.

"I figured I'd save some money," answered Craig.

The driver began to have some doubts about the validity of Craig's story but turned his attention to the hot, fresh cup of coffee that was placed before him. Craig bit into a grilled cheese sandwich and sipped his hot coffee. The coffee and food perked him up and he began to think more clearly about the events that landed him in a diner somewhere in Delaware. Occasionally, he would nod his head to acknowledge the fact that he was still listening to the driver, who was an incessant talker.

When he noticed money being exchanged by the cashier, his hands suddenly went to his pockets. Fortunately, he had three dollars tucked away in his wallet that he kept there for emergencies. He also had some loose change that his father had given him for lunch money that had remained unspent.

"You want anything else, kid?" questioned the driver. "Gotta get going soon. I have a schedule to meet."

"I'm ready when you are," Craig answered.

As Craig began to pull his wallet out, the driver grabbed his arm.

"You keep it son. You'll need it," the driver said knowingly. "I'll take care of this one."

Craig didn't resist the driver's offer, knowing that the lack of money would be a problem he would face very soon.

"Thanks a lot," said Craig gratefully.

The driver continued to be in a talkative mood as the truck pulled away from the diner, and Craig sat back and half-listened as he continued his saga. They drove for another hour before they came into the suburbs of Baltimore. During that hour, Craig was in intense thought about the next step in his runaway adventure. Where would he stay? What would he do? How would he eat? All of these unanswered questions continued to bounce around in his mind. His thoughts were suddenly interrupted by the driver's question.

"Where do you want to get off, son? This is the end of the line for me."

"Any place is fine," answered Craig.

"You better stay on the main highway," advised the driver. "You'll have a much better chance for a ride into Washington."

"You're right," answered Craig.

"When we get to the next rest area, I'll pull over and let you out."

Craig began to thank the driver for the ride and food as the truck pulled up to a small rest area.

"Good luck, son," said the driver. "The next time you run away from home, you'd better come prepared."

A smile flashed across his weathered face as Craig sheepishly thanked him again for the ride.

"So long, kid. Be careful," cautioned the driver as Craig stepped out of the truck and headed toward the small building that housed a rest room and some vending machines.

The truck sped off, and suddenly a lonely, scared feeling swept Craig's body. He shuddered as he entered the tiny building and headed for the men's room. A young couple was standing by one of the vending machines feeding change into it. After Craig had relieved himself, he looked in the mirror. The dark bags under his eyes revealed the stress and anxiety he had endured during this long day. It was 10:30 p.m. and here he was in some lonely rest area outside of Baltimore, Maryland.

He shuddered again as he exited the men's room and headed for a candy machine. The young couple was sitting on a long bench, munching on sandwiches they had retrieved from a vending machine. Craig fed some change into one of the machines and pushed the button. A Hershey bar fell out and he devoured it, suddenly feeling hunger pangs that had remained dormant up to this point. The couple was whispering to each other as Craig started on his second Hershey bar. He could hear a few words here and there, and when he heard "Washington" mentioned a few times, he decided to make his pitch.

"Excuse me, sir." Craig directed his request to the young man. "Are you going to Washington, DC?" he asked.

"Yes, we are. Why do you ask?" said the man in a slightly annoyed manner.

Craig detected the annoyance in his voice and changed his tone to a somewhat pleading one.

"I'm sorta stranded here and I need to get into Washington tonight," said Craig. "I certainly would appreciate a ride if you would accommodate me."

The young girl nodded to her partner, and he softened his tone as he responded.

"Okay, kid. We'll take you to Washington. We're eating something now. We'll be with you in a few minutes."

Craig thanked them both and went outside to wait for his next ride. The night air was chilly, and he fastened the top button of his jacket and constricted his body to maintain some body warmth. He watched the traffic zoom by the small rest area and wondered about his fate in the days to come. He was sure his father had contacted the police by now and that he was the object of an intense search by the small community. All of a sudden, the reality of his situation hit him squarely, and a few tears began to roll off his cheek. He began to feel sorry for himself and the predicament he found himself in. The thought of facing his father ever again was unbearable, and he resigned himself to the fact that to return home was no longer a viable alternative. He wiped away the moisture that continued to form on his cheeks and closed his eyes tightly in a futile attempt to stop the persistent tears. His thoughts were suddenly aborted by the abrupt command of the young man emerging from the rest area building.

"C'mon, kid, if you want a ride into DC," the shrill voice broke the silence of the night and Craig jumped to his feet, rubbed his wet eyes, and followed the couple to their waiting car.

"Hop in the back seat, kid, and watch out for the packages on the seat."

"Yes, sir," answered Craig obligingly.

The girl turned to Craig and smiled compassionately as the car screeched out onto the highway.

The drive to Washington was a relatively quiet one as the couple, for the most part, ignored their passenger and quietly discussed their trip. Craig was content to remain silent. He wasn't in the mood to answer questions or engage in banal conversation. His thoughts again began to focus on home and his father.

Running away isn't all that it is cut out to be, thought Craig. For the first time, a tinge of regret began to creep into Craig's cluttered mind.

Before he knew it, they were in Washington, DC, and for the first time since he had entered the car, the young driver spoke to Craig. "Where do you wanna get off?" he asked gruffly.

Craig looked out of the window and saw the Capitol building in the distance. He had seen it many times in pictures and in history books. It was something familiar to him in an area that was so unfamiliar and strange.

"Are you going anywhere near the Capitol?" he questioned.

"Passing right by it," answered the young man.

"That'll be fine," responded Craig.

The Capitol building was lit up in the night as Craig thanked the couple and waved as the car sped off. He looked around to get his bearings, and his eye caught the massive structure of the Capitol. He was impressed by it and stared at it for a long while, taking in all the wonder of it.

"Where to now?" Craig spoke to himself as a few people passed him on the sidewalk and glanced his way to look for the nonexistent listener.

The air was getting colder as the night hour became later and he became concerned about where he was going to spend the night. As he walked up Pennsylvania Avenue, a thought suddenly occurred to him. The back seat of an empty car would provide a relatively warm and comfortable bed for him for the night. The trick was to find one that was unlocked. He approached a line of cars and began to stealthily check the doors on each one as he passed by. All were locked and secured for the night, and his idea seemed to be doomed for failure.

Suddenly a stroke of luck! He found a large black Cadillac with the rear door unlocked. He scanned the area to see if anyone was looking and quickly jumped into the back seat, hastily slamming the car door behind him. He held his breath, momentarily ducking down between the seats to avoid being observed.

After he felt relatively certain that his entrance into the car had gone undetected, he slowly sat up and peered out of the windows, checking all sides for possible witnesses. He prayed that the car was parked for the night, stretched his body out to the extent possible, and closed his eyes, hoping to slip quickly into peaceful sleep. Traffic was light at that hour of the night and, with the exception of an occasional car humming by, it was quiet and relatively warm, in the car.

Sleep came, but it was fitful and nightmarish as he awoke several times abruptly and anxiously. With the exception of a grilled cheese sandwich and a Hershey Bar, Craig had not eaten anything substantial since the previous morning. Hunger pangs and an annoying stomachache kept him half-awake. He resigned himself to resting on the car seat for the remainder of the night. At the crack of dawn, he carefully slipped out of the car and walked briskly and, hopefully, inconspicuously away from it.

The gnawing hunger persisted and got worse by the minute. He turned into a side street and quickened his pace as he spotted a small luncheonette advertising bacon and eggs, coffee, and toast for $2.99. He entered the luncheonette and took a seat at the far corner of the counter.

"I'll have the breakfast special," said Craig as the young waitress took his order to the short order cook behind the screened enclosure.

Craig waited impatiently as the pleasant aroma of frying bacon and fresh toast reached him. He ate every scrap of food on the platter and scraped the residual egg off the plate with his fork. He was still famished but wisely decided to keep the remaining money he had left for another meal.

He couldn't afford a tip and surreptitiously slipped out of the luncheonette while the waitress was serving another customer to avoid the embarrassment.

Once out on the sidewalk, he hastily walked away from the luncheonette, wiping away some egg that had crusted around his mouth with his jacket sleeve. He had no idea of his location except that he was in the vicinity of the Capitol building. He decided to walk back toward the now familiar structure as the sidewalks began to crowd with the hustle of people on their way to work.

Craig felt less conspicuous and more comfortable as he walked along with the crowds. As he walked, he remembered that there were free tours of the Capitol conducted by government personnel. He remembered his social studies teacher telling the class about them and decided to spend his morning touring this magnificent government building.

As he approached the Capitol building, he noticed two uniformed policemen heading straight toward him. They appeared to be looking directly at him, and Craig tensed as he turned abruptly and crossed the street, away from the building and the patrolmen. After he crossed, he scurried away without looking back, expecting to be summoned by the voice of some legal authority. He was grateful when he felt safe enough to look back and saw no one following him.

He slowed his pace and breathed easily again, but decided to change his plans for the morning. He wondered whether he was being sought after by the authorities in Washington, DC. He knew his father had probably reported his absence to the police and that a search was likely taking place in and around his hometown. He finally decided that it was ridiculous to think that they would be on the lookout for him in DC. He walked for a few minutes before stopping to rest on a park bench. As he sat down, he noticed the tall, familiar-looking obelisk ahead of him. It was the Washington Monument, another historic landmark that he had seen so many times before in books, magazines, and TV. He rested for a half-hour, observing people as they passed by, wondering where they were all going in so much of a hurry. His sleep had been erratic and short the night before, and he began to doze off on the park bench, unaware that he had slipped down into a prone position on the bench.

"Hey, son, what are you doing sleeping in the middle of the day?"

Craig jumped up and found himself staring into the friendly face of a police officer.

"I'm going back. I promise, I'm going back," blurted Craig as the officer reached out to calm him down.

The friendly expression suddenly turned to a serious one as the police officer became aware of the anxiety and fear in Craig's voice.

"Calm down, son. Calm down," commanded the policeman. "Why aren't you in school?"

"I … I … I …" Craig couldn't think straight as he tried to clear his mind and provide some rational explanation for his truancy. "I'm off today," he blurted out.

The police officer realized he had a truant on his hands and beckoned Craig to follow him to a nearby police car that was parked by a government building.

"What school do you attend, son?" asked the policeman.

Craig knew he was caught and as he got into the police car, he blurted out the truth. When the officer realized he had a runaway on his hands, he radioed headquarters and drove off with a frightened, shaking young boy in the back seat.

"What ya' gonna do to me?" Craig questioned dolefully.

The young policeman calmly responded, "The first thing we're going to do is contact your parents, son. You're under age, and they will have to come for you. I have to release you to your parents' custody. By the way, why did you run away from home?" the officer asked inquisitively.

Craig trusted the officer and decided to confide in him. "I got drunk in school and my father had to come up to school to speak to the assistant principal, who suspended me. When I got home, I just couldn't face my father and on an impulse decided to run away from home."

The officer innocently asked him why he didn't approach his mother with the problem, and Craig sadly told him about their separation.

The police were very familiar with teenage runaway cases, and many were a direct result of broken marriage, family strife, etc. They were usually very sympathetic.

Craig felt much better when the officer led him into police headquarters and assured him that everything would be all right. The clerk, sitting at a desk in the corner, took all of the information and typed out a report. The young officer stood by with his arm over Craig's shoulder as he answered the numerous questions fired at him by the clerk. After the report was completed, the officer led Craig to the main desk and asked him if he wanted to make the phone call to his father.

Craig hesitated and decided it might be better if he spoke to his father first. As he dialed the area code, his hands began to shake and an empty feeling filled his stomach.

"Hello, Dad, this is Craig," his voice cracked in trepidation as he waited in anxious anticipation for a response.

"Where in hell are you? I've got the whole police force out looking for you. You'd better get your tail home on the double."

It was just what Craig expected, and he sighed despairingly.

"Let me speak to him," offered the police officer.

"Mr. Juncosa, this is Officer Bado from the Washington, DC, Police Department. That's right, sir, Washington, DC," he repeated. "We found your son very lonely and quite confused on a park bench here in Washington. We're all anxious to have him returned home as soon as possible."

Craig watched as Officer Bado nodded and noticed his expression change from a pleasant one to a serious and grave one. He knew his father was not pleasing the policeman.

"Yes, sir … yes, sir … okay, sir. Yes, sir, but we don't recommend that in this case. We would like you to be reunited as soon as possible and, most important, some acceptable agreement worked out between both of you. Okay, sir, if that's what you want, but we don't recommend it."

Craig was frightened as the officer slowly placed the phone down and looked ruefully at Craig.

"Your father refuses to come for you right now," said Officer Jerome Bado. "We'll have to place you in a children's shelter until you dad decides to come for you, Craig."

Craig bit his lip to keep the tears from rolling out, but he couldn't suppress them and he turned away to cry privately.

Officer Bado heard the tearful sighs and gently placed both hands on Craig's shoulders. He didn't say anything but wanted Craig to know that he cared. He did care and felt a deep empathy for Craig's dilemma.

The children's shelter in Washington, DC was a clean, well-supervised facility where many troubled kids passed through on their way to either rehabilitation or to further trouble, and in some cases, prison. Unfortunately, children were thrown together whether they were chronic truants or thieves and muggers. Craig was assigned to a room with another chronic truant runaway, along with a thirteen-year-old who had assaulted and mugged an elderly woman on the streets of Washington.

Jimmy, the runaway, immediately struck up a conversation with Craig, and they found that they shared many common problems. The other boy kept his distance and suspiciously eyed the newcomer and his newfound friend as they conversed.

"Why'd ya run away?" asked Jimmy.

"I got in trouble in school and was suspended, and I was afraid to face my ol' man," Craig answered gruffly.

He seldom referred to his father as his old man and it felt uncomfortable to do so, but he felt a certain pressure to use the vernacular he thought was expected from him.

Jimmy smiled inquisitively. "You mean you ran away just because you were suspended from school and you were afraid of your father? Man, I wish that was the reason I ran away. My father beats the hell outta me every night after he comes home drunk. My mother is so damn frustrated; she just stands by and cries. He hit me once too often and I decided to take off and get the hell away from that goddamn maniac. I figured before I kill him I'd better get outta that house and as far away as I could get. Man, I don't believe you ran away for that freakin' reason."

Craig listened incredulously to Jimmy's story and was embarrassed about revealing his reason for running away.

Craig looked over and saw the disheveled third occupant of the room leering at the two of them. He wanted to say something to him but for some reason couldn't muster up enough courage to introduce himself. The boy was a sorrowful-looking figure who appeared neglected, unkempt, and forlorn. Jimmy finally took the initiative and introduced Craig to the boy.

"Meet Clarence, friend, Clarence, this is Craig."

The two boys eyed each other, and Craig extended his hand in the direction of the boy. At first, a puzzled look crept onto Clarence's face. The look turned to a defiant one as he turned abruptly away from Craig's extended hand

and muttered something incomprehensible, acknowledging his gesture. Craig pulled his arm back, embarrassed, and stepped away clumsily and in a surprised manner. Jimmy tried to comfort him. "Once he gets to know you, he'll like you a lot better," Jimmy said encouragingly.

"I don't expect to be around here that long," said Craig apprehensively.

Jimmy smiled again as he went over to the simple, cot-like bed they provided for the occupants of the shelter. The room was cold and bare, with only the bare necessities. A clean white sink and small face mirror were tucked into one corner of the room. Three beds and a portable closet were the only items added to the austere room. Clean white towels and three small bars of institutional soap were placed near the sink. There was one window in the room that had a strange mesh like screen covering the outside of the window. Craig curiously walked to the window to examine the screen.

"What the hell is this?" queried Craig.

"This is a jail and those are the bars, my friend," responded Jimmy.

"You mean we're in jail?" Craig asked surprised.

"Well, it ain't no dance hall," Jimmy answered sarcastically.

Craig suddenly came to the realization that he was confined to this institution and that he was not free to come and go as he pleased. The feeling of being incarcerated was a new and somewhat terrifying experience for Craig.

He felt a wave of anxiety sweep his body and he began to break out in a cold sweat.

"They're a bunch of assholes in this place, kid. They don't give a shit about you or your troubles. They're a bunch of freakin' phonies."

The bitter, caustic voice of Clarence sent a chill up Craig's spine. He turned toward Clarence and obligingly nodded his head in agreement. Clarence waited for more of a response, and when it didn't come, he turned away from Craig, muttering obscenities about the shelter and everybody in it. Jimmy approached Craig from behind and quickly whispered into his ear,

"Cool it with this kid. He's a nut."

Craig walked to his cot and sat down heavily. He suddenly felt a profound longing for home. Even the severe reprimands he occasionally received from his father seemed to be mild compared to his predicament now.

"Chow time, c'mon, fellas, come and get it."

The voice of his assigned counselor reverberated throughout the floor as Craig raised his head and shook it, hoping to wake from a bad dream. But it wasn't' a dream—it was reality, and he was in a children's jail in Washington, DC.

As they followed the counselor toward the mess hall, other kids converged on them until some twenty of them entered the institutional mess hall together. Craig could hear curses and obscenities of every kind and he stayed as close to Jimmy as he possibly could.

Each boy grabbed a tray as they entered the dimly lit room and lined up in front of a counter similar to the one in his school cafeteria.

"Move your f—king ass, kid." A deep voice threateningly urged Craig to move forward in line.

Craig turned and looked up at a huge, handsome, rugged-looking black boy who stared belligerently at the fair-skinned blond boy in front of him.

"I said move it," the boy repeated angrily.

Craig obliged and almost knocked Jimmy over in the process.

"What the hell are you doing? Take it easy, huh?" Jimmy implored.

Craig apologized but stayed as close as he possibly could to Jimmy, hugging the rail separating the counter from the seating area. He breathed a sigh of relief when his tray was full, and he emerged from the line, quickly following Jimmy to a table in the corner of the room.

"I thought that kid behind me was going to bite my head off," he said nervously. "Did you hear what he said to me?"

"Just mind your own business and don't ruffle anybody's feathers and you'll be all right," answered Jimmy as they took their seats by a window.

Two other kids sat down opposite them and began devouring the steaming heaps of spaghetti on their trays. They ignored the two boys sitting opposite them, and Craig and Jimmy were pleased that they did.

They spotted Clarence sitting alone at a table in a far corner of the dining room. He was nursing the food on his tray and, from time to time, would glance up suspiciously as if he was being threatened by some unknown force hovering nearby. Craig looked sympathetically at him and thought about how lucky he really was. His father's strict ways and discipline seemed very mild and almost welcome to him now.

Jimmy nudged him and whispered in his ear.

"Look at that kid to your left. He looks like a cyclone hit him."

Craig turned his head as inconspicuously as possible and out of the corner of his eye saw the scarred and battered face of another boy preoccupied with his meal.

"Geez … what the hell could have happened to him?" he whispered back.

"Whatever it was, I certainly don't want to get in its way," Jimmy half jokingly responded.

Craig began to look around at all of the inmates of the shelter, and in a moment of disbelief, closed his eyes in an attempt to wish away the whole bizarre setting that lay before him.

"Anyone wishing to play basketball will meet outside the mess hall in fifteen minutes," the voice of one of the chief counselors rang out over the P.A. system.

"What do you say, Jimmy, you want to play some basketball?" asked Craig.

"Nah, I'm not a jock and I'm clumsy as hell," answered Jimmy. "You go ahead and play."

Craig decided some exercise might help him relax a little, and he enjoyed basketball.

"See ya later, Jimmy." Craig picked up his tray and emptied the refuse into a nearby trash barrel.

About twenty boys were standing in the corridor just outside the mess hall, waiting to play basketball. The only boy Craig recognized was the black boy who had intimidated him in the meal line. As Craig caught his eye, he looked away in order to avoid any further problems. He could feel the black boy's eyes penetrating him, and he moved behind another boy in an attempt to block his line of vision.

Craig had second thoughts about participating in a game of basketball with him, but decided it was foolish to be afraid. He followed the counselor to the small outdoor basketball court along with the other boys. Sides were chosen, and Craig found himself on a team opposing the boy. He would just stay out of his way and avoid any confrontation.

The game started, and he displayed some of his athletic prowess as he contributed significantly to his team's offensive play. A good fifteen minutes had passed, and some of the boys were tiring. Craig was in possession of the ball and drove up the middle in an attempt to make a layup shot. The black boy was blocking the middle, and Craig could not avoid the collision that occurred.

"You white son-of-a-bitch. I'll kill you for that."

Craig saw stars as he fell backward onto the court after receiving a solid punch on his fragile chin. He barely felt the kick that followed as he shook his head in a semi-conscious state. The other boys were holding the black boy, who was in a rage. Craig's legs felt like rubber as a few of his teammates lifted him to his feet and slowly walked him to the sidelines. He suddenly felt a sharp, shooting pain in his side and buckled momentarily, grimacing in pain.

"I'll get you later, you no good son-of-a-bitchin' white bastard."

The black boy's face was filled with hate as Craig lay on his back, legs up to his chest, clutching his side. Two guards grabbed the black boy and literally dragged him into the shelter.

Craig could hear the encouraging words of his teammates telling him to get up and shake it off. He was still groggy from the impact of the punch, and the soreness in his side was almost unbearable. Courageously, he attempted to stand on his feet but found his legs unable to hold his weight. He cautiously lowered himself to the ground again.

A stretcher was called for by a counselor, and he felt humiliated as all eyes were upon him as they carried him into the building and into the infirmary. The nurse was very gentle as she probed the areas that were painful, checking for broken bones. Relatively sure that no broken bones were evident; she led him to one of the cots in the office and directed him to lie down to rest and recuperate from his ordeal.

As he lay on the austere, cloth cot looking up at the off-white ceiling, he suddenly felt a strong compulsion to call Officer Bado and solicit his help in getting him out of this nightmare! Bado had left his name and number with Craig in an attempt to reassure him that he wasn't being abandoned. He knew that the boy was not an incorrigible or hardened juvenile and was reluctant to place him in the shelter in the first place.

There were certain designated times in the day when the boys had access to the phones and could make a limited number of monitored phone calls. The pain in his side began to ease, but his jaw was still extremely sore. He beckoned the nurse to his side and feebly asked if he could use the bathroom. The matronly nurse helped him to the bathroom and released his arm as he entered and closed the door behind him. As he sat on the commode, he began to rehearse the appeal he would make to Officer Bado the next morning. He had to convince the police officer to call his father again and convince him to make arrangements to release him and have him returned home.

"Are you okay?" questioned the nurse from outside the door.

"Yeah, I'll be right out," answered Craig, embarrassed.

Before leaving the bathroom, he looked in the small mirror hanging above the white enamel sink. What he saw looking back at him took him aback for a moment.

Dark circles rimmed his eyes, his hair was disheveled, and a red mark with a bluish tint blotched the left side of his face just above his chin. He washed his face and tried to comb his hair by repeatedly running his fingers through it. He opened his pants, tucked his shirt in, and headed for the door.

Emerging from the bathroom, he noticed the nurse walking toward him, holding out her hand to offer her support. Craig thanked her for the gesture and asked if he could leave to return to his room. She was reluctant to release him so soon, but finally acceded to his assurances that he was fine and did not need any further medical attention.

Jimmy was waiting anxiously by the door when Craig entered and headed for his bed.

"Are you okay?" asked Jimmy.

"Yeah, I'm fine. They had to take me to the nurse—it's procedure," answered Craig.

He didn't want to give the least impression that he was shook up by the experience.

Clarence was eyeing him curiously from his bed. He was amazed at how fast Craig had recuperated from the ordeal and suddenly developed a new respect for his roommate.

Jimmy noticed the grimace on Craig's face as he sat himself down on his bunk, trying desperately to conceal the sharp pain that shot through his side. He couldn't bend to remove his shoes. Instead, he used his opposite foot to slide off each shoe. He gingerly removed his shirt and took his pants off by dropping them to the floor and stepping out of them.

Jimmy realized the discomfort he was silently enduring and refrained from any further conversation with him. Craig appreciated his consideration as he slipped under the covers and quickly succumbed to much-needed sleep.

The morning came too quickly as the rays of sunshine streaming in through the window directly on his face hastened his awakening. Clarence and Jimmy were still sleeping as he quietly tiptoed to the bathroom. The pain in his side had diminished somewhat but was replaced by a severe soreness and tenderness. There were no clocks in the room, and he figured the time to be approximately 7:00 a.m. Phone calls could be made between 9:00 and 10:00 a.m., immediately following breakfast. Craig searched his pants pocket for the little slip of paper containing Officer Bado's number. He folded it and slipped it into his shirt pocket. The quiet of the early morning provided him with the opportunity to think clearly as he stood by the sunlit window. The morning traffic was beginning to get heavy.

Craig looked over at Jimmy, who was sprawled out on his back with his right leg hanging comfortably over the side of his bunk. His small, thin-lipped mouth and pug nose were rhythmically and slowly involved in the breathing process. Occasionally a sudden short snore would break the silence of his sleep and he would move abruptly to a seemingly more comfortable position. Craig scrutinized Jimmy's face and could almost see the inner scars that resulted from child abuse and neglect. He looked so innocent and incorruptible in his slumber. The harsh and abrasive voice that emanated from him seemed the antithesis of his boyishly cute countenance.

Clarence was rolled up into a tight, fetal position, with the covers almost completely covering his body. His position in sleep symbolically revealed a secret wish to return to his mother's womb.

Once again, moisture began to well up in his blue eyes as Craig turned away from the two sleeping roommates and held a clenched fist to his forehead in quiet despair. He thought about his father, his sister, Melissa, and his absentee mother. He tried to visualize his bedroom, the family room, and the comfortable chair in the living room. He longed for his special place in the weeping willow tree and pictured himself sitting snugly on his favorite branch looking over the traffic on Route 52A. The nostalgia that swept over him was bittersweet.

The harsh sound of the wake-up bell violently broke the serene silence of the morning, causing Craig to painfully jab the toothbrush into the side of his mouth. Clarence and Jimmy almost simultaneously pulled their blankets over their heads in a futile attempt to drown out the sound. The ringing continued for a good thirty seconds as Craig covered his ears and grimaced, impatiently waiting for the din to subside. When it finally stopped, a deep-voiced counselor announced the beginning of the new day and hurriedly repeated the brief morning invocation.

"Mornin', guys," whispered Craig as he replaced his toothbrush in its plastic holder.

"What's so Goddamn good about it?" retorted Jimmy in his inimitable abrasive style.

Clarence silently climbed out of his bed and headed for the john.

"I'm gonna make a phone call this morning to Officer Bado, Jimmy," said Craig. "I'm gonna ask him to please call my father and make another plea to him to get me out of this place and back home."

Jimmy listened politely as Craig continued to reveal his plans for the morning.

Craig completely forgot about his sore body as he devoured his breakfast and thought about the phone call he would make. He avoided any conversation with Jimmy and Clarence as he reviewed the plea over and over in his head.

It had to work, it just had to.

"All those who want to make any phone calls this morning, line up outside the lunchroom door in five minutes."

The voice over the PA system announcing morning phone privileges sent an exhilarating shock through Craig's body.

As he took his place in line, he rehearsed his plea again. By the time he dialed the Third Precinct's number, Craig had memorized his pitch to the police officer.

"Officer Bado, please." Craig waited in anxious anticipation for the mellow voice of Officer Bado.

"Hello." The exuberant and familiar voice of Bado brought a smile to Craig's face.

"Officer Bado, this is Craig Juncosa from the shelter."

"Hi, Craig. How's it going?" Bado immediately recognized the boy.

"Officer Bado, I want to go home. I know I made a mistake running away from home and being truant from school, but I realize my mistakes now and I'm ready to accept the punishment and amend my ways."

It sounded so rehearsed and practiced it brought a wry smile to Bado's face.

Craig continued, "Please call my father and relay my message to him. I know you can convince him to come for me."

Bado interrupted, "Listen, Craig, I will certainly try again, but I can't promise you he will respond to my suggestions. I will call him as soon as time permits. Right now, I have to attend to some paperwork, but as soon as I finish, I will try to contact him for you."

Bado could hear a large sigh of relief as Craig thanked him profusely for again interceding on his behalf. Misty-eyed and weak-kneed, Craig returned to his room and fell heavily onto his thin bed. You could hear the muffled cries coming from beneath the pillow that covered his head. No one was in the room, and the emotion-filled adolescent could no longer suppress the tears. They burst forward in almost torrential proportions as he removed the pillow and turned his head to breathe and allow the surge of tears to fully pour forth.

Officer Bado's call to Mr. J finally got through at eight that evening. Bado's exhortations, combined with Mr. J's growing guilt and fatherly instincts finally won out.

A young boy in distress would be coming home soon.

CHAPTER EIGHT
Home Sweet Home

Craig lingered in bed a little longer than usual, savoring the last remnants of sleep and warmth. The security of home so enveloped him that he felt a rush of pleasure and enjoyed the last few minutes nestled warmly under his covers.

The night before, Mr. J had remained silent from the time he picked Craig up at the train station until Craig sheepishly bade his father good night.

"We'll discuss this tomorrow, Craig. In the meantime, consider yourself grounded indefinitely."

The very stern voice of his father made Craig cringe as he retreated stealthily toward his room. He quickly shed his clothes and slid under the covers. Sleep was quick, deep, and welcomed.

The morning sun streamed through his window. It was Sunday, and Craig waited for the inevitable command from his father to "rise and shine." Mr. J was an avid churchgoer, and Craig reluctantly accompanied him to the nine thirty Mass every Sunday. Since the breakup, Mr. J visited the church several times a week to say small prayers for the restoration of his family. Craig would often find his father in deep thought, massaging his eyebrows in a meditative state. Craig would ask him if he was all right, and his father would answer with a slow nod of his head and mutter.

Craig never knew whether he was answering yes or no. What he did realize was that his father was extremely upset over the marital breakup and it was taking a toll on him.

Craig leaned over and glanced at his clock: 9:00 am and the familiar command to arise hadn't come yet. His father never let him sleep beyond 8:45 on Sunday mornings.

"Dad?" he squeaked out in a low voice.

No answer. Craig jumped out of bed and called again. No answer. He ran out of the bedroom and made a beeline for the kitchen—no sign of his father. *Maybe he is still sleeping*, he thought. He tiptoed toward the master bedroom. The door was ajar, and Craig peeked in.

"Dad?" he called again anxiously.

The bedroom was empty and the bed made. Craig ran to the front window and peered out to the driveway. The green pickup was parked in its usual spot, but the yellow VW was nowhere in sight. Craig's mind raced as he tried to figure out where his father had gone so early on a Sunday morning. He knew he was in for the confrontation of his life and had anticipated it from the time he had opened his eyes. His father's unusual behavior this morning unnerved Craig, and he began to worry.

An hour passed, and he sat nervously on the couch, still clad in his pajamas, waiting patiently for the sound of the VW in the driveway. His heart began to pound when he finally heard the very distinguishable sound of the VW. He peered out of the window and saw his father get out of the car. Another figure emerged from a car parked behind the VW. Craig didn't immediately recognize the hulking figure dressed in black walking behind his father toward the front door.

Father McClanahan was the young new priest who had recently joined the other priests at St. Vincent's Church. He was supposedly sent to work especially with the Catholic youth in Centerville. Craig had met him briefly in the beginning of the school year when they had a welcome party for the priest one Friday evening. He was a tall, handsome, appealing man with a deep, soft voice and a ready smile.

Craig ran into his room and put his robe on. He decided to remain there until he was beckoned by his father to come out. He knew instantly what he was in for as his father's stern voice finally commanded him to come into the living room. *I'm gonna be preached to*, thought Craig as he slowly headed for the living room.

"Good morning, Craig." Father McClanahan's smile flashed from ear to ear as he extended his hand in greeting. The priest's strong grip and warmth had a bit of a calming effect on him.

"Good morning, Father," answered Craig, his voice betraying the embarrassment he felt.

"Your dad invited me over to find out if I can be of any help to you, Craig," said Father McClanahan obligingly.

"I don't want to force you to talk if you don't want to, understand that.

"However, whenever someone runs away from home, there is usually something bothering him, and I thought I might be of help. Of course, your dad came to me on your behalf."

Craig's embarrassment finally revealed itself as a pinkish tint began to appear on his cheeks. He felt the warmth spreading and knew it was now evident to the priest and his father. He glanced over at his father, who was standing to the side, and could read his unspoken plea to accept the priest's counsel. He decided it would be in his best interest to consent.

Father McClanahan interrupted, "May I sit?"

"Sure, Father, have a seat," Mr. J said. "Can I get you a cup of coffee?"

"That sounds great," said Father McClanahan as he eased himself onto the couch.

Mr. J disappeared into the kitchen and was deliberately noisy to create the impression that he was leaving the two of them alone to converse freely. Craig felt uneasy with priests, and although Father McClanahan was easy to like, he still felt flustered and anxious. The priest broke the ice and began to discuss the upcoming football season with Craig. He wasn't particularly interested in football, but seized the opportunity to open the discussion on a light subject.

"It looks like the Giants might have a chance this year with the acquisition of those two defensive linemen from Atlanta, huh?"

Craig had no idea what he was talking about but nodded his agreement. The priest continued his analysis of the Giants' chances for a few minutes as Craig smiled and nodded at appropriate intervals. There was a long pause, and Father McClanahan's face suddenly turned serious as he prepared to change the subject.

"Your father is very concerned about you, Craig. He can't understand why you ran away from home, and he feels you might need someone to talk to. I was a young man once and can remember the pressures and problems that confronted me at that time. Sometimes it's good to talk it out with somebody other than your parents. I can be a lot more objective than your dad and might possibly be able to give you a few suggestions to help you work through your problems. I realize it's hard to verbalize the emotions that you feel, but sometimes it's good therapy to discuss them with someone."

Craig began to warm up to the amiable personality of the priest and felt a little more comfortable with him. However, his father's presence in the house gave him an uneasy feeling. The priest instinctively realized Craig's apprehensions.

"Suppose you come back to the rectory with me for a while, Craig," the priest suggested.

Craig immediately agreed, and Father McClanahan called Mr. J into the living room. "I'll take a rain check on that cup of coffee," said the priest. "Craig and I have decided to go back to the rectory, if that's okay with you."

"Sure, sure," replied Mr. J. "I've got a few things to attend to around the house. Give me a buzz when you're ready, Craig, and I'll pick you up."

The ride to the church rectory provided Craig with a few minutes to think about what he would say to Father McClanahan. The ride delayed any further discussion with Craig until they reached the austere-looking building that housed the priests of the parish. The priest decided to break the silence by discussing the weather. He wanted to maintain the dialogue that had begun in Craig's home.

The walk to the rectory from the parking lot was a long one, and Craig's level of anxiety began to rise as the thought of being alone with the priest began to unnerve him. What would he say and how probing would the priest's questions be? The deep, dark secret that lay behind the recent disruptions in his life still preyed tenaciously on his muddled mind. The recurring images and thoughts of the horrible events he witnessed wreaked havoc on his nerves, and whenever the compulsion to shed this burdensome secret surfaced, he grew frightened and tense.

Father McClanahan had a unique ability to get people to confide in him. He considered this God-given talent to be an extremely important quality necessary to competently fulfill his priestly duties. As Craig settled down into the comfortable leather recliner in Father McClanahan's office, that compulsion to tell all intensified. The simple and friendly-looking room provided the perfect setting for confessions. A wooden crucifix along with a large portrait of the Pope adorned the pastel blue wall above the priest's chair. A large, gilded Bible rested on the dark mahogany desk that the priest sat behind. The faint odor of incense permeated the small office, which had a strange, calming effect on Craig.

"Let's begin with a short prayer?" Father McClanahan suggested.

Craig instinctively bowed his head as the priest, with eyes closed and head raised, silently prayed for strength and help in dealing effectively with the young boy who sat across from him. The priest's eyes opened and he lowered his head, signaling to Craig an end to the prayer. Craig raised his head and looked pleadingly at the smiling priest.

Craig had decided to reveal his terrible secret to Father McClanahan, but with certain conditions. The priest was pleased when Craig initiated the dialogue.

"Father, if I confess something to you, will you promise me that you'll tell no one else."

Father McClanahan nodded approvingly and assured the boy of absolute confidentiality.

With surprising calm and composure, he described in detail the events of that fateful night and the subsequent confrontations with the boys who were responsible for the crime. A tightness began to develop in the priest's face and intensified as Craig recounted the experiences he encountered in the past weeks.

Father McClanahan was very familiar with the brutal and sickening details of the murder of Peter Stohler. He had celebrated the solemn funeral Mass dedicated to the dead boy and had delivered the brilliant and heartfelt eulogy for the bereaved parents and friends of the boy. If ever he wanted out from a situation during his years as a priest, it was now. Yet he felt a compelling responsibility to the adolescent who had been subjected to such intense shock and tragedy. A dull ache crept up his back and lodged itself in the back of his head. The priest grabbed his neck in a futile attempt to massage the pain away. It persisted and grew, and he struggled to organize his thoughts in preparation for the inevitable response the boy would be expecting at the conclusion of his confession.

There was no stopping Craig now as he blurted out all of his experiences, including the events of his runaway episode.

Father McClanahan wasn't expecting the abrupt end to Craig's story and sat dumbfounded for a few seconds. Craig eagerly awaited advice and words of wisdom. For a moment, the priest wished he were somewhere else and with somebody else, but quickly summoned his years of experience and education to deal with the situation at hand.

He cleared his throat, composed himself, and began what had to be an inspired response to the devastated youth who eagerly sought consolation. Father McClanahan slowly stood up and walked toward Craig. He tenderly placed his large hand on his shoulder and gently patted it as he began to speak.

"Craig, life is full of unexpected and sometimes overwhelming problems. God always gives us the strength we need to endure these problems. He never gives us more than we can handle, even though we sometimes think he's testing us to our breaking point. I fully understand the terrible dilemma facing you now, and although I can't feel what you're feeling, I understand and empathize. What I mean is, I'm trying to put myself in your place. As a priest, I am bound not to reveal the substance of your confession to anyone, and I will not do so. I wonder, however, if I can give you a few ideas and suggestions that might help you?"

The priest continued when Craig nodded in consent.

"What you witnessed was the worst of crimes—the taking of another's life. The boys who committed this crime will have to live with this for the rest of their lives. These poor souls will have a lifelong burden to endure, and sometimes this burden can be alleviated if they feel they are paying a price for their crimes. In other words, Craig, if … if they are caught and tried for their crimes, it sometimes helps them to bear this terrible burden."

Father McClanahan began to weigh his words carefully. The priest judiciously evaded this question for a while, believing it wise to further soften the boy before delivering this final piece of advice.

"God works in strange ways, and we sometimes never understand them. Right now, you feel like you're in a vise—damned if you do and damned if you don't. No one wants to snitch on his peers."

"Boy is that ever the truth!"

The priest had said the right thing, and Craig suddenly felt an increased confidence in Father McClanahan's counsel.

The priest continued, "The question you have to ask yourself, Craig, is whether what you witnessed is something that cannot go unpunished and unrevealed. The peer code you described to me earlier certainly places restrictions on you. To snitch on someone is one of the worst things a kid can do. I believe that is essentially what you told me."

Craig nodded again.

"However, is there ever a time when you might be doing someone a grave disservice if you don't snitch on him?"

"What d' ya mean, Father?" asked Craig. "What d' ya mean a grave disservice?"

"Well, let me give you an example of what I mean. You know that a certain friend is on heroin and is slowly killing himself and his family. He's stealing money to support his ever-increasing habit, and he looks sicker and sicker each time you see him. If he goes without help much longer, he will surely die or be arrested for theft. You have tried desperately to stop him, but to no avail. He just won't listen, and he has become so addicted to heroin that he is desperate. Your peer code tells you not to rat on him, but what will happen to him if you don't? Death, disgrace, jail, possibly murder. These are the options available if he continues on this self-destructive path."

Craig listened intently and began to understand Father McClanahan's intention.

"What would you do as a friend and person who cared for this poor soul?" The priest waited.

Craig lowered his head and began to quietly sob. Father McClanahan knew he had made his point and tried to console the boy, placing both hands on his lowered shoulders. The priest could feel his frail body jerking with each sob. He allowed Craig to cry it out, but remained in close contact to assure the boy of his support and understanding.

The thought of squealing to the police was unbearable to an adolescent who would have to face the consequences in school and in the community. How could he possibly continue to live in Centerville once he revealed his story to the police? What would the other kids say and do? He would be the focus of attention for months, maybe years. People would point at him and whisper. Questions would be fired at him by teachers, kids, neighbors. His life would drastically change. What would his father say and do?

A murmured and meek, "Help!" split the silence in the priest's office.

"Help me, Father. Please help me."

Craig's sobs turned to flowing tears as the full impact of what lay ahead of him became evident and dreadfully real. Father McClanahan opened one of the drawers to the mahogany desk and pulled out a box of tissue. He held out the box to Craig, who eagerly grasped a handful and began to dab his swollen and wet eyes. Silence reigned as Father McClanahan stood aside and allowed him to weep freely.

The tears released the pent-up frustrations and fears that he built up for so many weeks. The afternoon sun streamed through the lone window in the office.

Father McClanahan had no more to say. He felt a deep pity for the young boy who faced a most difficult dilemma, but he knew the decision had to be his. He had fulfilled his responsibility as a spiritual and moral counselor quite aptly, but he still felt a certain helplessness. Craig slowly lifted himself off the chair and headed for the office door.

"Bye, Father. Thanks for your help," Craig muttered feebly.

The priest grasped both of his arms and gently squeezed them. "How about a ride back to your house?"

"No thanks, Father," replied Craig. "I'd rather walk. I've got a lot to think about, and the walk will do me good."

The determination in Craig's voice was a positive sign to Father McClanahan and he stepped back to allow Craig to leave. The priest went to the window and watched Craig, head lowered, saunter off through the church courtyard. He whispered a small, simple prayer asking for strength for this young man who was faced with an incredibly difficult decision. He called Mr. Juncosa and advised him that Craig was on his way home.

CHAPTER NINE
High Anxiety

The headlines of the *Centerville Weekly* jolted Craig as he quickly retrieved the newspaper from his mailbox and ran to the front porch. He began to devour the story that had come to obsess him and had so altered his life.

Three Teens Charged in Boy's Death

MONROE – Three youths who have been suspects in the slaying of 13-year-old Peter Stohler of Centerville in October were indicted in the case yesterday.

Investigative sources said that the probe is continuing and that a possible fourth youth was involved. All three were questioned by police a week after Stohler's bruised body was found in a wooded area adjacent to the Calderwood Elementary School with strangulation marks on his neck. The sources said that Stohler came upon a gang of youths who were vandalizing a nearby house and they killed him to stop him from reporting them to police.

In a month and a half since the murder, police have repeatedly questioned youths in the neighborhood. Investigators who worked on the case said the toughest problem they had to overcome was the reluctance of neighborhood youths to give information to police about the suspects, their schoolmates. All three of the indicted youths attend Centerville Regional High School.

"Peer pressure was the major concern of several neighborhood youths who had information that might have helped police," one investigator said. "They were very reluctant to come forward, and their parents encouraged them to remain silent."

The parents and lawyers for the suspects charged police had illegally questioned them. In the six weeks since the murder, a Wood Street resident said that homicide detectives "were like part of the neighborhood" because they were around so much. However, no witnesses have come forward yet to substantiate the results of the intensive investigation.

A confession by one of the youths to police has become the basis for the indictments. District Attorney Charles Bowring urges anyone with information in the case to call a special police number.

Craig lowered the paper and momentarily rested his eyes and head against the porch column. His body was rigid and shaking as he returned to the newspaper article.

Several homicide detectives said that there was confusion in the October 6 questioning of the three youths because of a change in state law. The change allowed juveniles to be charged in adult courts for murder, but legal sources said that in September there were contradictory court rulings concerning a parent's right to be present during a juvenile's questioning by police. The issue was settled in late October, when the Appellate Division of the State Supreme Court reversed an Ocean County manslaughter case because a parent was refused permission to be present when her teenage son confessed.

Craig's head swirled as he glanced away from the article and tightly closed his eyes. Biting his lip, he suppressed the tears and gently closed the newspaper. It was an unusually warm day in November, and Craig was getting used to the indefinite grounding his father had imposed on him since his runaway return.

His father, in an attempt to fill Craig's idle time, had assigned him a number of odd jobs around the house on Saturdays. Today was garage clean-up day, however, the warm November sun was not conducive to work. Craig had decided to tell his father that he didn't feel well and had rested most of the day. Mr. J always succumbed to Craig when he complained of illness, and he knew it would work again.

His report card had arrived home, and all was discovered by his father: the failures, the inordinate number of absences, the negative comments by most of his teachers. His father's disappointment in him was manifested in a number of ways. He spoke only when absolutely necessary and, when he did, it was usually in a command or a question about his schoolwork or chores. In a way, Craig didn't mind the silent treatment he was getting. It gave him an opportunity to get his head together and reflect on the advice he had received from Father McClanahan.

Craig was biding his time in the hope that the police and the courts would try and convict the murders and he would be released from the awesome burden of having to snitch on other kids.

What preyed on his mind continuously, however, was the thought of Travis Graham, the fourth assailant, going scot-free. So far in the investigation, the so-called fourth suspect had not turned up and it appeared that the three indicted high school youths were not implicating him.

"How the hell are ya doin', Juncosa?"

The afternoon silence was broken by the raspy voice of Vinny Robinsky, who came lumbering up to the front porch.

"Hi, Vinny," replied Craig.

"Ya still grounded?"

"Yeah."

"Boy, you're really getting it good from your ol' man. How much longer do ya think it'll last?"

"I dunno, and I don't particularly care," replied Craig.

"Guess what, Craig? Vager was suspended from school for a week. Mr. Bacardi busted him for selling pot in the boys' room. Bet you're glad to hear that, huh?"

"Why the hell would I be so happy about that, Vinny?" replied Craig disgustedly.

"After he rabbit-punched you in the corridor! I'd be pissed off as hell."

"He's the kid who punched me? How did you find that out? Who was there when it happened?" Craig continued to fire questions at Vinny about the attack on him since the whole incident was a blur to him. Vinny filled him in on the details and Craig shook his head in disbelief.

"See you around, Craig. Are you going to Laura Donohue's party next week?"

"What party?"

Craig's interest was rekindled for a minute. He still felt something for Laura, and the sound of her name perked him up.

"Didn't ya hear about it? Her parents are goin' away and she's throwing a party. You probably can't go anyway with you bein' grounded and all. Sorry I brought it up. See ya."

Craig didn't answer as Vinny ran across the front lawn and headed down the street. Craig began to reflect on the brief relationship he had with Laura Donohue. Pleasant thoughts and memories helped to lift his depressed spirit. Laura had turned into a very pretty girl and she was very popular in school. Occasionally, she would approach him in the cafeteria and they would sit and playfully reminisce about their brief but intense courtship. At times, he felt she was condescending as she related how he was so love-struck that he did some "real stupid" things. He still enjoyed her company, and his heart still pounded a bit when he was with her.

When he asked his sister, Melissa, to interpret his feelings about Laura, she laughed and chalked it up to infatuation and puppy love. After that, he never again mentioned Laura's name and decided Melissa wasn't a very good confidant and advisor. Melissa had a steady boyfriend now and Craig saw very little of her. She still stopped in to visit from time to time, but her stays became short and abrupt.

"Hi, how's everything going? How's work, Dad? How's my little brother doing?" and then she was gone.

Mr. J had decided not to discuss Craig's poor showing in school with his daughter, and had even refrained from discussing the runaway incident with her. He didn't want to burden her with problems he had to deal with as a parent.

Instead, he looked to his close friend, Freddy, as a sounding board for his problems with his son. Freddy was a good listener and never passed judgment on Mr. J's handling of his son. Instead, he would nod in agreement, shake his head despairingly, and repeat what he knew Mr. J wanted to hear.

Craig's mother had not been informed of the runaway episode, and Mr. J decided to withhold that information from his estranged wife as long as possible. He knew she would probably blame him for his inability to provide proper supervision for Craig. He decided he didn't need the criticism from her. They were seeing each other occasionally and their relationship seemed to be steadily improving. Discussion of the children was a topic they both avoided in an attempt to keep their meetings conciliatory and promising. Instead, they laughed and reminisced about the good times they had and the funny things that happened to them. Mr. J would inform Craig whenever he saw his mother in an attempt to keep Craig's hopes alive that reconciliation was still possible.

Craig entered his room and put on a Billy Joel CD. His mother had introduced him to his music and he liked the lyrics to most of his songs. He removed his shoes, turned up the volume, and began to sing along:

"I don't need you to worry for me 'cause I'm all right. I don't want you to tell me it's time to come home. I don't care what you say anymore, this is my life. Go ahead with you own life and leave me alone …"

The words became very appropriate to Craig's mood, and he decided to play the song again. This time, he really got into the song and again began to sing loudly and dramatically.

The words "leave me alone, leave me alone" began to echo over and over again as Craig's frustration surfaced and spewed.

I gotta get it together. I just gotta get it together, he repeated over and over. *The decision is mine and I gotta make it myself. It's my life.*

CHAPTER TEN
The Victim

Peter Stohler was an itch. He was one of those kids who, for some unknown reason, grated on people's nerves. He was constantly appealing to Mr. Bacardi for help to get him out of jams. Mr. Bacardi was fed up with dealing with Peter's perennial problems with his peers. Peter's complaints ranged from being pushed and shoved in the corridor to being the victim of extortionists in the cafeteria.

Mr. Barcardi had recommended intense counseling to Peter's parents, who unequivocally denied that their son needed help. They were convinced it was the other kids who were responsible for their son's inability to relate positively to his peers.

"Peter is a good boy who always tries to do the right thing," Mr. Stohler would say. "The other kids and their warped parents are the ones who need help and counseling."

Mr. Bacardi was just plain tired of trying to deal with the Stohlers, and to the extent possible, he avoided contact with them. A day didn't go by when Peter didn't come up to him during the course of the school day with a fat lip, a bruised eye, or a red-blotched face with streaks of dried tears on his cheeks. To complicate matters, Peter wore braces and his orthodontist was kept busy straightening and repairing them after his many altercations and scuffles.

"What the hell is wrong with this school? Can't you people provide protection for my son from these animals that are constantly harassing him?" Mr. Stohler would threaten, condemn, accuse, and verbally attack the entire adult staff of the school on his many visits to Mr. Barcardi's office.

Mr. Barcardi would sit back in his swivel chair as the finger-waving father unleashed his wrath.

Peter would stand by with a very innocent and self-pitying look on his face. Mr. Bacardi knew that Peter instigated at least ninety percent of the confrontations he was involved in, but gave up in his attempts to convince Mr. Stohler of this fact. Instead, he played the humble public servant and assured Mr. Stohler that everything possible would be done to protect Peter from his peers.

Peter thought he could win Mr. Bacardi's favors if he reported on every kid who was violating a school rule or regulation.

Consequently, the Stohler boy's reputation as a snitch didn't help his relationship with the rest of the kids. Mr. Bacardi would tactfully advise Peter to mind his own business, but the adolescent never seemed to get the message.

Craig's only incident with Peter occurred in a gym class they shared. Peter was throwing a football to another student and Craig happened to be in the way. The ball bounced off his head, and for an instant Craig saw stars. Instead of apologizing, Peter began to chuckle mischievously as Craig tried to shake off the throbbing pain. When he discovered that Peter was taking it as a big joke, Craig saw red. The gym coach's quick intervention saved Peter from receiving yet another fat lip as he pulled the two boys apart and gently shoved them in opposite directions.

Craig was quick-tempered, but also quick to forgive and forget. The other kids urged him to challenge Peter to a fight and to call him out after school, but Craig didn't take the bait in spite of the constant prodding of his friends.

"The kid ain't worth getting in trouble for," was Craig's response. "Anyhow, I'd destroy him and probably would end up having to pay for a new set of braces," said Craig in a macho tone.

Craig's biggest fear, however, was the wrath of his father, who threatened to tan his hide if he got into trouble in school.

Peer pressure to fight was extremely strong and the risk of being branded as a chicken loomed large in Craig's mind. He withstood the pressure and eventually was able to convince the kids that he wasn't afraid of Stohler. He just didn't want the hassle with school authorities that would inevitably follow if he did battle with him.

Peter wisely avoided any further confrontation with Craig, knowing full well that the slightest provocation on his part would surely provide Craig with a perfect excuse to call him out.

Peter was a pampered young boy who had grown up smothered by his mother's protective wings. He had a serious case of asthma and on many occasions had come close to death when severe attacks came without warning. Mrs. Stohler had become paranoid about Peter's ailment, and her motherly instincts got the better of her as she desperately tried to monitor his every movement and action. This over-attention caused severe psychological problems for Peter, especially in his relations with other children.

His characteristics were manifested in an effeminate manner, and he was constantly chided by others. Fag and Pumpkin Eater were two of the favorite nicknames that Peter begrudgingly was forced to live with both in and out of school. Mr. Meyer had tried desperately to work with Peter and his parents to modify these characteristics but had failed to convince his parents of his need for intensive help and counseling. His parents' reluctance to agree to family counseling turned out to be catastrophic for Peter and them.

Peter lived a few blocks from Craig. They took the same school bus, and on many occasions Craig found himself sitting next to Peter. After the gym incident, Craig did everything in his power to avoid the Stohler boy and would even move out of his seat if by chance he found himself near Peter.

There had been a rash of vandalism and thefts in the neighborhood in the fall of that year, and the homeowners in the area had become extremely concerned that their home would be next. The police doubled their rounds at the urging of the local civic associations. Although there were no immediate suspects, the police had indicated that the nature of the thefts and acts of vandalism pointed to teenagers.

The continued problem finally led to semi-hysteria when the police were not able to apprehend the culprits. Neighborhood vigilante committees began to form. Mr. J was approached by the local civic association leader and was asked if he would be willing to patrol the neighborhood for an hour every other evening. Mr. J was a law-and-order man and was opposed to the vigilante concept. He explained his disapproval of vigilante groups to the leader, but expressed his sympathies and support for their cause.

Mr. Stohler was one of the vigilante leaders and, at a meeting of the civic association, called for more intense patrolling of the neighborhoods by homeowners. Mr. J again expressed his concern about the wisdom of such neighborhood action.

"What happens if there is a confrontation between suspects and one of us? What authority do we have to take the law into our own hands?"

Mr. Stohler responded by severely criticizing the police for their inability to apprehend the vandals and thieves, and referred to the American God-given right to protect life and property. A sense of despair and insecurity permeated the meeting as Mr. Stohler's emotional pitch appealed to the majority of fearful and frustrated homeowners. Mr. J could sense that in the people who crowded into the Calderwood Elementary School auditorium that evening. He decided to leave early, knowing that his more moderate and law-abiding approach was not going to prevail.

The incidents continued and became more frequent as more and more homes fell victim to the vandals and thieves. Vigilante committees roamed the streets at night on foot and in their cars. The police continued to urge the residents to leave the problem to them and assured them that the culprits would be apprehended. The people paid no attention to the pleas of the Fourth Precinct, and the search continued.

Peter Stohler pleaded with his father on that chilly October evening to let him accompany him on his evening vigil of the neighborhood. Mrs. Stohler was inalterably opposed to Peter becoming involved in this vigilante movement, but on that fateful evening, she succumbed to her son's pleading, and Mr. Stohler agreed to allow Peter to come along.

He decided to go on foot that night and told Peter to remain close to him as he began his rounds on the dimly lit streets. Peter was excited and shuddered at the thought of the adventurous trek through the neighborhood.

As they walked down a nearby dead-end street toward a cul-de-sac, Peter thought he saw a dark figure streaking across the side yard of a darkened house on the block. He immediately notified his father of his sighting.

Mr. Stohler stopped momentarily to allow his eyes to focus in toward the blackness of the home that Peter had pointed out to him. They remained perfectly still for a few minutes, with eyes and ears intense and searching. Mr. Stohler finally broke the silence by attributing the alleged sighting to Peter's vivid imagination. He continued to walk down toward the end of the street.

Peter asked if he could remain for a few minutes to further investigate his suspicions. His father reluctantly agreed, assured that Peter's excitement had gotten the best of his imagination. Peter nervously edged toward the darkened house. He crept up to the side of the house, surveying the area as he took each careful step. As he cautiously edged toward the rear of the house, he saw the all-night spotlights of Calderwood Elementary School lighting up the school grounds.

The school was approximately two hundred yards behind the house. A small beaten path through the wooded area led to the school grounds.

Suddenly, Peter tripped on an object that lie in his path and fell to the ground. He turned around to see what it was that caused his fall and caught sight of a portable TV laying face down on the lawn. Peter looked up toward the house and saw a shattered glass back door half ajar leading to the darkened house. His heart raced as he turned toward the street to alert his father to his discovery.

At that instant, he saw two figures streaking toward the path to the elementary school. Peter unthinkingly followed in pursuit. The light from the spotlights on the school penetrated the wooded area.

Peter increased his speed toward the figures emerging out of the wooded area and onto school grounds. He could now distinguish colors and saw a bright red shirt on one of the boys racing toward the school driveway. Peter was fast afoot and gained considerable ground on the culprits.

Suddenly, a figure shot out from the edge of the wooded area where Peter was emerging and grabbed his arm, spinning him around and against a lone tree guarding the entrance to the footpath.

"Travis, what are you …" Peter immediately recognized his assailant, who called out to the other boys.

"I've got the kid. Come on gimme a hand with him."

Three figures came bounding toward Peter and Travis, who continued to pin Peter against the oak tree.

"I know the kid. He's in my school," muttered Graham to the three older and larger boys, who huddled around Peter menacingly.

"Waste him," muttered the tallest of the boys. "He knows us now and we can't let him go."

Travis backed away for an instant and looked in a bewildered way at his fellow culprit.

"Waste him? What? Are you crazy?"

The look on Peter's face turned to terror as the large boy removed his belt and wrapped the end of it around his left hand. Travis's pleas went unheard as he backed farther away from the three boys who enveloped Peter and muffled his cries with a red bandana. Travis saw Peter's figure slump away from the tree and fall heavily to the ground. The boy with the belt coldly and deliberately retied his belt and moved away from the crumpled body that lay face down on the dirt path.

"Peter? Where are you, Peter?" the faint voice of Mr. Stohler broke the deathly silence of the moment and sent the four boys scurrying toward the rear of the school building.

Peter's body was found at 3:45 that morning by a neighbor who was helping the police search for the missing boy. The shocked and grief-stricken community was paralyzed. Neighbors and friends clustered together on the streets and at home, murmuring and weeping for the boy and his parents. Fathers took personal days from work and mothers ignored household chores as the terrified community mourned the death of the boy. The vigilante tactics of the community had resulted in a tragic and senseless death.

The next few days saw swarms of blue uniforms combing the wooded area behind the school for clues. There were no witnesses and no leads—or so thought the authorities and community. One boy, adjusting the chain on his bike unnoticed during the attack on Peter, had witnessed the macabre scene. Frozen with fear, he remained silent and still.

As the four boys scurried away from the murder scene, they caught sight of the lone figure sitting on his bike.

The spotlights on the school revealed his identity to Travis Graham as he raced away from the crime. For an instant, their eyes met and a cold chill shot up the cyclist's spine. Indeed there was a witness, and Travis Graham knew him. He was a schoolmate: Craig Andrew Juncosa.

CHAPTER ELEVEN
The Confession

Jerry consoled Craig in his own inimitable fashion, stroking and clasping the back of Craig's neck while muttering barely audible words of simple encouragement.

"Sooner or later, you gotta go to the police, Junky. You can't have this hangin' over your head forever."

Craig half listened to Jerry, being more content with the physical consolation than with words. Craig knew how concerned and deeply involved Jerry was in his dilemma, but for some inexplicable reason barely listened to Jerry's advice. Jerry's presence alone was enough of a natural tranquilizer to provide at least temporary relief from the terrible psychological burden that haunted Craig day in and day out.

"How about a Coke?" asked Jerry in a semi-enthusiastic voice.

He saw Craig was becoming consumed by his deep thoughts and was trying to bring him back to reality.

When Craig didn't answer, he knew he had temporarily lost him to his thoughts. He quietly strolled to the small radio on the kitchen cabinet and switched to a station playing soft, relaxing music. Words were no longer a useful device. Jerry concluded that the best he could do for the boy now was to simply sit with him and try to share some of his anguish.

Craig was rubbing his forehead with the palm of his hand, his face contorted and frowning. The soft, quiet music was the only thing that broke the morbid silence that existed between these two friends. Craig slowly lifted his head and peeked out at the wall clock from under his palm. It was 5:30 pm, and he knew he had to get home soon. Mr. J was expecting him for dinner and he didn't need any further chastisement from his father for being late.

"Gotta go, Jer," muttered Craig as he lifted himself from the kitchen chair.

"Thanks for listening, buddy. I really appreciate your help and friendship."

Jerry put his giant, freckled arm around Craig's shoulder and walked him to the door.

"Come on, I'll give you a lift home," said Jerry as he grabbed his keys to his car from the top of his small refrigerator.

Silence prevailed as Jerry drove Craig back to his house. His blank stare and extreme quiet deeply concerned Jerry. He began to hum a light tune, hoping to break the trance-like state Craig was in.

"Thanks a lot, Jer. See ya."

The solemn tone of Craig's voice made Jerry feel totally inadequate as Craig's confidant. Craig murmured his thanks again and headed for the front door.

Jerry drove slowly off, wishing he had more to offer in the way of advice and counsel for the troubled boy.

Heading straight for his room, Craig fell heavily face down on his bed. The tears began to flow again, and his muffled sobbing broke the solemn silence in his room. Mr. J was due any minute, and Craig knew he had to cry it out before his father arrived. The pressure was too unbearable. He needed the emotional release that crying provided.

The front door slammed heavily and shook the house as Mr. J entered.

"Craig? Are you home, son?"

"Yeah, Dad. I'm in my room changing. I'll be right out."

Craig tried to wipe the dried tear streaks on his cheeks with his undershirt. His eyes were reddened and puffed when he looked in the mirror. All the telltale signs of grief and terrible anguish covered his youthful face.

"How was school today?"

The booming voice of his father penetrated his frail body, and Craig mustered up a husky voice to answer, "Fine, Dad, just fine."

He wanted to get to the bathroom to wash his face before confronting his father. He opened his bedroom door and slipped quietly into the bathroom. He splashed cold water on his cheeks and eyes in hopes of clearing the signs of his grief. He combed his hair and tucked his shirt into his pants. His father would surely notice if he had to look at him, and Craig decided to remain in the bathroom until summoned by Mr. J. His hope to remain secluded in the bathroom was short lived as his father urged him out into the kitchen.

"Come on, son, give me a hand with dinner. I've got a KC meeting tonight and I haven't much time."

Craig reluctantly obeyed and walked slowly into the kitchen, trying to avoid a face-to-face greeting.

"Hi, Dad. How's it goin'? How was work today?"

Craig decided his best tactic was to keep his father preoccupied with answering questions. Mr. J's back was turned toward the stove as Craig entered the kitchen and began to set the table. His father obliged by concentrating on the pot of stew on the stove and answering Craig's questions.

"It's starting to get very cold and outside work will end soon," said Mr. J.

"Are you still working on that insurance building, Dad?" asked Craig.

"Yep, still on that building, but we'll have to move inside soon"

Craig kept firing questions at his father that he knew the answers to.

"Get me a beer, Craig, will ya? And pour some milk for yourself," commanded Mr. J.

Craig went to the refrigerator and pulled out a bottle of beer and the half-gallon of milk. He got two glasses from the cabinet and set them on the table along with the milk and beer. His father turned toward the table with the heated stew and their eyes met briefly. Craig shuddered momentarily, waiting for his father to comment on the way he looked. He hadn't noticed and Craig was temporarily relieved as they both sat at the table and began to eat dinner. The conversation continued during the course of the meal, and Craig did an excellent job of avoiding face-to-face discussion.

"Clean up, will ya, son?" Mr. J said as he wiped his mouth with a napkin and pushed back his chair. "I've gotta run. I'll be late for the K of C meeting and we're nominating new officers tonight."

"Sure thing, Dad. See you later."

Craig breathed a heavy sigh of relief as he heard the front door slam shut, and sat heavily on the recliner chair in his living room. He was tired from the emotional strain of the day and closed his eyes for a brief respite. He had homework to do but absolutely no motivation to tackle it. He slipped off into a deep sleep, and for a while was freed from the misery of his conscious state.

The doorbell jarred Craig out of his deep but fitful sleep.

He jumped out of the recliner, his heart pounding. When he realized it was the front door, the pounding subsided and Craig feebly responded to the visitor.

"Be right there."

Melissa stood at the doorway as Craig swung open the heavy front door.

"Hi, little brother. How are you?"

A faint but enthusiastic sisterly smile greeted him as Melissa brushed by Craig and entered the house. Craig was still in a stupor as his sister made the rounds of the rooms, checking things out as she usually did on her infrequent visits. She straightened pictures and moved knickknacks as she muttered something about the lack of a woman's touch in the house.

"Well, cat gotcha tongue, Craig? You haven't said a word yet," Melissa questioned as she continued her straightening routine.

"How's it going, sis?"

Craig's voice lacked the normal enthusiasm that Melissa was accustomed to, and she immediately detected the somber tone in her brother's voice.

"Are you okay, Craig? You sound like you just lost your best friend."

"I just woke up and I'm still half asleep," answered Craig in a more forceful voice.

"Where's Dad?" asked Melissa.

"He had to go to a K of C meeting tonight. He left about an hour ago."

Melissa finally stopped her room-to-room ritual and joined Craig in the family room. She sat heavily on the couch and sighed as she discovered her brother's disheveled appearance.

"You look like you just emerged from the eye of a cyclone," said Melissa, half-joking and half-serious.

"I was asleep," replied Craig, annoyed with his sister's constant criticism. "Lay off me, will ya, sis," Craig continued.

"I was just kidding," assured Melissa. "Don't get so uptight. Something is bugging you and I don't know what it is."

Melissa's sisterly instincts told her that her brother wasn't acting like himself lately. Even though her visits were brief and infrequent, she detected something different and out of character about Craig, and that concerned and puzzled her.

Craig immediately changed the subject and began to question Melissa about her new life. He was very good at changing the focus of attention as a diversionary tactic. Melissa took the bait and began to relive her busy week.

She was long-winded and loved to expound on the details of her daily experiences and problems. Craig settled back in his chair and nodded obligingly as Melissa chattered on. He would interject occasionally to reassure her he was attentive and interested.

Her saga seemed endless to Craig and his mind began to wander away from his sister's words. The urge to reveal his deep, dark secret to his sister began to emerge again. He began to weigh the pros and cons of letting his sister become one of the select few who shared his dilemma. *She'll blab to Dad for sure*, thought Craig. *On the other hand, if I get her to promise not to, she probably won't.*

She had kept secrets in the past, but this was serious and she might break her promise.

"You haven't heard a word I've said." Melissa's sharp retort jolted Craig. "What the heck is wrong with you, Craig? You always seem so lost in your thoughts."

"Hold it, Liss. Just hold it for a second." The tone in Craig's voice startled her.

"Liss, if you knew what I've been living with, you would understand why I'm so uptight and down. It ain't easy, damn it. It ain't easy."

Craig suddenly began to cry, and his sister rushed to his side to show her sibling support for her grief-stricken brother.

"Craig, oh, Craig, what the heck is bothering you? Tell me. I'll try to help you. Is it a girl, huh? Come on, you can tell me. What's the problem?"

The tears flowed freely as Craig buried his head in his lap and Melissa embraced him tightly. Wisely detecting the severity of his grief, she stopped talking and just held him and allowed him to cry it out. As the tears subsided, he began to shake uncontrollably. Melissa held him tightly and quietly began to whisper simple, consoling words in a desperate attempt to calm him down.

"Please, Craig, we can work it out. Believe me, we can work it out. Nothing can be that bad."

Craig slowly raised his head to reveal his swollen eyes. His voice cracked as he began to recount the horrible scene he witnessed. Melissa's face tightened and contorted as the full impact of Craig's situation hit her.

"My God, Craig, why didn't you report it to the police immediately? Why have you waited so long? You're talking about murder, do you realize that?"

Craig slumped back in complete despair. Instead of an empathetic ear, he was being preached to by his big sister. A strange feeling of ambivalence overcame Craig as his sister continued to nervously and unceasingly chastise him. Her words fell on deaf ears as Craig suddenly felt lighter and more peaceful. He had released a terrible, heavy burden that had weighed him down for weeks and weeks. The critical barrage from Melissa came as a strange and sudden relief and an almost joyous feeling permeated his body.

He was jolted back to reality when Melissa suddenly became silent and slumped back into the couch. Craig looked over at his sister and saw the frightened look in her blue eyes. He turned toward her, placing his hand on her arms.

"Liss," he began in a strangely composed tone of voice. "You've gotta promise me you won't tell anyone about this—you gotta promise."

Melissa felt his grip tighten as he made his plea for her silence.

"Let me work this out myself," he continued.

"I realize how serious this is and I gotta think it out and make the decision myself. Please don't tell Dad—please! He couldn't handle it now and it's just too much for him to take. He'll fall apart. He and Mom have been seeing a lot of each other lately, and I don't want to say anything that might … might, you know what I mean."

Melissa sat up and tried desperately to compose herself. The shock had so unsettled her that she felt faint, and a nauseated feeling crept into her stomach. Melissa was seldom at a loss for words, but the moment at hand rendered her speechless.

Craig became concerned with the unusual silence that gripped his sister.

"Are you all right, Liss?" He saw a pallor in her face that convinced him that she was extremely distraught. "Hey, sis, take it easy. It ain't the end of the world. I didn't do it; I was just a witness to it."

Melissa continued to stare blankly at the wall. The incredulity of it all was too much for her to take.

"Hey, listen, I would never have told you if I thought it would do this to you," Craig said apologetically.

Melissa excused herself and walked quickly toward the bathroom. Although it was only a few minutes, it seemed like an hour before Melissa came back into the family room. She seemed much more composed and the color had returned to her face. She cleared her voice and, in a relatively calm tone, began to advise Craig.

"You must realize how very serious this whole thing is. It's not like some small incident that happens in school with your friends. I realize the fix you're in, but you must understand what your responsibility is. A life has been taken by some ruthless kids. It's not like you're snitching on some kid who threw food in the cafeteria, Craig. You have a responsibility to Peter's parents and to society to go to the police."

"I never liked the damn kid, anyhow," screamed Craig. "He was a real faggot. Why the hell should I get involved?"

Melissa just looked at her kid brother as he tried desperately to rationalize what he knew was wrong. Underneath the anger, Melissa could sense her brother's real feelings. She knew Craig well. She knew that he couldn't justify to himself what he was saying. Wisely, she refrained from continuing the argument and tightly embraced him.

"Liss, what do I do? Please tell me. What do I do?" The pleading tone of Craig's voice filled her with deep sorrow and sympathy.

"Do what you think is right, Craig. Just do what you think is right."

They stood and embraced for a long while until her arms began to ache. As she relaxed her grip, Craig tightened his. She knew her brother had listened. She hoped he would do the right thing.

The sound of the phone sent a shock through both of them, and Melissa momentarily lost her breath. Craig quickly grabbed the phone and put it to his ear. He paused momentarily and, in a meek voice, greeted the caller.

"Hello?"

Melissa tensed up and held her breath as she waited to find out who it was.

"Oh, hi, Dad." Craig's voice returned to normal and Melissa exhaled in relief. "Uh-huh, uh-huh. Okay. Uh-huh, okay. See you later, Dad."

Craig hung up and for the first time in a long while a barely detectable smile crept onto his handsomely fair face.

"This is ridiculous. Every time the phone rings, my heart stops," said Craig.

Melissa smiled faintly in an attempt to ease the tension of the moment. "Yeah. I can imagine. That's why you've gotta unload this damn thing."

CHAPTER TWELVE
The Party

Flurries of snow began to fall outside. It was December, and the Christmas lights and the festiveness of the holiday season began to appear throughout Centerville. In years past, the Christmas season always filled Craig with joy and excitement. It was a time when even his father's rigid manner relaxed, and Craig always found it easier to talk to him during the holiday season. He became more genteel and soft. Craig would always take advantage of his father's vulnerability and ask for a lot of things he wouldn't normally ask for.

Vinny had reminded him again in school about Laura Donohue's party, and Craig began to feel an urge to go. Laura seemed unattainable now that she was becoming so womanly, but Craig still felt an excitement when he was with her and during the infrequent times when they spoke to each other. She was no longer dating Travis Graham, and Craig had heard that she was going with a high school junior.

It was a Wednesday, and Laura's party was Friday night. As Craig dressed after his gym class, he began to conjure up some ways to convince his father to let him go to the party. Craig jogged toward his school locker but slowed to a walk when he spotted Mr. Bacardi standing at an intersection in the corridor.

"How's it going, Craig?" asked Mr. Bacardi as Craig approached him.

"Fine, thanks," replied Craig as he continued to walk past the assistant principal.

Mr. Bacardi reached out and gently slapped his back as Craig turned the corner and picked up his pace. Mr. Bacardi was always friendly, even after dishing out punishment to students. Craig wondered about that.

His damn locker was stuck again as he pulled and pried on it. Some wise guy had vandalized his locker and since then he had trouble opening it.

Craig wanted to get out to the buses as quickly as possible so he could get a seat in the back of the bus with Vinny. Everybody wanted to sit in the back of the bus and there was a mad rush to get on first. Usually the smokers found refuge in the back and could get a few puffs in undetected. Craig didn't smoke but wanted to talk to Vinny, who always seemed to get a seat in the back, even though he didn't smoke either.

Vinny had gained even more weight and now waddled when he walked. Craig caught sight of Vinny and Roland walking side by side as he began to trot toward the circle drive area where the busses waited for the students.

"Hi, Vin," shouted Craig. "Wait up."

Vinny turned his pudgy head around and caught sight of Craig weaving his way through the crowd of students evacuating the building.

"Hey, Juncosa, what's up?" asked Vinny as Craig caught up to them.

Roland stood by as the two boys met and slapped hands.

"I want talk to you about the party Friday night," said Craig enthusiastically. "I'm gonna try to get my father to let me go. You did say it was an open house, didn't ya?"

"Yeah, it is," replied Vinny surprised. "I thought you said you didn't want go, man."

"I changed my mind, okay? Is it okay to change your mind?"

Vinny laughed as they reached the loading area and got a place at the front of the line. Roland took his place behind Craig, and Vinny listened attentively as they continued discussing the party.

"Who's goin'? Do you know?" asked Craig.

"What the hell's the difference who's goin'?" replied Vinny. "I'm gonna be there, and that's all that counts."

Vinny chuckled as he boarded the bus and made a beeline for the back seat.

The ride home was, as usual, a bumpy one, but for Craig it was an unusually bumpy ride. He wasn't used to the back of the bus, and his head began to throb from a combination of cigarette smoke and the jarring ride.

"How the hell can you sit back here all the time, Vinny?" asked Craig, annoyed.

"You get used to it after a while," replied Vinny. "Say, ya think your ol' man will really let you go to the party?"

"Yeah, I'll be there, no sweat."

Roland, who was sitting in front of Craig, turned around and offered a ride to the two boys.

"Hey, guys, my mother said she'll drive me over. If ya want, I'll ask her if she can pick you guys up, too."

"Lemme make sure I can go first, Roland," answered Craig.

"I gotta get my father in a good mood sometime between today and Friday. I'll offer to do some chore that has to be done around the house, and then I'll hit him with the question. Good idea, huh?"

The bus was approaching Craig's block, and he stood up. Roland quickly slipped into his seat next to Vinny as Craig turned to bid his friends farewell.

"See you guys tomorrow. Wish me luck."

When Craig stepped off the bus, he stood up on the curb for a second. As the bus resumed its route, he saw Vinny's pudgy nose pressed against the window at the back of the bus with two thumbs pointing up. Craig smiled as he acknowledged Vinny's encouragement and responded by raising his hand and shaking a fist.

He ran into his house and made a beeline for his bedroom. Throwing his books and jacket on his bed, he ran to the hall closet and pulled out the vacuum cleaner. He plugged it in and set it up for the right moment. He looked at the clock and figured he had about an hour before his father would arrive home from work. He had some math homework to do and decided to sit in the family room and do the ten problems assigned. Craig hadn't had much fun for weeks. As a matter of fact, it had been a nightmare and he was ready to explode. A loud, raucous party was just the kind of therapy he needed and, by hook or by crook, he was going to get his father's permission to go. He was still grounded, Mr. J was a man of his word, and when he said something, he meant it.

Craig's confession to Melissa had given him a lift and the needed strength to continue functioning as an adolescent should. He still had not made a decision, but his sister's encouraging words reinforced him temporarily, and he needed to get out with the kids for a while.

The rattle of the pickup truck in the driveway signaled Craig to action. He jumped up, closed his math book and loose-leaf, and ran to the vacuum cleaner. He switched it on and began vigorously vacuuming the carpet. Mr. J trudged through the front door with his lunch box under his arm. His nose and cheeks were red from the day's outdoor work. The whir of the vacuum cleaner caught his ears as he set his lunch box down and removed his heavy down work jacket. Craig continued vacuuming, not acknowledging his father's homecoming. He wanted him to see him so engrossed in his chore that he would be favorably impressed. It worked.

"Good to see you takin' the initiative, son," Mr. J raised his voice over the whir of the vacuum cleaner.

Craig looked up in a false surprise and welcomed his father home.

"Hi, Dad! How was work?" His ebullient greeting pleased Mr. J, and he patted Craig on the head as he headed for the bathroom.

Craig smiled sheepishly as he continued his work. When he heard the toilet flush, he increased the vigor of his chore. Mr. J was pleased as punch to see his son take on a responsibility so enthusiastically. He decided to let Craig finish up before asking him the routine questions about school. Craig continued vacuuming for another five minutes while carefully planning his plea for leniency.

Mr. J was standing at the stove when the sound of the vacuum stopped. Craig carefully wound up the vacuum cord and gently set it back in the closet.

"How was school, Craig?" the inevitable question came.

Craig enthusiastically replied, "Great, Dad. I got an A on a social studies quiz, and Mr. Kubek told me how much better I was doing lately." A little white lie couldn't hurt. His father beamed at the good news, and Craig knew the moment was right to pop the question.

"Say, Dad, ya think I could go out Friday night with Vinny and Roland?"

Craig saw the lines in Mr. J's face grow more pronounced, and he knew he was in for a battle.

"You're grounded, Craig, you know that," his father answered emphatically.

Craig detected a slight softening in his father's tone.

"I know, Dad, but I've been in for weeks and I'm losing touch with all my friends. I'll be home early, I promise."

Mr. J paused for a moment to digest Craig's appeal. He usually didn't concede to begging after he had made a decision, but Craig had planned well and caught his father in a vulnerable state.

"Well, you know I mean what I say, Craig, and you really botched things up. Not only that, but your grades have improved since you've been grounded, and I hate like heck to give in now when things are improving at school."

Craig had the response all planned.

"Mr. Kubek was discussing the need for young people to socialize with their friends. He said it's important that kids associate with other kids as much as possible. He said it's not healthy for kids to stay alone too much."

Mr. J smiled slightly as he looked over at Craig knowingly. "I'll bet he said that today. That's a good line, son. So good that I'll make an exception this one time."

"Does that mean I can go, Dad?" Craig sheepishly smiled as he turned around and headed for the refrigerator. "Wanna beer tonight, Dad?"

Mr. J nodded, and Craig's hands shook with joy as he pulled out the half-gallon of milk and a bottle of beer. Dinner was unusually good as father and son sat down to a meal of sirloin steak, baked potatoes, and sautéed green beans.

The cafeteria was alive with excitement. It was Friday and the kids were anxiously looking forward to a fun-filled weekend. Craig was sitting with Vinny, Roland, and a few of his other friends munching on a peanut butter and jelly sandwich. Vinny had just gone through two scooter pies and was starting on his third meatloaf sandwich.

"How the hell can you eat so much?" asked Joey Benavenga.

Vinny looked over at his antagonist and gestured accordingly. Benavenga was a burnout, but Craig liked him. He was a nice kid with a lot of problems at home, and Craig understood why he was hooked on pot. Benavenga was a frequent guest in the Pit along with Bobby Vager and Travis Graham, but he chose to hang around Vinny, Craig, Roland, and the others in school.

Vinny ignored his teasers and returned to the business of eating.

Roland piped up. "You guys need a ride tonight? My mother said she'll drive."

Vinny and Craig looked at each other and accepted Roland's offer.

"Hey, Roland, get me a milk, will ya?" ordered Vinny.

Roland obligingly jumped up and strode toward the milk line. Ms. Healey, the cafeteria aide, felt sorry for Roland. She didn't interfere but on occasion would ask

Roland why he let himself be used all the time. He always gave her the same answer.

"They're my friends and I can do what I please."

She would shake her head and continue her rounds.

Craig didn't like it either and never took advantage of Roland.

"Why the hell do you send him for your food, Vinny? That's cruel, man."

"Aw, come on, Juncosa. I like the kid, and anyway I'm one of the few kids who hang around with him."

Craig still didn't like the idea of using the kid, but decided not to get involved any further. Roland returned with the milk, and Vinny thanked him. Roland sat down satisfied that he could be of help to a friend.

He was a frail boy who was rather sickly looking and very susceptible to respiratory infections. He missed a lot of school days and consequently had a hard time keeping up with his studies. He had a good heart and was well-liked by the other kids but always taken for granted. He was content to stay on the fringes of the group. He got his recognition by fetching food, books, etc. for his friends.

"Hey, Robinsky, going' to the party tonight?"

The familiar raspy voice of Travis Graham echoed in Craig's ears. He looked up to see Graham grabbing Vinny's arm and pulling it up to his mouth in an attempt to eat a piece of Vinny's pie. Vinny pulled his arm away from Travis, muttering obscenities.

"Selfish bastard. You won't even give me a bite of your pie."

"Screw you," Vinny replied, and Travis repeated his question.

"Goin' to Donohue's party tonight, huh?"

Vinny nodded as he took a long drink of his milk. Craig deliberately turned away from Travis and began striking up a conversation with a kid next to him. Suddenly, he felt a knee slam into his side, and he grimaced in pain. When the pain subsided, he looked up and saw Travis walking away, laughing hysterically. A flush of anger gripped Craig as he jumped out of his chair. Vinny grabbed him before he could move away from the table and gently restrained him.

"Don't take him on, Craig. He'll murder you. It ain't worth it."

Craig's first instinct was to pull away from Vinny's grip, but when Vinny reminded him of the trouble he would be in if he fought Travis, he reluctantly sat down, his face hot and flushed with anger.

"That SOB will get his someday."

Vinny agreed with a nod of his head and tried to change the subject.

"Sue Vager is going to the party tonight. You like her, dontcha, Junk?"

Craig didn't answer as the pounding of his heart responded with a burst of adrenaline that shot through his body. Vinny detected the burning anger in Craig and continued in his attempts to divert him.

"Somebody was telling me that Laura Donohue has a real class basement with strobe lights, a bar, and a four thousand dollar sound system. Her old man must be loaded, huh, Craig?"

Craig wasn't listening. He was engrossed in plans of vengeance. He was suddenly convinced more than ever to blow the whistle on Travis Graham. He felt the soreness in his side as he got up in response to the bell signaling the end of his lunch period. As he walked to his next class, he was completely unaware of the other kids in the hall and bumped into a number of them on his way to his English class.

Craig was lost in angry thought as he took his seat behind Sue Vager. It seemed as though Travis Graham was deliberately provoking him. He was confused. Why would a kid that he had so much on prod him into turning him in to the police? He was the only one who could attest to the fact that Travis had opposed the ruthless attack on Stohler. He could save him from a murder rap. What the hell made that kid tick? The bell jolted Craig out of his thoughts as his English teacher took the cue and called the class to order.

It was a long afternoon, and when his gym class came to an end, Craig was relieved. He had promised Jerry that he would stop in to see him at Gabor's before going home. Jerry was keeping close tabs on Craig, knowing the state of mind he was in. He didn't feel like waiting around for the late bus, and was undecided about visiting Jerry.

He wanted to see him but finally decided to make it another day. He met Vinny on the way to his bus.

"You cooled down yet?" asked Vinny as they headed for the loading area.

"Yeah—the hell with him. I'm not gonna let that bastard get to me."

"That's the attitude, man. He ain't worth it."

As the boys entered the bus, Craig decided to sit up front to avoid the smoke and bumps that came with a seat in the back.

"See ya tonight, Vin. What time is Roland's mother picking us up?"

"Eight o'clock," answered Vinny as he strode to the back. Roland followed behind and confirmed the pickup time.

The bus ride home provided Craig with some time alone to think about the near confrontation with Travis. The kid was rotten to the core, and Craig felt a hatred that he rarely felt.

Craig disembarked from the bus and gave a feeble wave to Vinny and Roland as he walked slowly toward his house. The pickup truck was in the driveway. Mr. J had come home early. He was glad that he had decided not to visit Jerry. It saved him an explanation as to why he was so late coming home from school. When he entered the house, a strange silence met him. The usual noise coming from the kitchen as his father hurriedly prepared dinner was missing.

"Dad?" he called quietly and waited for a response. "Dad?" he said a little louder, but still no answer.

He headed for the bedroom and saw the door to his father's bedroom was closed but slightly ajar. He carefully and slowly opened the door and saw his father sprawled out, asleep. It was highly unusual for Mr. J to sleep in the afternoon and Craig became concerned. Mr. J moved slightly, reassuring Craig that he was indeed sleeping.

He cautiously closed the door and tiptoed into his bedroom. He didn't turn on his iPod or any music, but rather quietly set his books down and removed his jacket. He looked over at his alarm clock to check the time: 4:30 p.m. Craig wanted to shower and wash his hair before going to the party but decided to postpone his plans until his father got up. As he opened his closed door, he caught sight of a newspaper clipping partly showing from underneath his guitar case. He was suddenly reminded of his dilemma and cautiously pulled out the clipping. This was one of the recent articles that appeared in the countywide newspaper.

Youths Plead Innocent in Murder of Boy, 14

MONROE – Peter Stohler's mother wept and his father sat expressionless as three Centerville teenagers pleaded innocent yesterday to charges that they murdered the couple's 14-year-old son by strangling him with a belt.

After the arraignment in Norfolk County Court of Henry Barr, 16; Dean Howser, 15; and Frank Calandria, 15—all from Centerville and Students at Centerville High School—Mrs.

Stohler approached Calandria's parents in the courtroom and screamed words of bitter revenge at them. She was subdued by her husband, who led her quickly out of the courtroom.

Prosecutor Charles Bola told Judge Robert W. Fleming that Barr was the instigator of the murder and originated the idea of "wasting him." Bola also said that Howser had made a confession that police recorded on tape. Bola said that he will seek early trials for the three youths and that no lesser pleas will be offered. Bola sought $100,000 bail for each of the three, but Fleming ordered the youths released on $10,000 bail.

The indictment alleges that a fourth suspect, unnamed and still unknown, participated in the murder, which investigators have said occurred on October 3rd when Peter discovered the youths after they had burglarized and vandalized a neighborhood house.

D.A. Charles Bowring, who observed the arraignment, said the investigation is continuing to obtain the identity of the mysterious fourth youth. He urged anyone with information in the case to call one of two special telephone numbers: 555-8811 and 555-5532.

In the two months since the murder, police have questioned youths in the neighborhood repeatedly. Investigators who worked on the case said the toughest problem they had to overcome was the reluctance of neighborhood youths to give information to the police about the suspects, their schoolmates. Peer pressure was the major concern of several youths who allegedly had some pertinent information for police, one investigator said.

As a result of their lack of substantial information, the indictments are based on what many interpret as an illegally secured confession from Howser. Because of these improper interrogation procedures by the Norfolk County Police and the lack of eye witnesses to the murder, the suspects could go scot-free, said a prominent member of the local Civic Association in Centerville.

Craig was so engrossed in the article that he failed to hear his father's gentle tap on his bedroom door.

"Craig, are you in there?"

Craig instinctively slipped the article under his bed and jumped up, startled.

"Be … be right there, Dad. Getting dressed." He took a deep breath and shook his head rapidly to regain control of the present.

"Anything special you'd like for dinner tonight, Craig?"

His father usually didn't ask what his preference would be for supper, and Craig was a little surprised at this change in his father's behavior.

"Whatever, Dad. It doesn't matter. What was wrong, Dad? I noticed you were home early from work."

"I felt like taking the afternoon off. I was tired and just didn't feel like working any longer."

This was highly unusual for Mr. J, and Craig wondered if he was all right. There was a carefree elation in his father's voice that was uncharacteristic.

"By the way, son," he continued, "I saw your mother for lunch today and we have set a date to see the counselor we've been going to. We're going to arrange a date with him for a trial period."

"What kind of trial period?" asked Craig inquisitively.

"Mom's going to move back home for a while to see if we can reconcile our differences."

"You're kidding, Dad. You're kidding!" Craig flew into the kitchen and looked at his father ecstatically. "Do you mean it, Dad? Do you really mean it?"

"Yes, son, I mean it." Mr. J's tone reassured Craig that his father was in fact telling the truth, and he couldn't believe it.

"It's just on a trial basis, Craig, and we've both agreed to that, so don't get your hopes too high."

Craig didn't care. He knew that it was at least a serious attempt on their part to get together again. The thought of the two of them under the same roof again gave him a feeling of security he hadn't felt in many months. He now knew the source of his father's flippant attitude and he felt like screaming for joy. Craig fired questions at his father during their dinner. Mr. J could barely get a mouthful of food chewed and swallowed as he attempted to fill in Craig on the details of the discussion with his estranged wife during their lunch together.

Craig had completely forgotten about the party and would have missed it if it had not been for his father's gentle reminder.

"I thought you were going out with Vinny and Roland tonight.."

Craig instinctively looked up at the kitchen clock and rushed for the bathroom. He hadn't felt this happy in months and he was in the best of moods for a party. No time for a shower, but he had to wash his hair. Within minutes, he was blow-drying his hair in front of the full-length mirror in the bathroom. He slipped on a pair of clean jeans and a Pittsburgh Steelers' football jersey, not a moment too soon. He heard a car horn honk, bade his happy farewell to his father, and ran for the automobile that waited for him in front of his house.

"Hi, guys! Hello, Mrs. Betz!"

Roland's mother was in her late fifties. Roland was an unexpected child and she had just finished getting two other children out of high school when Roland was born. At first, Mrs. Betz resented the unexpected new addition. She was a tender, loving person and finally resolved to raise her new son as best she could. Roland found it difficult to relate to his mom and dad because of the vast differences in their ages. Mr. and Mrs. Betz were well-intentioned, but so far removed from the fads and fashions of the new generation that they found it hard to communicate with Roland.

Nevertheless, she was a nice lady who always volunteered to chauffeur the kids around when they needed rides. The boys remained relatively silent as Mrs. Betz took directions from Vinny to the Donohue house.

"Be careful, boys, and I'll pick you up at eleven thirty, okay?"

"Okay, Mom. Thanks for the ride."

"Thanks, Mrs. Betz."

The three boys gently closed the car door and stood on the curb, looking at the lit-up house that belonged to the Donohues. Their parents had not bothered to ask if Mr. and Mrs. Donohue were home, all assuming that they were. As they sauntered up to the front door, a green car raced by the house and screeched to a halt at the corner. Unbeknownst to the boys, one of its occupants was Travis Graham.

Laura greeted them at the door with a smile from ear to ear. A musical cacophony from the basement filled the house as Laura directed them to the basement stairs.

"Go down, boys. I'll be right there," directed Laura.

The basement was filled with smoke, and a faint acrid smell of marijuana greeted their nostrils as they entered the basement and looked around for familiar faces. Bobby and Sue Vager, Joey Benavenga, Kenny Haller, the Dunnedin twins, and many more familiar faces greeted them as they began to circulate.

Laura had insisted that no alcoholic beverages be allowed. All the liquor bottles had been removed from the bar counter top and replaced with ice and soft drinks. Pretzels, potato chips, and onion dip were also available. Here and there, paper bags were seen as some of the kids took swigs from the bags, which contained something other than soda. It was difficult to carry on a conversation with anyone as the music of a popular rap group blasted throughout the basement's built-in speakers.

Craig grabbed for a handful of potato chips as he nursed his Coke. Sue Vager had noticed Craig's arrival and was slowly making her way through the crowd toward him. He and Bobby Vager had since made their peace after the confrontation in the Pit and in school. They weren't the best of buddies, but they tolerated each other. Whenever they met in school, they would ceremoniously greet each other and continue on their way.

"Hi. Craig, how are you?" Sue finally reached Craig.

"What d' ya say, Sue! How are things going?"

Sue was cute, but he felt no longing for her like he had felt for Laura. They struck up a casual and rather banal conversation about school and teachers, with Craig straining to hear her over the blaring music.

Vinny and Joey Benavenga were close by, murmuring to each other about the various girls who were milling about. Vinny was a lot of fun, and the girls liked to be around him, but that was about it. He was popular because of his crazy manner and jovial personality. Roland, as usual, stood close to Vinny, but was not directly involved in their discussion. A few of the girls had found a corner and were dancing to the music as a group of boys watched and commented on their moves and femininity.

Laura finally came down, and Craig's heart skipped a beat as he watched her move through the crowd toward him. She had matured into a strikingly beautiful young woman, and he felt a strange uneasiness as she approached him.

"Glad to see you here, Craig," said Laura enthusiastically. "Enjoying yourself?"

"Great party, Laura. The music is great."

Craig didn't know what to say after this. He felt awkward and uncomfortable as Laura continued to smile at him, waiting for him to continue the conversation. His heart sunk as she moved on toward another group of boys huddled by the bar.

What a jerk I am, he thought. *I can't even keep a conversation going with her for two minutes.* He watched Laura's womanly figure weave away from the group of boys and toward the girls who were dancing in the corner. Laura and another girl began to dance rather sensuously, and Craig riveted his eyes on her as she gyrated to the music.

Craig looked around at the beautifully paneled basement and the expensive furniture and decorations that adorned the room. Laura had painstakingly decorated the room with red and green crepe paper and other Christmas decorations. The strobe lights flickering, combined with the music and kids dancing and laughing, made for a festive and exciting party.

He was talking to Joey Benavenga when he heard the familiar raspy voice of Travis Graham behind him. His heart seemed to bounce up into his mouth, and he felt and heard the pulsating of his heart in his ear. Instead of turning around, he walked away from the voice, leaving Joey Benavenga surprised and openmouthed.

"Where you goin', Juncosa?" asked Joey. "See ya later, huh?"

Craig walked to the other side of the basement and faced away from where he surmised Travis Graham was standing. He suddenly felt weak-kneed and slightly nauseous. He decided he would try to get upstairs to the bathroom for a while. What he didn't want was a direct confrontation with Graham. He knew it would be inevitable if they met face-to-face.

Graham, in his typical arrogant style, moved throughout the basement, favoring the girls with his winks and flirting gestures. Vinny saw Craig heading up the stairs and was about to call out to him when he spotted Travis coming toward him.

"What's up, Vincent baby?" questioned Travis as he playfully punched Vinny in the arm. "Quite the scene here, eh! Where's the booze and pot?"

Vinny decided not to answer as he shrugged off the light punch and halfheartedly laughed. Roland was standing by, as usual, and extended his hand to Travis. Travis looked at Roland amused and disdainfully slapped his hand away. Roland pulled his hand back timidly and backed up behind Vinny. Observing the whole thing, Vinny looked disgustedly at Travis and shook his head despondently. Travis moved on with a sardonic smile on his face. He towered over most of the other kids, and they moved aside for him as he spotted Laura and moved agilely toward her.

"Hey, Laura baby, how's my girl?"

Laura was still somewhat attracted to him but was becoming more and more disenchanted with his arrogance and conceit.

"Fine, Travis, how are you?" she answered coolly.

"I understand you're dating a junior, eh? Really getting up in the world, huh, kid?"

Laura wanted to walk away from him but felt a social obligation to at least give him a few minutes of conversation. When he went to place his hand on her shoulder, she politely shrugged it off.

Craig was grateful that he had reached the top of the basement stairs still undetected by Travis, and made a beeline for the bathroom. He passed an embracing couple on the living room couch and turned away, embarrassed, as the couple broke their embrace for a look at the intruder. He finally found the bathroom and scurried in, locking the door in an almost desperate manner. He leaned against the mirrored wall with his head raised and hands clenched tightly. It was minutes before he relaxed his clenched fists and lowered his head.

He saw his image in the mirror and shuddered. There he was, a frightened, pitiful sight, afraid to move, afraid to socialize, afraid to confront Travis Graham. A sudden burst of pride enveloped him as he took a deep breath, unlocked the door, and strode confidently toward the basement door. He passed the couple again. This time, they didn't bother looking up but continued their romancing.

Craig proudly negotiated the stairway and once again entered the smoke-filled basement. Vinny caught sight of him as he descended the last step.

"C'mere, Craig. Where the hell were you?" questioned Vinny curiously.

"I went to the john," Craig answered abruptly. "What's happening down here?"

Vinny didn't know it, but Craig was carefully searching the crowd for Travis Graham. If a confrontation with him was inevitable, he was ready for it. That SOB wasn't going to run his life. He was psyching himself into a state of readiness.

"Man, what's the matter with you?" Vinny inquired.

"What d'ya mean?" asked Craig.

"You look like you're a thousand miles away."

"Get off my case, will ya, Vinny?" Craig said angrily.

"Okay, okay, man. See you around."

Vinny walked away defiant and puzzled, shaking his head in disgust. Roland walked by looking for Vinny and spotted Craig standing alone.

"Hi, Craig. How's it going?"

"Good, Roland, good. How ya doin?" answered Craig impatiently.

Roland stood by Craig, content just to be with another kid. Travis Graham's looming figure came into view and Craig stiffened. He was coming straight at Craig and Roland. Craig prepared for the worst.

Completely ignoring Craig, he approached Roland and, without warning, landed a vicious unprovoked punch to Roland's mid-section. Caught completely by surprise, Roland fell forward, clutching his stomach and gasping for breath.

Craig stood dumbfounded for an instant and then instinctively and fiercely kicked Travis in the groin.

A blood-curdling shriek silenced the loud and raucous group. Only the din of the music pounding out a rock song could be heard as all eyes and faces turned toward the three boys. Craig was frozen in place as Travis doubled over in pain, clutching his groin desperately. Roland was still on the floor, face down, gasping for air.

"What the hell is going on?" The irate voice of Laura Donohue broke the silence as one of the other girls switched off the music.

A girl who had witnessed the entire incident grabbed Laura as she stalked toward Craig angrily.

"Hold it, Laura. I saw the whole thing. Travis came up to Roland and just punched him in the stomach for absolutely no reason. Craig kicked Travis, and he deserved it."

Roland sat up, his face ashen and fear-stricken. Laura was speechless as she turned away and began to cry. Vinny was at Roland's side, helping him off the floor and muttering obscenities about Travis. Craig was still frozen in fear and hadn't moved an inch since he landed the devastating kick to Travis's groin. Travis was in severe pain and unable to move. He rested on his knees, face down to the floor, groaning.

Kids began to quietly leave the basement and began calling their parents to pick them up. The party had come to an abrupt and untimely end as Laura continued to sob softly on the basement couch.

Vinny and Joey approached Craig, who was still in a state of shock, and urged him to follow them upstairs. Two girls were desperately trying to console and revive Travis, who remained almost paralyzed. Vinny and Joey pushed Craig and Roland up the staircase and toward the closet, where they retrieved their jackets. Craig was still in a state of semi-shock as Vinny anxiously helped him put his jacket on. The four boys quickly exited the house, which was suddenly empty and morbidly quiet.

Violence had ended the festive gathering, and Craig was inextricably involved.

Just what he needed—more trouble!

CHAPTER THIRTEEN
Panic

The telephone jarred Craig out of his uneasy sleep and he began to shake uncontrollably. He glanced at his alarm clock with the illuminated dial, trying to focus in on the time—3:00 a.m. He had to get to the phone before his father. Racing out of his room and toward the den, he met his father head on, as both had panicked looks on their sleep-swollen faces.

"I'll get it, Dad." Craig nearly knocked his father over in a desperate attempt to get the phone first.

He slowly picked up the receiver and held it to his ear, knowing who was calling. The raspy voice on the other end answered Craig's muffled and meek, "Hello?"

"We hear you put Travis Graham in the hospital, punk. Well, you just dug your own grave, Juncosa. The last time we met was just a rehearsal. The next time it will be the real thing. Bye, bye, punk. Sweet dreams."

Craig shuddered involuntarily as the phone clicked. The voice was demonic and ice cold. Craig's knees weakened and momentarily buckled. A sick feeling swelled in the pit of his stomach and slowly crept up to his throat. His father's voice broke the terror of the moment.

"Craig, who was it?"

Craig gulped and, in a barely audible voice, responded. "A crank call, Dad. J-just a crank call."

He could hear his father's garbled voice mumble angrily from his bedroom. Craig was still gripping the phone tightly, and the loud sound of a dead phone broke the nocturnal silence in the room. He slowly placed the phone on the receiver and sauntered toward this bedroom, still uncontrollably shaking. His father had already discounted the untimely phone call and was back in bed.

Craig sat on the edge of his bed as small beads of sweat formed on his brow. The back of his neck ached and he futilely attempted to rub it away. His mind was racing, and he could hear his heart pounding rapidly in his ear. Craig remembered his father's advice about how to relax and began to take deep breaths. Eventually, his heartbeat returned to normal and he could feel the tenseness gradually diminish.

He sat for a good half-hour, his mind lost in a maze of unrelated abstract thoughts. The demonic voice on the phone had frightened him, and, for the first time, he began to fear for his own life. These kids had murdered once. Why not again? He couldn't understand how they could continue to terrorize and threaten after their indictment. Evidently, they felt confident that they would be acquitted. He and he alone could turn the odds against them if he testified as an eyewitness. Yet they continued to harass, intimidate, and threaten him. Their strange and bizarre behavior dumbfounded him. He fell heavily back onto his bed in a desperate attempt to rattle away his painfully persistent thoughts.

There were two more days of school left before the beginning of the Christmas vacation. Craig visualized the terrifying situation he would face in school during that two-day period.

Cutting school was the only way to avoid a confrontation with Graham. He couldn't face another encounter with the murderers. If Graham returned to school on Monday, it was inevitable that he would confront Craig. Who knew what would happen?

He continued to take deep breaths, trying to calm his nerves and return to a blissful sleep. A good hour passed before sleep came again.

The crash of the front door closing startled Craig out of his sleep and he sat up abruptly. The winter sun was streaming into his bedroom, and he looked over at his alarm clock. It was Saturday morning. For the time being, he was safe at home with his father.

"Anybody home?" Melissa's voice broke the morning silence as Craig grabbed for his robe and headed for the bathroom.

"Be right there, Liss," Craig answered anxiously.

"Where's Dad?" asked Melissa.

"Dunno," garbled Craig as he washed the sleep out of his face.

Mr. J was in the backyard, pumping out the idle water that had accumulated on the pool cover. He was a man who believed in keeping busy and very seldom slept beyond 6:00 a.m., even on the weekends and holidays. Melissa walked up to the closed bathroom door and tapped gently on it. Craig opened the door.

"Did you tell Dad?" she whispered anxiously.

"Shh, shh." Craig placed his finger up to his mouth. "Where's Dad?"

"He's not around; obviously you didn't," Melissa answered, annoyed.

"I'll be right out."

Craig hastened his bathroom rituals and opened the door. He grabbed his sister's arm and led her into this room, closing the door behind them.

"You're hurting my arm, Craig, What the heck is wrong with you?"

Craig released his tight grip and apologized, "I'm sorry, Liss, but … but things are getting bad."

"What's the matter?" she asked.

Craig related the phone incident, and Melissa listened intently.

"If you don't tell Dad, I will!" Melissa's emphatic tone made Craig cringe as he once again pleaded for her silence with the finger-to-mouth gesture.

"I'm not going to be quiet!"

Melissa raised her voice again as the backdoor slammed and Mr. J entered the house. She suddenly became quiet when she heard her father enter. She left his bedroom, gritting her teeth in anger at Craig's failure to take her advice.

"Hi, Dad."

Craig heard Melissa's tone change to a warm, friendly manner and knew, for the time being, that she was not going to follow through on her threat.

"Hello, Melissa, good to see you."

Mr. J's voice was pleasant as he welcomed his daughter. Whenever she visited him, he was always pleased. Since Melissa left the house and took an apartment with her girlfriend, her relationship with him improved considerably. The old adage "Absence makes the heart grow fonder" seemed to apply. This renewed relationship with her father made her very happy. She felt a new closeness to him as he embraced and kissed her.

"How's my beautiful girl doing these days?" Mr. J asked proudly.

"Great, Dad, just great," Melissa answered enthusiastically.

"I've got something to tell you, Melissa, that I hope you'll like to hear," said Mr. J in an almost excited tone.

Melissa waited impatiently for his revelation.

"Your mother and I have decided to give it another try. She'll be moving back home next week."

Melissa's face broke into a dazzling smile and she became speechless as she again embraced him. She did so with such fervor that Mr. J felt his eyes become moistened. An uncontrollable urge to cry swept over him. She held him for minutes as he attempted to suppress the tears that began to roll down his ruddy cheeks.

Craig had watched the entire episode from behind the wall leading to his bedroom, and he too began to cry. Mr. J wiped his eyes and cheeks, embarrassed, as Melissa gradually released her tight embrace. She stood back, red-eyed and smiling proudly at her father. The scene was so tender and moving that Craig couldn't stop the joyful sobbing. He ran into the bathroom and washed his face again. He was both happy and sad. Something good was happening to his family, and something terrifying was happening to him.

A large pimple had formed on Craig's cheek, and he began to laboriously squeeze it. Craig hated the eruptions that began to appear with increasing frequency on his face. He would spend hours trying to get rid of them by squeezing and washing them. At times, he would make things worse by leaving red blotches on his face from the constant effort to remove or hide them.

He stayed away from sweets as much as possible, but the small pimples continued to appear in spite of all of his efforts to prevent them.

His voice was beginning to crack, and at times his father would playfully mimic him by raising and lowering his voice. Craig would smile, embarrassed, and immediately stop any conversation he happened to be engaged in at the time. The adolescent juices were beginning to flow. He could feel and see evidences of the emerging man.

His fair complexion and blond hair concealed much of the facial hair that was becoming increasingly thick and dense, especially over his lip. He had contemplated shaving the hair over his lip, but decided against it when he realized how conspicuous it would be to his family and friends. He would do anything to be spared the teasing and taunting that would accompany his first shaving effort.

Craig was content in remaining as inconspicuous as possible during this stage of his life. *I'm going to have a helluva time doing that now*, thought Craig, as he was reminded of his ordeal. That panicky feeling that he was experiencing so often these days suddenly returned. He lifted the toilet seat abruptly to urinate.

"Hey, boy, are you up yet?" Mr. J's exuberant voice echoed throughout the house.

Craig answered feebly, "Be right there."

He slipped on his jeans and sneakers and headed for the kitchen where Melissa and his father were joyfully sharing a pot of coffee.

"Morning, Dad."

"It's almost afternoon, Craig," his father jokingly responded.

Melissa looked up at Craig, and her face turned solemn for an instant as she was reminded of her brother's serious problem.

"Want an egg or something?" Mr. J asked happily.

"Nah, I'm not too hungry this morning, Dad. I'll just have a cup of tea or something."

Craig didn't like coffee and couldn't understand how adults could be so addicted to it. Tea was a lot more tolerable, and from time to time he enjoyed a good, hot steaming cup of it.

"Sit down and join us, son. I was just telling your sister about the plans your mother and I have made. We both decided that we really didn't work hard enough on our marriage to make it work, and we hope to save it this time around."

"Your mother and I have an appointment with Father McClanahan tomorrow after the eleven-thirty Mass. We'll be meeting for breakfast first and I thought it would be nice for both of you to share breakfast with us tomorrow."

"Sure, Dad. We'd love to," answered Melissa.

Mr. J looked at Craig, waiting for a similar response from him.

Craig looked up from his cup and halfheartedly smiled.

"Yeah, it would be great, Dad."

Craig hadn't seen his mother for about a month. His preoccupation with the terrible problem confronting him had all but inured him to the once-joyful anticipation he felt whenever his mother visited him. He just couldn't feel the natural peace he once felt in his mother's presence. The gnawing feeling in his stomach had now become an all-too-familiar feeling. It seemed to always interfere with any feelings of happiness that infrequently came along. Panic and anxiety had now become the dominant feelings in his life. It was devastating and very damaging to a young emerging man.

"I'm going to get a haircut today, kids." Mr. J broke the silence of the moment, and began to clear the empty cups from the table.

"I'll take care of those, Dad," Melissa insisted.

"Thanks, Melissa. I'm going in to shower. See you tomorrow. Meet us here at the house at eight."

"Okay, Dad. See you then," Melissa answered enthusiastically.

She turned to Craig again and whispered to him, "You're lucky Dad is meeting Mom tomorrow and I don't want to ruin the meeting, or I would have told him."

The ominous tone in her voice made Craig cringe as she continued. "You had better tell Dad everything and go to the police, brother of mine. Do you realize how serious …"

"Shut up! Will you … just shut up!"

Craig's pent-up emotions erupted into hysteria as Melissa leaned back in her chair in surprise.

"What's the matter out there?" Mr. J's booming voice from the bathroom jolted both of them.

Melissa answered, "Oh nothing, Dad. Just a friendly brother and sister argument."

"This is supposed to be a joyful day—no more arguing."

Craig was still steaming inside as he pushed away from the table and ran quietly to his room. Melissa sat expressionless for a few minutes and began to empathize with her poor brother's terrible situation. She quietly cleared the table and gently placed the coffee cups and saucers in the dishwasher. After brushing her hair and touching up her makeup on the hall mirror, she quietly slipped out of the house and headed for her apartment.

"See you later, son." Mr. J headed for the front door as Craig turned down the volume on his CD player to answer.

"Okay, Dad."

He heard the pickup truck roar down the street and turned the volume up as high as he could without distorting the sound. He lay back on the bed with both hands covering his young but troubled face. As the rock music blasted out its rhythm, Craig suddenly had a strong urge for a drink. His father kept a supply of liquor in the dining room for houseguests and other visitors. He didn't drink but would do so socially when he was entertaining.

Craig went into the dining room and surveyed the varied bottles of liquor in the cabinet: vodka, gin, scotch, and assorted liqueurs. He didn't like the taste of most of them but remembered someone telling him that vodka was tasteless and you couldn't smell it on your breath. He reached for the bottle, removed the cap, and took a big gulp. As he swallowed it, he felt a severe burning sensation seeping down his chest and into his stomach. He ran for the kitchen sink and gulped down a large glass of water. His eyes teared and his breathing was labored as he stood and propped himself over the sink, waiting for the burning sensation to subside. Gradually, it did, and a warm, sort of pleasant and now familiar sensation began to spread throughout his body. Craig smiled sheepishly as he returned to his room, where the music continued to blare.

For the first time all day, he felt relaxed and relatively calm. As the music played on he became lost in dreamy thoughts about Laura Donohue. A gnawing feeling of desire spread through his young body. It was quite a contrast to the horrible feelings of anxiety and fear that so persistently enveloped him.

The effects of the alcohol lasted a long time. In a semi-stupor, Craig played CD after CD of his favorite music. For a moment, the urge to consume some more vodka returned, but the thought of his father returning home shortly stopped him. Good sense prevailed. Anyhow, he was content to savor the good feelings he was now experiencing, and remembered the terrible ordeal he had endured when he drank too much Southern Comfort.

The euphoric feeling came to an abrupt end as he heard the screeching ring of the phone. He switched off the music and ran into the family room. As he approached the ringing phone, he froze momentarily and stared woefully as the phone continued its unrelenting and methodic clamor. He slowly lifted the receiver and gradually raised it to his terror-stricken face. His hand shook uncontrollably as he placed the receiver to his ear and listened.

"Hi, punk. How's your weekend going?"

The same demonic and creepy voice sent a cold shiver up his spine.

"Enjoy whatever is left of it, Juncosa. See ya Monday. Don't forget to go to church."

Craig held the phone tightly to his ear. "You son of a bitch. You better stop calling this house or—"

Click. The caller hung up, and Craig yelled into the receiver, "You miserable bastards. You … you … you."

He dropped the receiver and fell to the floor, thrashing in uncontrollable terror. The alcohol in his system had dissipated rapidly, and the sobering effect of another traumatic phone encounter with the caller was too much for him to take. He remained on the floor for a long while, continuing to mutter obscenities and threats to the unknown caller. Panic had set in, with an inevitable confrontation drawing closer and closer.

CHAPTER FOURTEEN
Reconciliation

Sunday morning. As Craig raised his head in response to Mr. J's call to arise, a dull throbbing sensation forced him to lay back on his pillow. He stared blankly at the bedroom ceiling and routinely answered his father's beckoning.

"I'm up, Dad."

He had endured a nightmarishly broken sleep that night, and his first impulse was to turn over and return to sleep. His impulse was short-lived as he remembered the breakfast reunion that was planned for the morning. His mother and sister would be joining him and his father for what was hoped would be the beginning of a reunited marriage and family. Craig would normally have been ecstatic over this event, but his life was now dominated by the crisis he faced. Each day and incident brought the inevitable confrontation closer. The anxiety that gripped Craig for weeks was now turning to terror and fear.

"Come on, Craig. We've got a breakfast date with your mother and sister."

The exuberance in Mr. J's voice was rare, and Craig realized how important a day this was for his father. He didn't want to ruin it for him as he reluctantly struggled out of bed and headed for the bathroom.

The mirror revealed the fear and frustration in his face. His eyes and cheeks were puffy, and dark circles seemed to be etched under his youthful eyes. He splashed cold water on his face and tried to rub away the puffiness. The strain of his ordeal and the frightening experiences of the last few days were taking their toll on his young body. The usual sparkle in his blue eyes had dulled, and his monotone voice betrayed his agony. Craig washed his hair and began blow-drying it when he once again heard his father's voice.

"Hurry it up, son. They'll be here any minute."

"Right, Dad."

Mrs. Juncosa looked absolutely stunning as she hugged Craig with a maternal fervor.

With her delicate hand on his shoulder, she gently pushed him back, and in a motherly manner, surveyed her son. Her radiant smile faded as she immediately detected the strain in his face. Her motherly instincts told her something was wrong.

"Are you feeling okay, Craig?" Her gentle voice and sincere concern felt good to Craig.

"I'm fine, Mom." He tried to change the subject and diverted her attention to something else.

spread throughout his body. Craig smiled sheepishly as he returned to his room, where the music continued to blare.

For the first time all day, he felt relaxed and relatively calm. As the music played on he became lost in dreamy thoughts about Laura Donohue. A gnawing feeling of desire spread through his young body. It was quite a contrast to the horrible feelings of anxiety and fear that so persistently enveloped him.

The effects of the alcohol lasted a long time. In a semi-stupor, Craig played CD after CD of his favorite music. For a moment, the urge to consume some more vodka returned, but the thought of his father returning home shortly stopped him. Good sense prevailed. Anyhow, he was content to savor the good feelings he was now experiencing, and remembered the terrible ordeal he had endured when he drank too much Southern Comfort.

The euphoric feeling came to an abrupt end as he heard the screeching ring of the phone. He switched off the music and ran into the family room. As he approached the ringing phone, he froze momentarily and stared woefully as the phone continued its unrelenting and methodic clamor. He slowly lifted the receiver and gradually raised it to his terror-stricken face. His hand shook uncontrollably as he placed the receiver to his ear and listened.

"Hi, punk. How's your weekend going?"

The same demonic and creepy voice sent a cold shiver up his spine.

"Enjoy whatever is left of it, Juncosa. See ya Monday. Don't forget to go to church."

Craig held the phone tightly to his ear. "You son of a bitch. You better stop calling this house or—"

Click. The caller hung up, and Craig yelled into the receiver, "You miserable bastards. You … you … you."

He dropped the receiver and fell to the floor, thrashing in uncontrollable terror. The alcohol in his system had dissipated rapidly, and the sobering effect of another traumatic phone encounter with the caller was too much for him to take. He remained on the floor for a long while, continuing to mutter obscenities and threats to the unknown caller. Panic had set in, with an inevitable confrontation drawing closer and closer.

CHAPTER FOURTEEN
Reconciliation

Sunday morning. As Craig raised his head in response to Mr. J's call to arise, a dull throbbing sensation forced him to lay back on his pillow. He stared blankly at the bedroom ceiling and routinely answered his father's beckoning.

"I'm up, Dad."

He had endured a nightmarishly broken sleep that night, and his first impulse was to turn over and return to sleep. His impulse was short-lived as he remembered the breakfast reunion that was planned for the morning. His mother and sister would be joining him and his father for what was hoped would be the beginning of a reunited marriage and family. Craig would normally have been ecstatic over this event, but his life was now dominated by the crisis he faced. Each day and incident brought the inevitable confrontation closer. The anxiety that gripped Craig for weeks was now turning to terror and fear.

"Come on, Craig. We've got a breakfast date with your mother and sister."

The exuberance in Mr. J's voice was rare, and Craig realized how important a day this was for his father. He didn't want to ruin it for him as he reluctantly struggled out of bed and headed for the bathroom.

The mirror revealed the fear and frustration in his face. His eyes and cheeks were puffy, and dark circles seemed to be etched under his youthful eyes. He splashed cold water on his face and tried to rub away the puffiness. The strain of his ordeal and the frightening experiences of the last few days were taking their toll on his young body. The usual sparkle in his blue eyes had dulled, and his monotone voice betrayed his agony. Craig washed his hair and began blow-drying it when he once again heard his father's voice.

"Hurry it up, son. They'll be here any minute."

"Right, Dad."

Mrs. Juncosa looked absolutely stunning as she hugged Craig with a maternal fervor.

With her delicate hand on his shoulder, she gently pushed him back, and in a motherly manner, surveyed her son. Her radiant smile faded as she immediately detected the strain in his face. Her motherly instincts told her something was wrong.

"Are you feeling okay, Craig?" Her gentle voice and sincere concern felt good to Craig.

"I'm fine, Mom." He tried to change the subject and diverted her attention to something else.

CHAPTER FOURTEEN
Reconciliation

Sunday morning. As Craig raised his head in response to Mr. J's call to arise, a dull throbbing sensation forced him to lay back on his pillow. He stared blankly at the bedroom ceiling and routinely answered his father's beckoning.

"I'm up, Dad."

He had endured a nightmarishly broken sleep that night, and his first impulse was to turn over and return to sleep. His impulse was short-lived as he remembered the breakfast reunion that was planned for the morning. His mother and sister would be joining him and his father for what was hoped would be the beginning of a reunited marriage and family. Craig would normally have been ecstatic over this event, but his life was now dominated by the crisis he faced. Each day and incident brought the inevitable confrontation closer. The anxiety that gripped Craig for weeks was now turning to terror and fear.

"Come on, Craig. We've got a breakfast date with your mother and sister."

The exuberance in Mr. J's voice was rare, and Craig realized how important a day this was for his father. He didn't want to ruin it for him as he reluctantly struggled out of bed and headed for the bathroom.

The mirror revealed the fear and frustration in his face. His eyes and cheeks were puffy, and dark circles seemed to be etched under his youthful eyes. He splashed cold water on his face and tried to rub away the puffiness. The strain of his ordeal and the frightening experiences of the last few days were taking their toll on his young body. The usual sparkle in his blue eyes had dulled, and his monotone voice betrayed his agony. Craig washed his hair and began blow-drying it when he once again heard his father's voice.

"Hurry it up, son. They'll be here any minute."

"Right, Dad."

Mrs. Juncosa looked absolutely stunning as she hugged Craig with a maternal fervor.

With her delicate hand on his shoulder, she gently pushed him back, and in a motherly manner, surveyed her son. Her radiant smile faded as she immediately detected the strain in his face. Her motherly instincts told her something was wrong.

"Are you feeling okay, Craig?" Her gentle voice and sincere concern felt good to Craig.

"I'm fine, Mom." He tried to change the subject and diverted her attention to something else.

"Did you lose weight, Mom?" You look much thinner than you did the last time I saw you."

Mrs. J's vanity got the best of her and she smiled again and graciously thanked her son for the compliment. The tender silence was interrupted by Melissa as she enthusiastically clapped her hands and summoned the reunited family.

"I'm starving. I don't know about anybody else. I can smell those pancakes. Let's go!"

The local pancake house was jointly selected, and they headed for the front door, Mr. J and Melissa leading the way arm in arm. Mrs. J wrapped her arm around Craig's neck and pulled him toward her as they followed father and daughter to the yellow VW.

Wreaths and outdoor lights decorated most homes as they traveled toward town. The Christmas holiday was rapidly approaching. It was an appropriate time for a broken family to reconcile its differences.

Mr. J's face was beaming as they selected a table in a secluded corner of the restaurant and sat down to a meal as a family for the first time in a long while. Melissa, Craig, and Mrs. J all ordered pancakes. Mr. J ordered his usual: sunny-side-up eggs, bacon, and home fries.

Coffee was poured for them and the waitress disappeared into the kitchen to place their orders.

Mr. J folded his hands in front of him and began his rehearsed speech.

"Well, here we are again as a family should be: together." He looked admiringly at his wife and continued, "Mom and I have decided to get together again. We have been seeing a marriage counselor and priest for the last few weeks and we think we can work out the differences and problems that separated us. We need your understanding and patience, and especially your support."

He looked at both Craig and Melissa as he almost pleadingly solicited their cooperation.

"Mother will be moving back with us in the next few days, and we all have to readjust to her return."

Mrs. J interrupted the serenity of the moment with a little humor. "I get the bathroom first." They all chuckled, and the tenseness that permeated the meeting seemed to dissipate.

"What your father is trying to say is that things will not be entirely normal for a while. Our relationship was strained for a long time, and there will be a period of readjustment for all of us. But we'll make it work—I know we will."

Her reassuring words brought a radiant smile to Mr. J's face as their breakfast orders were placed on the table. Melissa rubbed her hands.

"Mmm, can't wait to dig into all those calories."

Mrs. J laughed, good-naturedly poked Melissa in the stomach, and remarked on her increased chubbiness. Light conversation and nostalgic reminiscing continued throughout their morning meal. Some degree of normalcy returned to their relationship as they finished the meal and prepared to attend Mass together. Craig had remained unusually quiet during breakfast and his mother noticed it.

"Something is bothering you, Craig. I can tell. What is it?"

"Nothing, Mom, nothing. I'm happy that we're together again, that's all."

His mother knew he was not himself but decided to drop the issue for the time being as they began their drive to church. Craig was fidgety during the entire Mass and couldn't wait to get out of the church. He was lost in thought when Mass ended. Melissa gently urged him to leave the pew.

"Let's go, Craig—it's over," she implored.

As the crowd filtered out of the church, Craig saw a number of kids from school and was reminded of the unnerving experiences that might be waiting for him in school the next day.

How could he possibly go to school after the incident with Travis Graham? Graham would surely seek him out and challenge him to a fight.

"Lost in thought again, Craig?" asked his mother as she caught Craig with a distant look in his eyes.

Mr. J dominated the conversation on the way home. He was so excited about the family reuniting that he completely overlooked the turn that led into the neighborhood. Mrs. J gently reminded him of the error; embarrassed, he turned the car around and headed for home.

After kissing his mother good-bye, Craig made a beeline for his bedroom and left his mother and father and Melissa by the front door. Mrs. J expressed her concern over Craig's strange behavior.

"Something is drastically wrong with Craig, Frank. He just isn't himself. Do you have any idea what's wrong?"

Melissa looked away knowingly as Mr. J answered, "He's been having trouble in school lately, and I'm also concerned. I hope it's just adolescent pains; you know how tough this age is on kids. Remember what we went through with Melissa?"

Melissa didn't hear her father's remarks as she walked toward the closet to retrieve her coat.

"Well, see you tomorrow, Frank. I've got a lot of junk and suitcases that I need to pack and get ready to come home. I'll call you later."

Mr. J interrupted, "I'll take the day off tomorrow and come to pick up your things. Don't worry about it."

"There's no need for that, Frank."

She was interrupted immediately, "Hey, this is the most important event in my life outside of our marriage and the birth of our children. I'm taking the day off!"

Mrs. J smiled appreciatively, kissed him gently, and said her good-byes. Mr. J waved to his wife and daughter as they drove away. His face hadn't shone with such joy for many years as he closed the door and headed for the kitchen. He felt almost like a kid and was compelled to jump up and click his heels with comical elation.

Craig could hear his father whistling a joyful tune as he began preparation for their traditional Sunday meal. Craig wasn't at all hungry as he switched on his radio and dialed his favorite FM station. He turned up the volume when the DJ announced that a selection of Billy Joel songs would be coming up. He liked Billy Joel and could relate to the messages conveyed in his songs. As the music blared, he stretched out on his bed and hummed along, keeping the beat with his right hand on the side of the bed. He became lost in the music, which provided the only effective escape from the haunting dilemma that was becoming a terrible obsession.

Snow flurries began to fall and Craig surveyed the small flakes falling gently outside his window. As he looked out, he caught sight of his favorite willow tree standing naked in its winter dormancy. Without its leaves, it did not provide the secret sanctuary it offered him in the spring and summer, when the green foliage enveloped it. He saw his favorite branch looming high above the ground, a reminder of the many days and nights that he perched on it in complete solitude and privacy, contemplating love and life.

Thoughts of his runaway experience suddenly popped into his head and he wondered about the fate of Jimmy and Clarence, his roommates in the shelter. Fond memories of the helpful Officer Bado also crept into his thoughts. He shuddered as he recalled the bitter experience with the boy who attacked him so viciously in the basketball game.

It all seemed so long ago and far away, even though only a month or so had elapsed since then.

He remembered the meeting with Father McClanahan after his return home and the words of encouragement he had offered to Craig in the rectory office. He could hear his husky but consoling voice offering bits of priestly advice and comfort in his hours of despair.

His other confidant, Jerry, suddenly came into the scene as he recalled the many visits to the Gabor Horse Farm during and after school hours. He could see his big, freckled arms and large frame tending to the needs of the horses while Craig looked on and listened to his simple but profound statements on life. Craig envied the privacy and serene solitude that Jerry so carefully guarded in his life. His quiet and non-eventful existence was the source of the peace and tranquility that Jerry valued so much. Jerry had been Craig's only constant source of strength in the past few anxiety-filled months. Were it not for his encouragement and support, Craig would have succumbed to his terrible ordeal soon after his shocking experience.

A loud knock on his door brought Craig back to the present, and he jumped out of his bed and lowered the volume on his stereo.

"Craig. Hey, boy, dinner is on. Let's go. You can't hear a damn thing over the loud music blaring."

"Be right there, Dad," Craig answered apologetically.

He tucked his shirttails in his pants and ran his brush carelessly through his blond hair.

Mr. J was sitting at the kitchen table waiting for Craig when he sauntered into the kitchen and took his seat across from his father. He wasn't hungry, and the pot roast that lay in his plate with the potatoes, broccoli, and salad did not look very appetizing. After a briefly muttered prayer, his father dug ravenously into his meal. Craig began picking away at the meat, consuming small bits at a time.

Mr. J was preoccupied, devouring the food and going for seconds. He didn't notice Craig's aversion to the meal, and Craig was just as happy that he didn't. Mr. J was insulted when people didn't eat his carefully prepared food. He took pride in the culinary skills he had developed since the breakup with Mrs. J and gloated with satisfaction when people commented on his good cooking.

Craig was conjuring up ways to get out of eating his dinner without insulting his father.

"Dad, I'm just not hungry today. I'm not feeling too well," he blurted out.

Mr. J was unusually forgiving and responded, "What is it, your stomach, son?"

"No—yeah, yeah, my stomach is bothering me," Craig reconsidered after he saw his father's sympathy.

"Well, what d' ya think of Mom's return home?" asked Mr. J jovially.

"Great, Dad. It's just great."

Craig attempted to answer as enthusiastically as possible, but his father detected a certain reluctance in his voice and pursued the issue.

"Are you sure you're happy about it, Craig? Something in your voice is telling me that you aren't sure." Mr. J's expression suddenly changed to a serious one.

"No, no, Dad. Are you kidding? It's great!" This time, Craig made sure he sounded enthusiastic and elated.

Mr. J looked at him for a long while, waiting to see some indication of his sincerity, and finally turned away, still unsure of his son's response. The tenseness of the moment was unnerving to Craig, who didn't want in any way to take away the pure elation his father was experiencing.

What a jerk I am, he thought. *I can't even share the happiness that Dad feels.* He suddenly realized how obsessed he was with his problem and how he couldn't even feel the natural high that would normally be felt by a boy whose mother was returning home after a long absence.

"Dad, I have to do some homework that's due tomorrow. I'd better get to it."

The uncomfortable feeling that they both felt stayed with them as Craig excused himself and quietly retired to his room. He fell face first on his bed and attempted to muffle his sobs in his pillow. The worst was yet to come, thought Craig. Tomorrow was Monday and there were two days left of school before the Christmas holiday began. He would have to face his tormentor again and God only knew who and what else.

CHAPTER FIFTEEN
Confrontation

Craig managed to get to his first period class undetected by Travis Graham. A few kids had approached him at his locker to question him about the fight with Travis on Friday night. Craig nervously brushed them off and scampered to his homeroom . His heart was racing as he reached his first period class and rushed to his seat. He felt safe for the time being.

The bell rang, signifying the beginning of first period, as students were still chattering about their weekend. Craig sat silently, trying to remain inconspicuous as possible. A few students huddled in one corner of the room momentarily looked up at him and continued whispering. He could feel the tension in the air and knew that something had to happen before the end of the day. How could he possibly avoid a confrontation with the Graham kid the entire day? His ears and cheeks were flushed and his heart continued to race as the teacher settled down the class and began the day's lesson.

"Hey, Juncosa," whispered a fellow student sitting behind him. "I heard you put Travis Graham in the hospital Friday night. He's in school, ya know."

Craig shrugged his shoulders and waved off any further queries from the student.

His teacher began to lecture, and students hurriedly opened their notebooks and began scribbling notes. Craig went through the motions of opening his notebook, but instead of taking notes, he began doodling, his mind completely preoccupied with the impending confrontation with Travis Graham. He didn't hear a word Miss Clark said as he continued his nervous drawing.

"Is that the way you take notes, Mr. Juncosa?"

He looked up, startled, and saw the young teacher looking down at his notebook, her hands on her hips and a wry smile on her face. He felt all eyes upon him, and a warm rush of blood began to spread from both ears toward his fair-skinned cheeks.

"Are you with us, Craig?" Miss Clark flashed a pleasant smile and returned to the front of the room and continued her lecturing.

Craig felt like crawling into the nearest hole as a few prying eyes watched him fidget in his seat. As the lesson progressed, he felt a slight easing of tension as most of the students became engrossed in the lesson. He didn't hear a word Miss Clark was saying but kept his eyes and head focused on the teacher for fear of being reprimanded again.

His mind raced as he conjured up ways of avoiding a confrontation with Graham. *I'll stay after each class and talk to the teacher until the halls are clear and then go on to my next class*, thought Craig. *No. I can't do that. Mr. Kubek doesn't give passes to students leaving his class and I'll be late. Wait, so, I'll be late. Who cares? Damn it, damn it.*

"What's that, Craig? What did you say?" Miss Clark stood staring at Craig, who was inadvertently mouthing his confused thoughts.

"Oh. Oh, nothing … nothing. I was just thinking aloud about what you said."

Craig found himself the center of attention again.

The bell saved any further inquiries from Miss Clark as the students scampered for the door on their way to their next class. Craig sat passively watching the crowd filter out of the classroom.

"Are you okay, Craig?" asked Miss Clark as she walked toward him with a concerned look.

"I'm … I'm fine, Miss Clark," stuttered Craig. "I have a little headache."

Miss Clark was a compassionate person. She urged Craig to take his time getting to his next period and that she would give him a late pass.

"Thanks, Miss Clark. I appreciate it."

He was able to avoid a meeting with Graham for the time being. He stood up slowly and approached the teacher.

"I'm okay now. Can I have a late pass to my next period?" Craig asked politely.

Miss Clark wrote out a pass and handed it to Craig.

"Hope you feel better, Craig. Would you like to go to the nurse's office?"

"No. It's okay," he muttered as he headed for the door, momentarily paused, and surveyed the emptying corridors.

Satisfied that no one was left in the corridors, Craig headed for his second period class at a brisk pace.

His next class was on the other side of the long building, and he began a slow jog down the carpeted corridor. As he turned the corner into C Wing, he caught a glimpse of a figure darting behind a column and stopped dead in his tracks. His heart raced and he held his labored breath momentarily as he fixed his eyes on the large, steel column that hid the figure. Craig instinctively turned around and began to walk slowly the other way. He looked over his shoulder in time to see two kids racing toward him, their long strides quickly closing their distance. Craig instinctively dropped his books and began racing toward the red exit sign that led to the outside rear of the school.

He had recognized Travis Graham immediately, but did not know who the other boy was.

The adrenaline that shot into his body propelled him at breakneck speed as he headed for the woods leading to the Pit. When he reached the edge of the woods, he looked back only to see his pursuers gaining ground on him.

He was oblivious to the branches and bushes that ripped into his clothing and skin as he made no effort to avoid them but instead ran headlong into all obstacles. He skirted past the clearing near the Pit, which fortunately was unoccupied, and headed toward the split rail fence that enclosed the Gabor farm. Just as the fence came into sight, his foot caught the top of a dead stump and he sprawled headfirst onto the cold, hard ground.

He felt no pain as the terror of the moment rendered him totally unfeeling. The hard fall had knocked the wind out of him and, when he arose, he suddenly felt weak and dizzy.

Breathlessly, he called out for Jerry in a desperate attempt to beckon for help as he stumbled toward the fence. He could not go any farther as he fell heavily on the ground. He turned over on his back, his head resting on the lower rail of the fence, to helplessly watch his pursuers pounce on his breathless body. Travis Graham reached him first and stood menacingly over him, straddling his collapsed legs. He called to his friend, who was close behind.

"The little bastard is right here and all set for pluckin'."

A cold, wrathful smile parted Travis's lips as he waited for his accomplice to reach them. Craig closed his eyes and prayed that the pain would not be too severe.

Suddenly, a loud thud and a spine-chilling shriek split the agonizing silence, and Craig opened his eyes to see Jerry's large body looming over the fallen Graham boy.

Travis was seizing his head in pain, his knees touching his chest, and rocking back and forth on the ground. The other boy had wisely scampered back toward the school when he saw the size of Travis's attacker.

Jerry's eyes were beet red, and he had a look on his face that frightened even Craig. Jerry was hardly recognizable to Craig, who knew him only as a gentle and peaceful giant of a man.

Craig reacted swiftly and rationally to the situation.

"Stop, Jerry, stop. That's enough! You'll kill him."

He grasped the enraged giant around the waist just as he was about to stomp on the fallen Graham boy.

"Please, Jerry, you'll kill him!"

Craig's pleading words and backward tugs on Jerry's waist suddenly registered. The gentle giant backed away from the pitifully contorted body of the boy who, moments before, was standing triumphantly over his prey.

"Jerry, please leave it alone now. You'll just get yourself in a lot of trouble. Please!"

Some normalcy returned to Jerry's face as he turned toward Craig and extended his large hand toward him.

"Are you okay, boy? Are you okay?" Jerry's voice was hardly recognizable to Craig, and he knew that Jerry had momentarily lost all control. Craig grabbed his hand and squeezed tightly.

"I'm okay, Jerry. I'm okay," he repeated reassuringly. Craig held his hand tightly and waited with bated breath for Jerry to return to his rational self.

Travis was still holding his head and sobbing loudly and painfully. He had straightened out his legs and was now lying in a prone position on his back, his hands covering his bruised face. Travis's sobbing had now become short, convulsive sniffles.

Jerry, who was almost calm, turned toward Travis with a concerned look on his face. He realized the severity of the situation and approached the boy to inspect the extent of his injury. The left side of his face was severely reddened as Jerry gently removed Travis' hand from his head. Jerry looked closely at his eye and was satisfied that no serious damage had been done.

"You got no right attacking Craig, kid, and you're lucky Craig pulled me off of you or you wouldn't be in such good shape. Now, get the hell outta here before I change my mind."

Jerry extended a gentle hand to Travis, who refused it and got up on his own. He stood momentarily, leering at the freckled giant, and then turned and began slowly walking away from the scene.

Jerry and Craig stood watching as Travis's lanky body loped carelessly through the underbrush and toward the school building. Satisfied that he was far enough away, Travis turned toward the two obscured figures near the fence and yelled out, "Hey, Juncosa. Don't think you're safe now. There's always another time and another place." He refrained from mentioning Jerry, being quite afraid to rekindle the volatile wrath of the redheaded giant. As he increased the distance between them, he continued his barrage of threats.

"You're gonna be so sorry kid, and you ain't gonna have your buddy around to help."

He finally made reference to Jerry feeling fairly assured that he had enough distance between them. Travis's figure disappeared in the woods, but his voice still carried. Bold obscenities directed to both Craig and Jerry now reached their ears.

Jerry grasped Craig's arm and gently urged him to follow him back to the barn. They scaled the split rail fence and walked toward the big red building. They were both silent as they walked, knowing that words at this point would be meaningless. Jerry placed his large, muscular arm around Craig's neck and shoulders. He squeezed tightly—his way of comforting the frail, blond boy who he cared so much for. Craig felt secure and safe as they trudged into the barn. Jerry sat heavily in the old dilapidated armchair that he used for stolen moments of relaxation in between tending to the needs of the horses. He motioned to Craig to pull up a stool. Jerry took a deep breath and lay his head back on the vinyl headpiece of the chair. He stared quietly at the barn ceiling as Craig remained still and quiet to allow his friend to be alone with himself for a few minutes. He knew how enervating the experiences must have been for Jerry, and felt a little guilty about involving Jerry in his problems.

"Hey, Jer," he whispered in a quivering voice. Jerry remained still, and Craig began softly.

"I'm sorry for getting you involved in this whole big mess. I shoulda never told you about it. I just needed someone to talk to and … and …"

"Forget it, kid," Jerry interrupted. "Just forget it."

Craig detected a slightly angry tone in Jerry's voice and decided to heed Jerry's words. They both sat quietly, distracted only by the sound of the horses snorting and pacing uneasily, as if aware of the tension in the air.

A good fifteen minutes elapsed before Jerry stirred from his semi-prone position on the reclining chair. Craig heard the squeak of the old chair and lifted his head. Jerry's normal tone of voice returned.

"Listen, kid, you'd better get back to school or you'll be in a lotta hot water with your teachers and your father. Those kids won't bother you again today."

Craig was afraid to disagree with him and decided to bid him farewell. He had no intention of returning to school but decided it was wise to leave Jerry alone.

"Thanks for helping me, Jerry. I really appreciate it."

Jerry nodded halfheartedly, and Craig stole quietly out of the barn and headed for the woods. Once into the woods, he walked toward the VA hospital.

When he reached the road, he quickly surveyed it in both directions and crossed quickly. On the other side, he began to jog toward the VA hospital and the extensive grounds that surrounded it. He decided not to chance walking on the public roads for fear of being seen by someone he knew. Instead, he began walking on VA grounds, deciding to get home via the paths and back roads of the town. A few times he had to cross various roads in order to get to another path, and tensed up when cars passed by.

He finally reached his neighborhood and caught sight of Mrs. Lyons sweeping the front walk of her house. He waited behind a tree until she went in, and made a beeline for his side door. Once inside his house, he breathed a sigh of relief and headed for the bathroom. After relieving himself, he looked in the mirror and saw his disheveled and torn clothing. Small scratches and dried blood dotted his lower arms and, for the first time, he felt a throbbing sensation in his right ankle. He removed his shoes and socks and looked at his swollen foot and ankle, comparing it with his left foot. He removed his shirt and pants, throwing the tattered shirt in the garbage and his pants in the hamper. He took some ice out of the freezer and applied it to his swollen ankle as he sat on his bed in his underwear.

The shock of the experience had rendered him a little numb. He sat quietly on his bed, trying to reduce the swelling with the ice pack. His mind was blank, and he welcomed the emptiness as a blessing. The last thing he wanted to do was dwell on the events of the chaotic morning. Satisfied that he had succeeded in reducing the swollen ankle, he emptied the ice pack in the bathroom sink and returned to his room.

He decided to get dressed and pulled out a clean shirt and a pair of Levi's from his dresser drawer. He looked at his clock and decided to take a short nap. There was one more day of school before Christmas vacation, and his thoughts began to flow again. The Christmas vacation was thirteen days, including two weekends, and he felt fairly sure of escaping the wrath of his father and the school for at least that period of time. He'd worry about it when vacation was over. For the time being, the most important thing was to keep out of sight and away from Travis Graham and his fellow culprits.

He lay back on his pillow and began to doze off. Fragmented thoughts raced through his mind as the events of the day were painfully relived. He was in a semi-sleep state when the doorbell rang. The piercing sound of the bell sent a shock through his prone body. He momentarily lost his breath as he jumped up and instinctively glanced at his clock: 2:30 p.m. Who could it possibly be at this hour of the afternoon? Again, the bell sounded and Craig reluctantly headed for the front door. His voice cracked as he asked, "Who's there?"

No answer. Again he inquired as his heart began to pound. His first inclination was to swing open the door and confront the unknown caller, but he suppressed the urge when he realized the possible consequences of doing so.

Instead, he ran to the living room window and craned his neck to get a glimpse of whoever stood in the small alcove outside the front door.

Again the bell sounded, along with two quick raps on the door.

This time, the caller momentarily stepped back from the door, and Craig caught a glimpse of a frail young man holding a small box.

Craig ran to the front door and slowly opened it.

"Good afternoon, sir. Did you know that it is written that the end of the world is almost here! Can I have few minutes of your time …"

Craig couldn't believe it! He was both angry and happy as he stood on the threshold staring at a man who was selling him religion!

"No, thank you. I'm … I'm not interested. I'm … I'm very busy, sir. No, thank you."

The man was completely oblivious to Craig's rejections and just continued to ramble on and on. It was difficult for him to say no, and he just couldn't slam the door in someone's face, so he decided to listen to his spiel.

"Did you ever feel like you were all alone in the world and no one cared?"

The young man seemed so sincere and concerned that Craig began to listen. It all sounded so relevant to Craig's terrible problem that he wondered if the stranger standing in his doorway knew about it.

"Don't despair—the Lord is always with you. Just turn you life over to Him and all of your anxieties and fears will be alleviated."

Craig was so thankful that the caller was friendly that he listened patiently and almost became truly interested in the message the man was espousing. The man handed him a booklet and asked for a small donation. Craig reached into his pants pocket and pulled out some loose change. He handed it to the man and began closing the door.

"May I see you again, young man?"

Craig nodded affirmatively and continued closing the door.

He returned to his bedroom, clasping the small booklet the caller had left with him. He was just so relieved that it was not a hostile visitor.

His frayed nerves were like exposed electrical wires; the sound of a phone, the bell, and unexpected noise all jolted his young body. He realized just how tense and wound up he was. Things had to change—they just had to.

CHAPTER SIXTEEN
Willow, Weep for Me

Everything was happening at once! Christmas vacation, Mom coming home, Travis Graham pursuing him, Craig was so confused. There was a strange ambivalence and a bitter sweetness about all of these events happening at once. The only place where he could digest all of this and be able to think clearly and rationally was on his favorite branch in the willow tree. Craig had cleverly planned his truancy and made a beeline for the weeping willow tree as soon as he heard his father's pickup truck rattle down the street and out of the neighborhood. He had spent a good hour in the woodshed waiting for his father to leave for work. It felt good to get out in the air.

It was a cool, crisp December day, but the sun was shining as Craig climbed the huge willow tree. The leaves had long since fallen and it did not provide the privacy and green refuge it did in the warm months. When he reached the spot where two large branches crossed and formed a natural seat, he stopped climbing. He sat down with his feet dangling high above the ground. His private spot that no one else knew about! It was nice to have a place that was all yours, and that you shared with no one. The crisp coolness of the December day would have chilled most anyone sitting high up in a tree, but for Craig it was completely comfortable.

He watched the traffic on 52A and took out his pocketknife and began carving his initials into the main branch: C. A. J. As he carefully carved, his thoughts began to make sense. Mom would be coming back home this evening and they would have to make her feel welcomed and at ease. He had still not forgiven her for leaving and it would be difficult to cover up the deep resentment he felt. He had been close to his mother before the breakup, and it was a shattering experience for him when she walked out on the family. He had lost a lot of respect for her, and it would be hard to hide this fact.

As he continued whittling, his thoughts began to stray. He recalled what Officer Bado had said to him while he was being transported to the children's shelter.

Will it ever pass? thought Craig. *How will I ever get out of this mess in one piece? This is not like some ordinary problem, like failing a subject in school or getting caught cutting class.*

This was big! Murder!

He shivered as the word murder came to mind. With all the people in the world, he had to be the one witness to the murder of Peter Stohler. And all because his stupid bike wasn't working right! If only he had stayed home that night.

Craig heard the eleven thirty train pass by, its loud warning whistle shattering the crisp winter air as it approached the Centerville station. Hunger pangs began to uncontrollably grip his stomach, and he decided that a thick peanut butter and jelly sandwich might be just the thing to relieve this feeling.

He artfully shimmied down the large trunk and loped toward his side door. Once inside, he headed for the kitchen and the refrigerator. He poured himself a large glass of milk and began making two sandwiches.

Settling down at the kitchen table, he began devouring the sandwiches. He caught sight of the previous day's newspaper lying carelessly on the cutting board by the kitchen sink. Craig hadn't looked at the newspaper for days, and he anxiously grabbed it and began perusing each page for articles on the Stohler murder. He had stopped collecting the newspaper clippings when his father noticed the cutouts from the newspaper. He didn't want to do anything that would in any way raise suspicion. A small article on page twenty caught his eye.

Stohler Suspect Says Police Coerced Him

MONROE – In a surprise move, Henry Barr, one of the boys indicted in the murder of 14-year-old Peter Stohler, told reporters that neither he nor his other indicted friends had any part in the brutal October murder of the boy. Barr, 17, claimed he had been coerced by homicide detectives into making a tape-recorded confession. Barr said that eight days after the murder took place, he was stopped in Centerville by detectives.

"Three detectives got out of their cars and said, 'Are you Henry Barr? Get out of the car. We're taking you to the precinct.'

Another guy told me to get out of the car. He grabbed me by the arm and threw me in the patrol car. I said, 'I have to tell my mother where I am.'

"*He said, 'Get in the car.' I didn't have a choice."*

Barr said he was taken to a room at the Second Precinct in Centerville and questioned by Detectives Anthony Diamond and Ray Minard. "He (Diamond) kept asking me questions. 'We know what you did. We have witnesses who said they saw you kill Peter Stohler.' I said, 'You're crazy.' They were telling me that the other two boys (he refused to name them) had confessed and they had all kinds of evidence. 'You'll go to jail for forty years to life ... never walk the street again ... never see your parents again.' I was scared. I didn't know what to do or say."

Later that day, Barr said, he, Diamond, and Minard went to the school, where the detectives told him what to say in a confession they wanted to tape. He said he recited the confession and repeated it later in the day when his parents were summoned to the police station.

Craig dropped the newspaper on the table as he swallowed the last morsel of the second sandwich. He washed it down with a last gulp of milk and sat motionless, contemplating on the small article he had just read. He looked up at the kitchen clock and noticed the time. His father sometimes came home for lunch if he was working nearby, and Craig decided to return to his sanctuary in the willow tree.

He quickly scaled the tree and straddled the two branches carelessly. A horrid thought came to his mind. It was very possible that these kids would go free because their constitutional rights were violated. If the judge and jury bought their story and the taped confession was not allowed to be introduced as evidence, they could be acquitted.

There were no witnesses. He could be the vital link that would determine the outcome of the trial.

Oh, God, why me? He felt a tingling sensation begin to creep up his leg, starting in his dangling feet. He changed his position on the branch in an attempt to ease the sensation. Once again, the urge to run far away from the whole mess became strong, and for an instant, he considered it. He remembered the words of Father McClanahan.

"You can't run away from your problems forever. Sooner or later, you've got to face them."

Sure, it was easy for him to say that, but he isn't the one facing it, Craig thought resentfully.

Everybody had advice for him. It sounded so easy, but none of them had to face the consequences. What the hell did they know! He looked down at his clenched fist and noticed a whiteness begin to creep into his knuckles. He took a deep breath and released his grip.

Tears began to drip down his cheeks, and he felt relieved as he allowed them to fall. He looked down at the weeping branches of the willow tree and felt an unusual closeness to the inanimate wood hulk he was sitting in. Caressing the large branch that trailed up from his seat, he could almost feel the tree react empathetically to his sad touch.

It was going on three o'clock when Craig decided to leave his high perch. As he jumped to the ground, he patted the large trunk thankfully and headed for the house. Mr. J had not come home for lunch and it was safe to return to his room. Mr. J had said something about his mother coming home today, and Craig decided to wash up in case she did arrive. He was still amazed at his lack of excitement about the return of his mother and felt a little guilty about it. He rationalized that his lack of enthusiasm was a result of the anxiety he felt. When this whole thing was over, he could feel normal again.

It was going on 3:30 pm and he suddenly heard the familiar roaring sounds of the school bus discharging its passengers at the selected corners of the neighborhood. As the kids got off, the bus, they let out shrieking yells: "Yeah! Yeah!"

Craig was confused for a minute but finally realized what the reveling was all about.

Christmas vacation had started and the holiday season meant fun, presents, and no school for almost two weeks. Craig went to his window and watched the younger kids scamper for their houses, still yelling their hurrahs. He waited until all of them were inside and the joyful din of their young voices subsided. Thank God! He had a two-week reprise from his ordeal and he felt a rush of relief and joy. His new Billy Joel CD sat precariously on his chest of drawers, and he decided to celebrate his vacation with a little music.

"While in these days of quiet desperation, as I wander through the world in which I live I search everywhere for some new inspiration. But it's more than cold reality can give. If I need a cause for celebration or a comfort I can use to ease my mind, I rely on my imagination …"

It was 5:30 pm when the front door opened and Mr. J announced his arrival home from work. Craig heard quiet chatter and came to the conclusion that his mother had accompanied him home.

It was a strange feeling to hear both his parents' voices again in the same house. It had been many months since his parents had lived under the same roof together, and Craig had become quite used to the quiet serenity of home. Gone were the caustic words, nasty looks, and uneasiness that prevailed in the house when his parents were battling. When Melissa left, it changed the whole atmosphere, and Craig had quite a time adjusting to an all-male household. Once again, it was a bittersweet experience for him as he simultaneously mourned the absence of his mother and sister but reveled in the newfound peace that permeated the house.

"Hello! Craig, are you home?"

The familiar voice of his mother echoed throughout the house as she greeted her long-estranged son. Craig swallowed, brushed his hand through his soft, blond hair, and came into the family room with a semi-sincere smile etched on his face.

"Hi, Mom, I'm here, good to see ya! Welcome home!"

They embraced for a long time, and for the first time in months, Craig felt a stirring in his heart. Mrs. J squeezed him tightly, and he could feel moisture on the side of his face that touched his mother's cheek. She was sobbing softly and continued to hold him until she could regain some composure and face him without breaking down completely.

Craig broke the emotion of the moment by playfully tugging on his mother's skirt and whispering, "I can't breathe, Mom."

She stepped away and looked at the still smiling face of her son. All three began to laugh, and Mr. J invited them all into the kitchen for a champagne toast. For this occasion, even Craig was invited to participate in the toast. A pop of the cork and the sparkling wine was poured into three pre-chilled champagne glasses Mr. J had stored in the refrigerator just for this occasion. Craig noticed a fourth one sitting on the table and assumed Melissa had also been invited. Melissa was just in time as a rap came on the front door and his big sister announced her arrival.

"One big, happy family again, how nice" she shouted as she entered the kitchen and hugged and kissed everyone. "Welcome home, Mom."

Melissa grasped her mother's hands and gripped them tightly as she extended her warm greeting and sincere wishes. Mrs. J's eyes began to moisten again as she turned away from her daughter and began nervously fidgeting with her watch.

Mrs. J was not usually one to become overly emotional, and she was a bit embarrassed by her lack of control in front of her children and husband. Mr. J recognized his wife's uneasiness and rescued her from the uncomfortable situation, refilling her champagne glass and making another toast. This time, Melissa joined in after Mr. J poured a glass for her. Craig liked the dry taste of the champagne and held his glass out for more. His father smiled wryly and succumbed this one time.

"That's enough now, Craig," he admonished gently as he refilled Craig's glass.

It went down like water as Craig drained the contents of the glass and gently set it down on the kitchen table.

"What's for dinner, folks?" Melissa jokingly inquired.

Mr. J had already set the oven for the fifteen-pound turkey that he had purchased. The pre-cooked turkey only needed to be warmed thoroughly. At first, he planned to take the entire family out to dinner, but when he thought about it, he decided a dinner at home would be more appropriate.

"We'll be eating in about a half hour," answered Mr. J as he turned the stove burner on under a pot of his famous creamed spinach and gravy. Sweet potatoes and Mr. J's special cranberry compote were also on the menu. Craig noticed that his father had previously prepared everything just for this momentous occasion.

Mrs. J made mention of the new culinary skills that her husband had acquired in her absence. They all laughed when she suggested that he permanently assume the job as head cook in the household. Mr. J smiled and requested Melissa's assistance in setting the table for the special meal.

"Sure, Dad," said Melissa as she motioned to Craig to follow her into the dining room.

"What d' ya think, brother of mine? Ya think they'll be able to mend their marriage and make it work this time?"

"Shh." Craig admonished his sister who didn't know how to whisper. "They'll hear you." Melissa smiled and asked Craig to help her set the table. As Craig was retrieving the dishes from the china closet, Melissa asked him about his problem.

"When are you going to deal with that, Craig?" she asked.

"With what?" Craig replied.

"You know exactly what I mean. You can't keep this thing going much longer. I just read in the newspaper yesterday that …"

"Will ya shut up, please," Craig implored. "Please drop it, huh? I don't want to think about it tonight."

Melissa decided it wasn't the most appropriate time to discuss it. They both remained silent from then on until the table was set, and then both went into the family room, where Mr. and Mrs. J were whispering to each other. They aborted the conversation when the children entered the room.

They reminisced about the funny things that had happened to them during their years together, and even Craig chuckled at some of the mishaps and amusing incidents that were called to mind by his parents. They kept the conversation light and humorous until Mr. J excused himself to tend to the meal.

"I bought a Christmas tree today and I was hoping that we could decorate it tonight after dinner," Mr. J said from the kitchen.

Melissa had a date planned for the night, but decided to break it when her father requested a family decorating party. She excused herself and went into her parents' bedroom to make a phone call.

For the time being, Craig forgot about his problem and began to enjoy the reunion celebration as they all sat down to a delicious turkey dinner. The occasion turned out to be very happy and pleasant. Craig couldn't remember the last time they sat down to a meal as a family without some nasty or sarcastic comments being exchanged.

After dinner, the tree was dragged into the house, and Craig and Mr. J propped it up on a stand while Melissa and Mrs. J tended to the dishes.

Just like old times, thought Craig as he held the tree straight while his father adjusted the stand that was attached to the base of the tree.

They all joined in hanging the lights and the Christmas bulbs as Melissa started a sing-along of Christmas carols. Mr. J's face beamed with joy as the family shared in the traditions of the Christmas holiday. A feeling of love had returned to the Juncosa home, and everyone could feel it. Craig had become so inured to life without a mother that he had forgotten the secure feeling and pleasant experience of family life.

When Mr. J switched on the Christmas lights as the finale of the decorating party, everyone applauded loudly and Mr. J disappeared into the kitchen to fetch another bottle of champagne.

He sure must be happy, thought Craig. Mr. J never overindulged and he was certainly going all out tonight. Once again, he toasted the reunited family as they all drank heartily.

"Champagne goes bad if you keep it refrigerated after you open it," said Mr. J.

That was a cue for everyone to come with glasses for a refill. Even Craig was invited for a glass, and he knew that his father was absolutely ecstatic. They reveled and laughed until Melissa interrupted with a loud yawn.

"I gotta work tomorrow, folks!" she exclaimed. "Where's my coat?"

Craig was feeling all warm inside and decided then and there that he really liked champagne.

Following Melissa to the hall closet, he gently helped her on with her coat as she looked in amazement at her brother, who suddenly had become a gentleman.

"Who said chivalry is dead!" she exclaimed as Craig adjusted her coat collar.

Mr. and Mrs. J beamed with parental joy to see their two siblings acting civil with each other.

"Wouldn't it be nice if we were always so thoughtful and considerate toward one another?" said Mrs. J.

Mr. J seconded the motion and put his muscular arm around his wife's waist. Melissa kissed and hugged everyone again and headed for the front door, elated over the whole evening.

"Good night."

"Night, sis."

"Good night, Melissa."

"Night, Mom and Dad, Craig. Thanks for a wonderful evening."

They watched Melissa drive off before switching off the outside light and locking up for the night. They all yawned almost simultaneously, and Craig got the hint.

"Night, Mom. Night, Dad."

Mrs. J grabbed Craig again and hugged him tightly. She said nothing, but Craig knew what she meant. She was glad to be home and glad to be reunited with her husband and son. Needless to say, Mr. J looked ten years younger as he stood beaming from ear to ear.

Craig quietly closed his bedroom door and switched on the small lamp on his bedside table. He heard his parents enter the master bedroom, gently close and lock the door. He smiled knowingly and began to undress. He wanted to hold on to the total joy of the evening as long as possible, and jumped immediately into his bed.

For the first time in many months, he felt that things would be all right some day. Even his dreaded dilemma seemed somewhat resolvable. The champagne had relaxed him, and instead of curling up tightly in a fetal position, he lay stretched out comfortably on his back and awaited his only escape: sleep.

CHAPTER SEVENTEEN
The Breaking Point

It started out as a relatively happy Christmas Day for the Juncosa Family. After the initial reunion of parents and children, a rather difficult period of readjustment was experienced by all. Mr. and Mrs. J were very careful with each other, and an uncomfortable atmosphere prevailed in the house.

As they all sat down to their Christmas dinner, Mr. J asked for a period of silence and prayer. Craig could see the tightness in his father's lips and knew he was not yet at ease with his reunited spouse. Conversation was light and rather boring during the meal as everyone avoided any subject that might be construed as controversial.

Craig remembered the volatile arguments and temper tantrums that existed before the breakup and was content that discussions and conversations remained non-threatening and banal.

A letter had arrived home the day before Christmas from the school reporting Craig's absences on the last two days before Christmas vacation. Fortunately, he had intercepted the notice before his parents had a chance to see it. He felt relatively safe that they wouldn't discover it until after the vacation.

Mrs. J was still a beautiful lady and had shed a few of the unsightly pounds she carried before the separation. She looked stunning in her new Christmas dress, and everyone commented on her appearance. Her blond hair was loose and flowing, giving her a youthful look, and Mr. J kept looking at her with an admiring glow on his rugged face.

In a previous discussion, Mrs. J had been designated to be the spokesperson for a little presentation they had prepared for the dinner table. She cleared her throat and began.

"Your father and I are together again, and we both feel a responsibility to you." She nodded to Melissa and Craig individually and continued, "Marriage is a very difficult commitment to make, and people must work at it. It's not something you can take lightly or take for granted. Daddy and I had our disagreements and problems, as all people have, but our mistake was we failed to clearly communicate our concerns to one another. To make a long story short, we are now talking things out rather than clamming up when something bothers us. We learned from the counselor we are seeing that we must do this if the marriage is going to work, and we are committed to making it work this time. It will take a little time, but we are determined. Let's make a pact right now with each other. If something is bothering you, let's talk about it. The rules are simple:

don't pass judgment on what the person is saying. Listen and accept the feelings that the other person has. Don't criticize or put down each other."

It sounded so rehearsed that Craig chuckled to himself. He wondered just how long the pact would last, especially after they discovered his truancies. He was tempted to reveal his secret to them at that moment and hold them to their word. He thought better of it when he remembered it was Christmas Day and not the most appropriate time to tell his story. Everyone agreed to the pact, and they finished their dinner high-spirited and congenial.

Dessert time was Craig's favorite part of the meal, and his mother had baked one of her patented apple pies. Just as he was about to dig into it, his father brought up the dreaded subject.

"Looks as though those kids who supposedly murdered the Stohler kid are going to trial in two weeks. I wonder if they're going to get off on a technicality."

Craig cringed. Melissa glanced at him and noticed the tenseness in his face.

"What do you mean, get off on a technicality?" Mrs. J inquired.

"Well," said Mr. J, "according to the paper, the police illegally questioned those kids without their parents' knowledge. There were no witnesses and all of the evidence so far is circumstantial."

Craig almost screamed out what he was thinking: *I saw the whole damn thing ... I saw it all!*

"You mean to say those little hoodlums will go free because the police botched up the investigation? I can't believe that!"

"It's true, dear. Unfortunately, it could happen."

Melissa remained morbidly silent throughout the whole discussion, occasionally looking at Craig for some indication of his thoughts.

"What do you kids think?" asked Mr. J after noticing the unusual silence from both of them.

"I … I dunno, Dad," Craig quickly chimed in before Melissa could speak. "The kids in school say they'll probably be convicted even though they were illegally held by the police."

Craig had verbalized what he so desperately wished for.

"Not necessarily," Melissa interrupted. "The way things are going now with the big push for rights of the accused and everything, I wouldn't be a bit surprised if they get away with it."

She looked directly at Craig when she finished her statement. He knew what she was thinking.

Craig couldn't take it any longer and excused himself to go to the bathroom. As he carefully closed the bathroom door, he could hear the remainder of the conversation.

"They'd better come up with some new evidence or those kids will be walking the streets the next day."

Craig sat heavily on the toilet bowl and covered his face with his hands. He leaned over to try to ease the cramps that began to gnaw away at his stomach. He knew that

Melissa was very close to telling her parents about Craig's involvement, and the thought was too much for him to bear.

"Please, sis, please don't," he whispered pleadingly.

The day was ruined for him, and he just couldn't face them again. He decided to feign illness to escape the probing eyes of his sister and the possible wrath of his parents if she told them. Melissa would instantly know what he was up to, so he decided to avoid facing her again.

"Dad? Dad?" he called.

"What is it, Craig?"

"I'm not feeling too well. I'm going to lie down for a while."

Mrs. J immediately stood up and rushed toward his room.

"What's the matter, Craig?" she asked with motherly concern.

Craig was face down on his bed and replied, "Mom, my stomach hurts. I have cramps.

Must have eaten too much or something. I'll be all right—just want to lie down for a while."

Mrs. J approached him and stroked his head solicitously. It felt good to have his mother there, and he acknowledged her gentleness by moving his head higher on the pillow so she could more easily stroke and caress his head and back. She felt very guilty about leaving him and was determined to make up for her long absence. She realized how much more her absence affected Craig then

Melissa and, after discussions with her husband, decided she would give him a lot of attention. She stayed with him a long time, and Craig began to feel a little uneasy about faking his illness. Mr. J and Melissa had long since cleared the table and were sitting in the family room.

"Mom, go ahead and join Dad and sis," Craig implored. "I'll be all right, don't worry."

Mrs. J patted his head and went to join her husband and daughter.

He could hear the voices coming from the family room, but couldn't quite make out what was being said. His curiosity got the best of him, and he stole quietly out of his bedroom and into the adjoining hall. From there, he could hear the conversation. When he heard the words "New Year's Day," he breathed a sigh of relief. They were off the subject of Peter Stohler, and Melissa had not blurted out what she knew.

From that point on, Craig was not interested in what was being said and he quietly tiptoed back to his bedroom. He carefully closed the door and flopped on his bed. He was thankful when he heard Melissa head for the coat closet. She would be leaving soon, and he was safe for another day.

"Bye, Craig. Merry Christmas!" Melissa shouted from the hallway.

"Thanks, sis, see ya," He ran from his room to hug his big sister. Melissa backed away and looked disdainfully at her brother, who was so young and stupid. Craig turned away quickly and walked to the front door. He opened it and held it open while Melissa kissed her parents and thanked them for the holiday meal. As she passed Craig, she leered at him. Craig sheepishly acknowledged the leer by nodding his head in a thankful manner.

"Lock the front door, Craig," his father commanded.

He was momentarily startled by his father's sharp command, but breathed a sigh of relief when he heard Melissa's car rumble away.

"Okay, Dad," he replied.

It was a little past midnight, and Mr. J made the rounds and customarily checked the doors, stove, and the lights before retiring.

"Your mother and I are going to bed, Craig. We're very tired and we've got to pick up a lot of Mother's belongings tomorrow."

"Good night, Dad. Night, Mom. Merry Christmas."

He embraced both his parents. His mother squeezed him unusually hard and held him for a long time.

She whispered in his ear, "I'm so happy to be back with you."

If felt good to hear his Mom speak affectionately again. For so long, she had a terrible hardness to her voice that disturbed him. Finally, she sounded again like the mother he knew as a small boy. Craig strolled to his room with a boyish grin on his face. The wretched ringing of the phone shattered the silence of the moment, and Craig nearly fell to the floor as he turned and dashed toward the family room. Not on Christmas Day—those bastards! He was breathing heavily as he lifted the receiver and meekly answered. His voice was barely audible and he cleared his voice and repeated, "Hello?"

"Craig? Yes, this is Melissa. I …"

"What the heck are you doin' calling this hour of the night?" Craig angrily interrupted.

"Will you be quiet and see if I left my reading glasses there. I can't find them and I think I left them in the kitchen. Could you check for me, please?"

"Who is it, Craig?" his mother's faint voice came from the bedroom.

"Melissa, Mom. She left her glasses here. Everything's okay. Don't worry," he yelled back.

"Hold it, I'll check," he said annoyingly.

He nearly cracked the phone receiver, dropping it abruptly on the small end table. He found her glasses on the kitchen cabinet and returned to the phone.

"Yeah, they're here. You scared the living hell out of us calling at one o'clock in the morning."

Melissa knew why he was inordinately frightened by late phone calls and sarcastically answered, "If you would do what you're supposed to do, you wouldn't be afraid of every damn sound you hear."

She quickly changed the subject. "Do me a favor, please. Put my glasses in the mailbox so I can pick them up tomorrow morning on my way into the city."

"Okay."

Craig hung up without as much as a good-bye. He grasped the leather glass case and ran outside to the mailbox. Depositing the glasses and case into the mailbox, he looked out into the cold night and a shiver shot up his spine.

Across the street was parked the sports car, or an exact replica of it, that stopped him on River Road. *No, it couldn't be*, thought Craig as his eyes began to focus in on the darkness that partially hid the car. He backed slowly toward the house, his eyes riveted on the steel object. When he reached his front door, he quickly stepped in and slammed the door shut.

"What's going on down there?" Once again, his mother's faint voice reached his ears.

"Nothing, Mom, nothing, I'm going to sleep now, good night."

He tiptoed toward his bedroom and, once inside, closed and latched the door, something he seldom did. He cringed as he tried to visualize the car and passengers that terrorized him.

I must be getting paranoid, thought Craig as he began to undress. *It couldn't be—no, no not on Christmas Day!*

As he talked to himself, he convinced himself that his imagination was getting the better of his good sense. He remembered what Melissa had said about his being frightened of everything and immediately dismissed the gruesome thought from his confused mind.

It kept coming back as much as he tried to forget it, and Craig became annoyed. *Gotta check it out again before*

I go to sleep, thought Craig. *I can't sleep unless I know it's not the same car.*

He quietly stole out of his bedroom and edged his way through the black darkness of the house. As he came into the living room, the light from the December moon streaming through the large picture window eased his straining eyes. He edged carefully toward the window. He peered around the left corner of the window and looked out at the darkness. He waited until his eyes focused and strained to look toward the corner where he had seen the car.

Nothing … not a damn thing. Am I going crazy or what? he thought. He had seen the damn car and now it was gone. He kept staring into the night, hoping to get a momentary glimpse of that car he knew he saw; nothing … just the blackness of the night with the moon beaming down through the window. Craig edged away from the window and sat heavily on the couch. He shivered and crumpled up in a fetal position as his body began to shake uncontrollably.

He lay there for ten minutes, his knees tightly up against his chest. He could hear his heart beating rapidly.

Gotta get to sleep, thought Craig. *This thing is driving me nuts. Gotta get to sleep.*

He edged his way out of the moonlit living room and into the blackness of the hall. He felt for the doorknob on his bedroom door and quietly entered his room, clenching his teeth in a futile attempt to block out the creaking sound of the closing door. Satisfied that his parents hadn't heard anything, he released his hand from the knob and stole quietly toward his bed.

Sliding under the sheets and double blankets, he pulled the covers over his head and bunched his pillow up so his head was propped up but fully covered by his sheet and blankets.

Thank God it was my imagination, thought Craig. *Boy, I need to get my head together or I'll end up in a loony bin.*

It wasn't until 3:00 a.m. that Craig finally got to sleep. Just a few minutes before his eyes closed, a red sports car idling quietly in front of the Juncosa house waited for its three passengers. They had just finished painting a large black skull and crossbones across the garage door.

CHAPTER EIGHTEEN
The Decision

Craig gulped nervously as he began reading the article in the *Norfolk News*.

MONROE – A detective testified yesterday in county court that the parents of a Centerville youth questioned about the death of 14-year-old Peter Stohler were not notified that their son was in police custody because the youth did not request that they be called.

Thomas Hill, a detective assigned to the Norfolk Police Department's homicide squad, testified that Dean Howser, 15, of 42 Lafayette Drive, Centerville, was picked up for questioning the afternoon of Oct. 23, and held for about four hours before his parents were notified.

Hill's testimony came during the second week of a hearing to determine whether a confession allegedly made by another defendant in the case, Henry Barr, 16, of 22 Carver Drive, Centerville, can be used at a trial. Dean Howser, Henry Barr, and Frank Calandria, 15, of 13 Grove Street, Centerville, are charged with second-degree murder in connection with the Oct. 3 murder of Stohler, also of Centerville.

Lawyers for the defendants, John Cassette and Mark Cohn, have charged that the youths were picked up by police and held incommunicado for several hours. The lawyers want the confession invalidated on the grounds that it was illegally obtained. Prosecutor Charles Bola has argued that the confession was legal.

Under examination from Cassette, Hill testified that he questioned Howser about the murder for about four hours. He said that Howser's parents were not notified that their son was in police custody because he never asked that they be called. Cassette charged that the precinct engaged "in a big cover-up" in an attempt to fool the parents of the suspects into believing that their children were not in custody. Detective Hill denied the charge. The youths, plus a possible unknown fourth person, are charged with killing Stohler after he saw them burglarizing a local home. They allegedly strangled him with a belt. The hearing is to continue today.

Craig dropped the paper on the floor near his bed and began to pray that the evidence would be allowed in the trial. Even if it was, Travis Graham could go free if the other three did not implicate him in the murder. He lay back on his bed, staring at the ceiling. He could feel his heart beating rapidly and was powerless to control his growing anxiety. It was Thursday, the twenty-eighth of December, and school would be resuming in five days. The thought of returning to school and facing Graham again was almost inconceivable. He began to wish he could make time stop so it would never come.

Mr. J had been the first to notice the black painted skull and crossbones across the garage door. When he told Craig, it substantiated his sighting of the red sports car on Christmas night. He shuddered at the thought of being so close to that car and its occupants that night, and barely heard his father's strong condemnation of the lousy youth of today and their lack of respect for people and property.

Mr. J had reported the vandalism to the police, and Craig was present when they arrived to take information from his father. He looked frightened as Mr. J angrily told the police of his discovery of the black symbol on his garage door. This prompted one of the police officers to comment to Craig.

"What's the matter, son? You look afraid. Don't worry about it. Probably a few drunk kids out for some kicks. Thank God they didn't do more extensive damage. You can always repaint the garage door." Mr. J was indignant with the officer's casual attitude toward the whole incident, but suppressed a strong desire to comment. Instead, he walked away in a huff, mumbling mild obscenities about the lack of concern by everyone, including the law. As Craig turned to follow his father back into the house, the young police officer called to him. "Are there any kids who are after you or giving you a hard time in school, son?"

Craig was startled and looked confused before realizing why the officer had asked him the question. "No … no," Craig answered, shaking his head. "There's no one out to get me. Why do you ask?"

The officer shrugged his shoulders. "Well, sometimes kids who are trying to get back at another kid will pull pranks like this. You know what I mean." The officer smiled faintly at Craig as he turned and walked back to the patrol car that was still idling in front of the house. Craig could hear the police radio blaring reports to headquarters between loud and prolonged periods of static.

The whole police scene so unnerved him that he became nauseous and made a dash for the bathroom. He locked the door, and as he passed the mirror over the medicine cabinet, he saw his ashen face reflected as he made a beeline for the toilet bowl. Whenever Craig became nervous about something, he always had troubles with his stomach. He was a prime candidate for an ulcer and wondered whether he already had one as he bent over the toilet bowl and wretched. Nothing came up, but he stayed in this position until the nauseous feeling subsided.

Fairly confident that the feeling had passed, he moved toward the door, glancing again at his face as he passed the mirror. He stopped and approached the mirror to get a better look at his face and noticed his cheeks being drawn farther and farther in. He was losing weight and could ill afford to lose anymore with an already slim frame. Since the incident, he found it difficult to finish a meal and skipped lunch many times in school—when he was there. His father had noticed his gaunt look and had commented on his appearance. "You'd better get some weight on you, Craig. You're beginning to look like one of those kids on the World Hunger posters. What's the matter? Are you feeling okay?"

Craig would always slough it off and assure him he was perfectly all right. Even his mother commented on his appearance when she was with him, and he began to get annoyed at their constant nagging.

"I'm okay. Just leave me alone. God, what do I have to be, two hundred pounds?"

Mr. and Mrs. J got his message and refrained from any further comments but privately expressed their concerns to each other.

Vinny and Roland were supposed to come over to the house on December 30. He had invited them over during a weak moment in school, and he was embarrassed to call them and cancel it. He was in no mood to entertain two of his friends, and the thought of Vinny and Roland coming for the entire day bothered him. He just couldn't tolerate Vinny's crazy antics and Roland's whining.

However, Craig was one to fulfill his commitments to his friends and had resigned himself to spending the day with them. He had received a number of games and a carved chess set for Christmas, and he figured he could occupy a good deal of the time introducing his two friends to the new games. Maybe he could get Vinny and Roland to play chess together. That way, he would be able to get a brief respite from them.

He continued to conjure up possible things to do and ways that would minimize his involvement. He knew Vinny would probably want to play football or something, and the last thing he wanted to do was to get involved in any strenuous activity. He just didn't feel up to it. He finally decided to forget about it and play it by ear.

He had received a pair of jeans for Christmas from his parents, and they didn't fit. Craig decided to take his bike and ride down to Gerard's Department Store to exchange them. Sitting around and thinking about his damn problem didn't help a thing. He figured that if he kept occupied, his mind would function better. He jumped on his bike and headed for town.

As he passed Nick's Pizza Stand, he saw a few of the neighborhood kids sitting on the open porch attached to the pizza stand. They were pointing at Craig as he passed by, and he wondered why he was being talked about. Again he wondered if he was getting paranoid about the whole mess he was involved in.

He parked his bike in front of the store and secured it to a nearby utility pole with his bolt lock. As he walked toward the entrance of Gerard's, he noticed a red sports car emerging from the narrow alleyway by the storefront. He instinctively lunged for the door handle of the store, threw it open, and nearly fell into the store.

Everyone in the store turned to look at the clumsy youth who had just entered. Craig felt the blood pour into his cheeks and the accompanying hot flush. As nonchalantly as possible, he strode toward the section marked Boy's Jeans.

One of the store employees, a college girl, stopped him and inquired about the package he carried.

"Oh, sorry I … I want to exchange a pair of jeans my parents bought me for Christmas," Craig stammered.

"Please leave the package at the counter, sir," the girl replied.

He followed the girl back to the store counter and sheepishly handed the package to her. She placed it under the counter and urged him to seek out a different pair. Craig returned to the boys' section of the store and began to sift though the jeans that hung invitingly on the pipe racks. When he came across his size, he removed a pair from the rack and brought it up to the counter.

This time he got a good look at the young girl who was preoccupied with taking care of another customer. She was a pretty brunette with long, shoulder-length hair. She had a tight sweater on that revealed a voluptuous figure, and Craig momentarily felt a stirring of desire, a feeling that for so long had remained dormant due to the overriding anxieties that controlled his recent life. He didn't notice the customer leave and was caught staring at her bosom.

"Can I help you?"

Craig once again felt the flush of embarrassment creep into his cheeks as he quickly handed the jeans to the girl. She had a faint smile on her face as she rung up a return on the old pair and packaged the new pair in a fresh paper bag.

"I hope these fit. You can try them on, you know, if you like, in the back of the store."

She pointed to a set of curtains in the back of the store.

Craig politely refused her offer.

"No, no, thanks, I'm sure they'll fit. My parents just didn't know my right size."

"Okay, have it your way," she said sarcastically.

Craig grabbed the package and hurried for the store entrance. He glanced back to get a last look at the beautiful salesgirl and caught her looking directly at him, a broad, devilish smile across her pretty face. He turned and quickly opened the door to leave when he caught sight of the red sports car again. He slowly closed the door and remained inside the store, looking out. He didn't turn around but stood close to the door, hand on handle, staring out. He recognized Travis Graham sitting on the passenger side, his long arms draped over the sleek red door of the sports car. Travis was staring at the doorway, but evidently couldn't see Craig due to the sunlight on the glass doorway. Craig realized that he couldn't be seen and gradually moved away from the door.

The salesgirl had witnessed his bizarre behavior and she began to wonder about Craig's mental state. He glanced momentarily toward the counter and caught the girl looking at him with a rather perplexed look on her face. He passed by her and offered the best excuse he could possibly think of at the time.

"I wanna look at some shirts. I just remembered that my father told me to pick out a shirt I wanted."

"Go right ahead," the girl interrupted. "You don't have to explain to me."

Craig grinned halfheartedly and strode toward the shirt rack. He simulated deep and careful analysis of each shirt he looked at, but his mind was elsewhere. *How the hell am I going to get out of this place without those guys seeing me?* He was sure they would remain there as long as was necessary, and he suddenly felt trapped and totally helpless. Maybe there was a rear door to the store, but how was he going to get to it without being noticed by the store employees? They would think he was trying to steal something and he would be in more trouble. Damn it, why did he leave the house? Now he was in some fix.

He edged toward the center of the store so he could get a better view of the rear to see if there was an easy exit. He noticed a lit-up red sign that said "Fire Exit" and began to walk slowly toward it. Thank God there were other customers in the store and he could walk unnoticed toward the red sign. When he reached the door, he momentarily turned around to survey the situation.

Fortunately, he had gone unseen so far and felt confident that he could get out. The door had a panic bar on it similar to the doors in school, and Craig carefully reached for it. He glanced back again to make sure he wasn't being observed. Depressing the bar and pushing at the same time, he swung the door open and quickly exited.

A small alleyway led to the back road of the shopping center and Craig ran pell-mell for the woods bordering the road. Once inside the woods, he paused to catch his breath. His heart was racing, and the beats were hardly distinguishable. It was more like a flutter, and he sat on the cold ground to catch his breath.

Craig decided to jog home after his long rest in the woods and cut through the church cemetery. He picked up his pace as he got closer to home and was running at top speed when he reached his front door. He flung open the door and ran in, removing his jacket as he sped through the hallway toward his room. Home sweet home, safe from the wrath of his tormentors, safe for the time being, anyway.

A frown crept onto his face as he sat on his bed, removing his sneakers. He had left his new jeans in the store and his bicycle outside the store. *Damn it! Damn it!* They're just going to have to stay there for a while. There was absolutely no way that he was going back to Gerard's. He'd worry about retrieving his bike later. The sound of the doorbell broke Craig's concentration.

"What ya say, Vinny? Hi Roland, come on in guys!" Craig welcomed his guests for the day with false enthusiasm. They trudged into the house, Roland obediently following close behind Vinny.

"How ya doin', Craig?" Vinny bellowed in his own inimitable style. "Here's your paper. It was sitting on your front lawn. You got a lazy paperboy. Did ya see the headlines? It's all about Peter Stohler's murder and the kids who dunnit."

Craig cringed as he thanked Vinny and glanced quickly at the headline:

Defense in Stohler Murder Wants Confessions Excluded

"These kids are in Centerville High. I know the Calandria kid. He's good friends with my brother," Vinny said.

Craig answered obligingly, "Is that right?"

"Yeah, my brother says the other kids are real nuts and one of the kids has a red sports car. He says the kids' parents have all kinds of money. They'll probably buy their kids out of it."

Roland chimed in at that point, "Ain't no way money is gonna get them out a this jam they're in. If they murdered Peter, they'll get the chair."

Vinny replied annoyed, "There's no electric chair in this state. Don't you know that, Roland?"

Craig wanted to get off the subject and interrupted, "Hey, guys, let's do something, huh? Let's get off this morbid crap!"

"Yeah, good idea," Vinny agreed. "What ya wanna do, Craig?"

"You guys know how to play chess?" Craig inquired.

"Yeah, yeah," both answered simultaneously.

Craig was looking for a way to catch a glimpse of the newspaper article. Here was a perfect opportunity. "I got a new chess set—all carved pieces—for Christmas. You guys play and I'll play the winner. I gotta go to the bathroom." Craig dug the set out from under the Christmas tree and set it on the dining room table.

"You guys start; go ahead." Craig excused himself and strode quickly toward the bathroom with the newspaper under his arm. He sat on the commode and began to devour the headline article.

MONROE – The defense attorney for Henry Barr, indicted in the murder of Peter Stohler, vehemently argued for the exclusion of a taped confession made to police by his client. The grounds for exclusion are that the confession was made under duress and without proper parental notification that Henry was being held for questioning by the police. The tape was played at a pretrial hearing in Norfolk County Court, where the defense is challenging the confession's validity and attempting to have it dropped as evidence.

The tape is being challenged by defense attorney John Cassette on the grounds that Henry Barr was illegally questioned without his mother or lawyer present. He also contends that the police used coercive and threatening tactics to elicit the confession from him, according to Barr. Henry allegedly told his mother and his attorney that the police used threatening and coercive tactics when they questioned him.

"They told me that I would be put in solitary confinement for a month and that I wouldn't see the light of day for years if I didn't give them the information they wanted. One of the detectives grabbed and squeezed my arm when I hesitated to give other names to them," said Barr.

"These strong-arm tactics used by the police on young teenagers were barbaric and seriously damages the integrity of what is supposed to be a civilized law enforcement agency," *said Defense Attorney Cassette. "If this evidence is allowed to be introduced in a court of law as legally procured evidence, it will be a most serious travesty of justice."*

Prosecutor Charles Bola discounted Barr's account of his questioning as fabricated and incredible. The pretrial hearing has been going on for several days, and a source close to District Attorney Charles Bowring indicated to news reporters that the decisions reached in the pretrial hearing will be vitally important to the outcome of the trial.

Craig stopped his voracious reading to gasp for air. He had been holding his breath the entire time, and the last few sentences that he read severely unnerved him. He had become extremely proficient at understanding legal terms and understood every word he read. It was frighteningly clear to him now that things were not good. He read the last sentence, folded the paper, and put his head between his knees in sheer frustration.

Testimony before Norfolk County Court Judge Robert W. Fleming is to resume tomorrow.

"Hey, Craig, what the hell did ya do, fall in?" Vinny's raspy voice echoed throughout the house.

"Be right there, Vin," replied Craig nervously. He flushed the toilet and quietly joined his two friends in the dining room.

"Are you okay, Craig?" Roland asked in his whining voice. "You look sick or something," he continued.

"I'm fine, fine. How'd you guys make out? Who's winning?" Craig changed the subject quickly.

"Roland took my queen, like a jerk. I missed a move and didn't see his bishop."

Roland smiled, gloating, and Vinny kicked him lightly in his shin to let him know that he caught him.

"Don't be so sure you got me, Roland. I can still win this game, so don't get cocky," Vinny warned.

Craig sat down next to Roland and urged them to continue. His eyes were fixed on the chessboard, but his mind was elsewhere. Craig began to seriously consider the pros and cons of coming forward and revealing his morbid secret to the police. Just the thought of it sent his heart beating quickly, and he felt a faint flush in his cheeks.

He started with the pros. These kids had committed a brutal and vicious crime and he alone witnessed it. His testimony would provide the ironclad evidence to convict them. He remembered what Father McClanahan had said. Those kids would have to live the rest of their lives with this on their conscience and they would be free to commit similar crimes again. They also would be free to terrorize and intimidate other people. Who knew what else they could or would do?

He then contemplated the cons. He would be targeted by them and by their friends, and he would be afraid to walk the streets or go to school. Other kids would point at him and call him a snitch, and he would become known throughout the town and county as the kid who testified in the Stohler murder trial. Newspaper reporters, police, and the media would want to interview him.

He could feel the perspiration begin to form on his forehead, and he quickly wiped it away. Roland and Vinny were totally engrossed in the chess game and didn't notice when Craig quietly stood up and tiptoed out of the dining room. Tears were flowing as he quickly strode to his room and closed the door. He ran to his bed and buried his head in the pillow in an attempt to muffle the sobs.

The decision was too difficult for Craig to make. He knew that to make it would result in dire consequences, regardless of the choice. The only wise alternative was to remain silent and hope that justice and the courts would prevail. Once again, he began to rationalize reasons why he should stay out of the whole mess. It was none of his business and he never liked the Stohler kid anyway. Why the heck should he stick his neck out for something he wasn't even involved in?

It was purely coincidental that he was there when the crime was committed. He had nothing to do with it and the whole damn incident was somebody else's problem. Convinced that he had finally made a decision, the tears subsided and Craig stole quietly to the bathroom to splash water on his swollen eyes and cheeks.

Luckily, Vinny and Roland were still engrossed in the chess game and he had time to compose himself and wipe away the remaining signs of his anguish. Craig remembered that he had challenged the winner of the chess game and began to conjure up excuses to get out of the match. He just wasn't up to a game of chess and he had to get out of it gracefully and without suspicion.

"Checkmate!" Roland's voice cracked over Vinny's grumbling.

"Come on, Craig; you're next," Roland triumphantly proclaimed.

"Listen, fellas, I'm not feeling too well. I ... I think I have a virus or something. I just upchucked and maybe you guys ought to go home. I'd hate like hell to have you catch the darn thing. It makes you feel miserable as hell."

Vinny and Roland looked up at Craig and both detected the red eyes and blotchy cheeks on Craig's fair skin. It gave credibility to Craig's claim, and they simultaneously stood up to move away.

"Get away from me, Craig," Vinny announced loudly. "I don't wanna get no virus for New Year's. Why the hell didn't you tell us before we came?"

"I didn't want to disappoint you guys, but I'm really feeling lousy. I thought maybe it had gone away, but it hit me again. I'm sorry, guys."

Craig did an excellent job of convincing his two friends of his ailment, and they both grabbed their jackets and headed for the front door.

"You wanna call your parents to get a ride?"

"No. No, thanks, Craig, we'll walk home," Vinny responded nervously. "Hope you're feeling better, Craig. See ya around."

It worked like a charm as his two friends quickly exited his house. Craig was thankful that he hadn't offended them in any way. Mrs. J was out shopping and he was alone again. Although he welcomed the serenity that usually accompanied being alone, he felt a pang of anxiety. He could clearly hear the hum of the refrigerator motor and the oil burner clicking on and off.

An occasional voice from outside broke the deafening silence of the house as Craig decided to take a walk. It was a crisp December day with flurries of snow drifting down and swirling in the occasional gusts of wind. He walked around the block twice before deciding to head for the willow tree in his backyard. As he climbed the tree and straddled his favorite branch, he looked out over Route 52A. Traffic was light with an occasional tractor-trailer truck whizzing by and swirling up the light snow flurries that began to accumulate on the roads.

This nightmare, that he had lived with for so long, had taken an enormous toll on his physical appearance and stamina. He began to shiver uncontrollably in the tree, but refused to climb down. There were times before the incident occurred when he sat on this branch in much colder weather and never reacted to the chilling wind. He had lost a lot of weight and his face revealed the agony of his dilemma. Drawn cheeks and a peaked, sickly look became the object of his parents' concern, and Craig had done all he could do to convince them that he was all right and didn't need to see a doctor.

Shivering in the tree, Craig began to pray for help.

CHAPTER NINETEEN
A Friend in Need

Craig ran for the front door as he heard the thump of the newspaper hurled from a moving bike strike his front stoop. The headline, "Teamster Strike Settled," had no relevance to him, and he began to quickly thumb through the newspaper. On page three, he caught sight of the name that had become so commonplace in the newspaper in the last few weeks.

"How about some breakfast, Craig?" Mrs. J was busy in the kitchen. It had become an obsession with her since her return home to try to fatten up her son.

"Okay. I'll have some cereal, Mom. Be right there—have to go to the bathroom."

Craig was in no mood for food but decided to appease his mother rather than refuse and listen to her lecturing. He rushed to the bathroom and locked the door behind him. Sitting on the commode, he began to read the article that glared out at him in black, bold headlines.

Stohler Murder Trial Opens

MONROE – Almost three months after the murder of 14-year-old Peter Stohler, three Centerville youths went on trial yesterday for what the prosecutor called the most "heinous and vicious killing in the county's history."

Craig cringed as he anxiously read on.

Assistant District Attorney Charles Bola told the jury that Stohler was murdered by three (or four) teenagers (a possible fourth youth is still an unknown factor) after he saw them burglarize a neighborhood house. Peter, the child of Mr. and Mrs. Stohler of Centerville, was found strangled to death on the morning of October 4. Bola's comments came at the start of the murder trial of Henry Barr, 16, Dean Howser, 15, and Frank Calandria, 15, all of Centerville and all students at Centerville High School. All are being prosecuted as adults. An unidentified possible fourth suspect is the subject of an intense investigation by the Norfolk County Police Department. The indictment was a result of a taped confession allegedly made by Henry Barr to Norfolk County Police. Judge Robert W. Fleming ruled in a pretrial hearing that Barr's confession was obtained illegally and under duress. As a result, this important piece of evidence will not be allowed to be introduced in the trial.

Craig slumped back on the toilet seat and dropped the newspaper on the bathroom floor. He closed his eyes and grabbed his forehead in despair. What he had dreaded for so long had finally happened. "Damn it—damn it to hell!" he blurted out as he massaged his forehead. He picked up the crumpled newspaper and continued reading.

John Cassette, the attorney for Henry Barr, who police have said confessed to the murder and implicated the others, angrily told the jury that homicide detectives had made a sham of the investigation and "had violated every civil right on the books" to obtain confessions from the boys. Cassette further characterized the investigation as "Gestapo like and totally un-American." Attorneys Mark Cohn and Daniel Hoot, representing the other two youngsters, waived opening statements to the jury.

"Craig, your eggs are getting cold." Mrs. J's voice startled Craig as he dropped the newspaper and jumped off the commode. Mrs. J had totally disregarded Craig's request for cereal and had prepared a large breakfast of bacon and eggs, toast and milk. His stomach was one big, tight knot, and he knew there was absolutely no way he could possibly consume the meal. He slowly opened the bathroom door and stole quietly to his room. Taking the entire newspaper, he carelessly shoved it under his guitar case. He ran his fingers through his disheveled hair, tucked his shirt into his pants, and headed toward the kitchen.

"Mom, I told you I just wanted cereal. Why did you make eggs for me?" His annoyed response surprised Mrs. J. Since her return home, Craig had gone out of his way to be overly polite and considerate toward his mother.

Mrs. J was uncomfortable with his attitude, knowing he had been putting on an act. When she heard his annoyed voice, she smiled. Back to his old self, she thought. She was glad that Craig was beginning to feel comfortable with her again.

"Come on, son. You need a good, hearty breakfast on a cold December morn. I made your favorite: Canadian bacon."

Craig strode into the kitchen and kissed his mother good morning. "Morning, Mom."

"You sound like you lost your best friend," Mrs. J said. "Have a good breakfast and you'll feel much better."

"Mom, I just don't feel like eggs this morning," Craig complained.

Mrs. J knew enough not to force him to eat and reluctantly removed the eggs from his place at the table. She decided that she would eat them and began to pour some cold cereal for Craig. Though he still had no desire to eat, he chose to force the cereal down rather than argue again with her. Mrs. J looked closely at her son and a concerned frown spread across her pretty face. She said nothing but turned away, troubled and deeply upset. She detected a terrible anguish in her son's face as only a mother can, and for the first time became totally convinced there was something drastically wrong with him. She would discuss it that evening with Mr. J, but for the time being she had to try to brighten his day. "How would you like to take in a movie this afternoon, Craig?" Mrs. J asked enthusiastically.

Craig hesitated for a moment, not expecting this kind of invitation from his mother. He wouldn't be caught dead at the movies with her. If any of the kids saw him, he would be the laughing stock of the school. "Nah, thanks, Mom I appreciate the offer, but … but I'm … I'm not feeling up to it today. I ... I have a headache. I think I'm coming down with a cold or something."

Craig made up excuses and reasons as he went along. Mrs. J didn't buy his excuses, but realized that he might not want to be recognized with his mother at the movies. She promptly rescinded her invitation. "There's nothing good playing, anyhow."

She knew something was gnawing away at Craig but she couldn't put her finger on it. She decided to tackle her apprehensions head on. "Craig, can I have a word with you?"

"What is it, Mom?" Craig turned and faced his mother as she pulled a kitchen chair out and offered him a seat. Craig looked a little puzzled, but accepted her offer. Mrs. J pulled out the chair across from him and sat down with folded hands on the kitchen table. Craig knew he was in for a lengthy lecture and was in absolutely no mood to sit and listen to his mother's advice, but he had no choice.

She began, "Craig, there is something called motherly instinct that no one else has but mothers. It sort of tells them something about their children that no one else recognizes or is aware of."

Craig began to listen carefully. *She can't possibly know anything about the incident, can she?* She continued, "My instinct now tells me that something is bothering you a lot. You're just not yourself. Daddy tells me and I can also see it that you have lost a lot of weight lately and you just don't look good."

Craig waited with bated breath for her to continue. "Craig, what is bothering you? I know something is on your mind and that it is hurting you. Whatever you tell me, I will keep confidential, I promise, and maybe I can help you resolve it." She stopped and waited, looking directly into his eyes with a soft, compassionate look on her face.

Again, he was tempted to blurt out everything to his mother. "Mom, Mom. I … I just don't feel too well. It's nothing, probably growing pains or something."

For a minute, Mrs. J thought he was ready to disclose the source of his anxieties, and she was right. Craig started to reveal his terrible ordeal, but reconsidered just in time. She had caught him at a very vulnerable moment, but something inside prevented him from confiding in his mother. Anyhow, he figured Melissa had already spilled the beans to her and she was just trying to get the story from him. Craig became confused and abruptly excused himself from the table, clumsily kicking the chair as he stood up. "Craig, please stay here and talk to me—please!" Mrs. J implored.

"I'm … I'm not feeling well, Mom. Please believe me, I'm just not feeling well, that's all it is. Now, get off my back." His voice angered gradually as he turned away from his mother and headed for his bedroom.

Mrs. J knew she had lost for the time being and didn't pursue him. Instead, she turned toward the sink and began cleaning the few dishes scattered in it. Craig heard the clattering of dishes and was relieved. He quietly latched his door and fell heavily on his bed.

The familiar rumbling of the front door woke Craig out of his afternoon sleep. He heard his father greet Mrs. J and begin his ritualistic toolbox cleaning and organization. The day's end for Mr. J consisted of a good half-hour of cleaning and organizing the tools of his trade. They represented his bread and butter, and he treated them with high regard and possessiveness. He constantly reminded Craig of the importance of organizing oneself. "Without organization, one cannot function effectively in this society." These words were uttered over and over by Mr. J, and Craig would nod each time his father said it.

"Dad is always saying the same damn thing to me," he complained privately to his sister.

"Over and over again. I've heard the same things a million times. I wish he'd find some new sayings."

Melissa would laugh and remind Craig of her ordeal with Mrs. J when she was growing up. "You remember Mom and her constant harping about my clothes. 'That makes you look sleazy; it's not becoming. You look like a floozy!' That's what I heard over and over again."

Craig would chuckle, remembering his mother's favorite sayings and admonitions. As Craig reminisced about the years when everyone was together, he felt a longing to return to those peaceful days when his biggest concern was who he would get in the next pack of baseball cards he bought. Things had certainly changed for him.

He suddenly felt a desire to see his buddy, Jerry. Of all the people he knew, Jerry was his favorite person. He always listened intently and most of the time was non-judgmental.

Occasionally, he would smile innocently at Craig and gently ruffle his soft, blond hair with his big, freckled hands. Craig felt a certain closeness to him that gave him the strength he needed to continue. Without the gentle giant's consoling and understanding, he knew he would have broken a long time ago.

"Dinner, Craig. Let's go, son." Mr. J's voice rumbled, and he responded quickly.

"Be right there, Dad."

An uneasy quiet permeated the dinner table, and Craig felt a little uncomfortable. Both his parents were glancing at him from time to time, and the usual dinner conversation was absent.

He felt their eyes on him every time he looked down at his plate, and he decided to finish his food quickly. "Don't eat so fast," Mr. J admonished.

Craig looked up obligingly and deliberately slowed down. Recently, Mrs. J had been talking to her husband about her concerns and he was trying to analyze Craig to substantiate her apprehensions. Craig knew the questions would begin to fly soon, and he was more determined to leave the table as quickly as possible. "Dad, I promised

Jerry, you know the guy who works for Gabor's Farm that I would go over to see him tonight. Is it okay if I go for a few hours?"

Craig looked pleadingly at his father. Mr. J looked toward his wife for approval, and when she nodded, he answered, "Okay, but be home by ten o'clock. And how are you going to get there?"

"I'll walk. It's only a couple of miles," Craig answered.

"Come on, I'll give you a ride over."

"No, it's okay, Dad. I want to get some fresh air. I haven't been out today and I need some exercise."

"Okay, you call when you're ready to come home and I'll pick you up in front of the farm. Is there a phone you can use there?"

"Okay, Dad. If Jerry doesn't drop me off, I'll call, okay?" Craig kissed his mother and strode quickly to the closet to retrieve his down jacket.

"See you later, Mom and Dad."

Once outside, he breathed a sigh of relief and took a deep breath, taking in the cold night air. It cleared his head and he immediately felt better. Anticipating his meeting with Jerry, Craig began to jog toward Route 52A. He didn't stop until he got within a mile of the horse farm. He continued walking at a brisk pace and arrived at Gabor's farm breathless but refreshed. It was getting dark as he walked toward the light in the north barn. Jerry always stayed with the horses until about 7:00 pm, when he would leave for some dinner. He startled Jerry when he entered the barn, and the big, gentle man smiled sheepishly at his young friend. "You scared the heck out of me, Junky," he said. "Why didn't you give me some warning, you wise guy." He grabbed Craig by the seat of his pants and lifted him off the ground, suspending him momentarily before gently lowering him. Craig smiled faintly at him and straightened his pants.

"How are you doin', Jerry? How was your Christmas? By the way, Merry Christmas!"

Jerry had no family, and holidays were lonely and rather sad for him. He was happy when they were over and didn't like to dwell on the memories that holidays brought back. "Thanks, Craig. How was yours?"

"Fine, fine, Mom is back home now, and my father seems much more content. He's not as uptight as he was when she wasn't there."

"Great Craig, that's good news, I'm happy for you. So all in all, you had a good day. Get anything good for Christmas?" Jerry asked.

"A chess set and some clothes. I needed them for school."

"Good. Glad you got what you wanted," Jerry replied. They continued to discuss trivial matters for a while, and when they ran out of things to say, Craig looked down at the dirt floor of the barn and stared blankly at it. Jerry knew about his terrible problem and wanted desperately to give him the right advice. "How are things going with that thing you witnessed?"

Craig looked up and with a doleful look responded, "Not good, Jerry. I mean bad, real bad." Jerry's expression changed to a concerned one as he sat down on a stool to listen to Craig's lamenting. "The judge in the murder trial is not going to let the jury hear the taped confession made by the Barr kid."

Jerry was a little more familiar with the case since Craig had become involved in it. "Don't worry about it, Craig. They're pretty sure those kids did it and, even without that evidence, they'll get them. You'll see. Don't fret so much. You'll get yourself sick as hell."

Craig looked up at his adult friend and saw a flicker of sincerity in the stable hand's eyes and he felt a little better. "Do you really think so?" Craig asked in a childlike manner.

"Sure thing, Craig. Justice is usually pretty darn accurate." Jerry reached for the most sophisticated words he could conjure up to try to impress his little friend.

Jerry continued. "If somebody is guilty of a crime, they're usually convicted. The courts of law know what they're doing, and juries are right on their verdicts 99 percent of the time."

Jerry looked for an approving expression on Craig's face. When he saw a glimmer of it, he placed his large arm over his shoulders and hugged him. "Come on now, relax. Give me a hand cleaning out old Jasper's stall." He walked Craig to the stall and handed him a pitchfork. "Let's see how you can use that tool, Junky. I'll make you a super stable hand yet."

The levity in Jerry's voice had an elating effect on Craig, and he enthusiastically began pitching hay. Alongside his gentle friend, Jerry's mammoth size dwarfed the fifteen-year-old, and they looked almost comedic side by side tending to the horses. "Last one, kid, and we go to my place for a nice, cold drink." They hurried through the last stall, and Jerry locked up the barn door. "See you tomorrow, steeds." The horses seemed to respond to Jerry's farewell with a few muffled neighs.

"What do you want, kid: Seven-Up, Coke, or root beer? I went shopping yesterday and I'm all stocked up."

"I'll take a root beer, Jer. Thank you," Craig answered.

Jerry went to his small refrigerator and pulled out two cans of soda. He set them down on the table and fetched two chilled glasses from the freezer. "I like my soda glasses chilled, especially with root beer."

"Hey, Jer, do you really think those kids will get convicted without that piece of evidence?"

Jerry looked down at him with a wry smile on his face. "What did I tell you, huh? You weren't even listening to me."

"Yes. I … I … just wanted you to assure me that they won't get off scot-free. I'm scared, Jerry. I'm scared stiff! Why me?"

Jerry stopped him by cupping his hand over Craig's mouth and holding up his can of soda, "Drink and shut up! Would I ever lie to you, Junky? Believe me, everything will work out. Now drink your root beer and relax."

Craig decided to get off the subject when he detected a slight anger in Jerry's voice. They both reminisced about the days they spent in the north barn tending to the horses and talking about trivial things: the happy, carefree days when they laughed and romped around the barn engaging in hay fights. As Jerry spoke, a slow dimpled smile began to creep across Craig's face. He had forgotten how to laugh, and for a moment he was lost in the pleasant memories of their frolicking and horseplay. The hour sped by, and before Craig knew it, the curfew set by his father neared. Craig checked his watch and interrupted Jerry's chatter. "Gotta get going, Jer. My ol' man said to be home by ten. Think you can give me a lift home?"

"Sure, kid," Jerry responded. They both hopped into the pickup truck and sped off in the direction of Craig's house. Jerry continued to talk as he drove; trying to keep Craig in the jovial mood he had him in. Craig listened politely, but the thought of going home and being alone again conjured up negative thoughts of what was waiting to face him there. He bid his farewell to Jerry, who gently patted his back as he emerged from the pickup truck. "Keep the old head high, kid. Remember what I told you—everything will work out."

Craig smiled meekly and waved as Jerry sped off, leaving a little rubber on the street. As Craig turned to walk toward his front door, he caught a glimpse of a small car parked on the opposite corner. His eyes had not yet focused in the dark, and he continued to stare at the car. Some overhanging evergreen bushes blocked the back portion of the car and only the front of it was exposed. As he stared, his eyes began to adjust to the darkness, and he breathed a sigh of relief. The car was either dark green or black, and, for an instant, Craig's legs felt rubbery as he turned and walked toward the front door. An eerie feeling crept into his body and he felt a sense of urgency to get into his house and lock the door behind him.

"That you, Craig?"

"Yeah, Dad, it's me," Craig replied.

"Mom and I are calling it a night. We're both tired. I would suggest that you get to bed, also. A good rest will do you good. Make sure everything is locked and secured, and switch off the front light."

"Okay, Dad. Night," Craig answered. He tiptoed to his room and switched on the night light in the hallway leading to his bedroom. He had been getting up frequently during the night and urinating, his nerves getting the best of him. He gently closed his bedroom door and changed into his flannel pajamas. Once under the covers, he buried his head under the double pillow and closed his eyes to try to hasten sleep.

Wild and erratic thoughts flashed through his head as the moment of truth was becoming so frighteningly close.

CHAPTER TWENTY
The Moment of Truth

Stohler Suspect Says Police Coerced Him
MONROE – In an unexpected move, Henry Barr testified in his own defense yesterday, asserting that neither he nor his other indicted friends had any part in the brutal October murder of 14-year-old Peter Stohler. Barr, 16, claimed that he had been coerced by Norfolk County detectives into making the confession that was taped by his interrogators.

That assertion spurred Prosecutor Charles Bola to ask that the previously suppressed tape recording be played for the jury. Judge Robert W. Fleming said that the ruling handed down during a pretrial hearing would stick and that the alleged taped confession would not be allowed to be introduced as evidence. He reprimanded Bola for insisting on the taped confession after the emphatic ruling made by Fleming and warned him not to mention it again during the trial.

Bola noted that, according to a 1971 U.S. Supreme Court ruling, if a defendant appears as a witness and makes statements to the police, the earlier statements can be used to impeach the defendant's credibility—even if those statements have been suppressed.

A few minutes after Barr began testifying, Mrs. Stohler, Peter Stohler's mother, started crying and stomped out of the courtroom. The Stohlers moved to California after Peter was slain; they returned to Norfolk County at the start of the trial.

Barr testified that he and two other friends, Dean Howser, 15, and Frank Calandria, 15, both of Centerville High School, were drinking some beer at Calderwood Elementary School on the evening of Stohler's death, but left the area and went to Calandria's garage to finish the six-pack an hour before the Stohler boy was murdered. "I never saw Peter Stohler. Frank and Dean got into my car and we drove to Frank's house. We parked the car in front of his house and went into his garage to finish the six-pack of beer. It was too cold outside."

The prosecution has alleged that when they were observed by Peter Stohler burglarizing a nearby house, they surrounded him, and, using a belt or a strap of some sort, strangled him to death.

Craig quivered uncontrollably as he relived the gruesome scene he witnessed on the dismal October evening. It was January 7 and he was back in school. The topic of conversation in school since his return from Christmas vacation was the murder trial. Craig couldn't get away from it. Whenever he tried to change the subject with his friends, they would inevitably return to it after a few minutes. It was stifling for him, and he yearned to be away from the school. His attendance was being closely monitored by his parents and the school, and cutting out was virtually impossible. The pallid look on his face became almost permanent, and whenever he heard anyone mention the word *acquittal*, he shuddered and grew paler. If these kids were acquitted, they would go free, and he knew they were the murderers. The brutal assault and murder of Peter Stohler would go unpunished.

As he walked toward the cafeteria in a semi-stupor, Craig could hardly hear the cacophony of loud voices and clattering lockers that surrounded him. Vinny knew something was really bothering Craig, and he kept his distance, choosing to leave him alone until he was ready to socialize again.

Since school had resumed after vacation, Travis Graham had not attended one day. Craig was relieved each day he saw Graham's name on the absentee list. Craig was quite sure that even if he did come to school, he would avoid a confrontation with him during the trial period.

"Craig, can I see you in my office for a second?" Mr. Bacardi's hand grabbed his shoulder from behind and his heart almost stopped.

As he turned to acknowledge the assistant principal's request, his legs gave out momentarily and Mr. Bacardi reached quickly to catch his fall. When he saw Craig's ashen face, he grabbed his arm and nearly carried him to the nurse's office. The other kids looked strangely at Craig as he was being half-dragged toward the office.

"Are you okay, Craig?" Mr. Bacardi finally asked as they neared the nurse's office.

Craig was speechless and could only nod as they entered the nurse's office. He gently sat Craig down on a chair and approached the school nurse. Craig couldn't make out the dialogue between the two school officials. The nurse finally approached Craig and told him to roll up his left sleeve. She also inserted a thermometer under his tongue.

As she took his blood pressure, she began questioning him. "Craig, did you take anything today?" Craig looked up with a puzzled look on his face and she repeated the question, this time more emphatically. "Did you take anything today: pills, alcohol, anything? I need to know."

Her stern voice shook him out of his stupor and he shook his head vigorously.

"No. No. I haven't taken a thing, I swear!"

She read his blood pressure, pulled the thermometer out of his mouth, shook it, and read it. Mr. Bacardi was standing with his arms folded authoritatively, awaiting the verdict from the nurse. She approached him and whispered again. This time, he listened more attentively and heard the words, "He might be on something; his pressure was a little high." He couldn't hear anything else but was sure of one thing: he was suspected of some form of drug abuse.

After nodding to the nurse, Mr. Bacardi approached Craig and summoned him to his office. Craig followed obediently behind, conjuring up his defense. The door closed behind them and Mr. Bacardi offered Craig a seat.

Mr. Bacardi's austere office reminded him a little of Father McClanahan's office at the church rectory. He looked around and noticed some family pictures on the assistant principal's desk. Mr. Bacardi was searching for Craig's file, and when he finally found it, he cleared his throat and began. "I asked to see you about your attendance record, Craig, but it seems you're not feeling too well and I wonder if you would like to tell me anything."

Craig looked puzzled and replied, "What do you mean, Mr. Bacardi?"

"Craig, I don't have time for game playing. You're in enough trouble with your truancies and horrible attendance record. Do you realize you almost fainted in the corridor when I approached you?"

Craig had his answer ready. "I didn't have breakfast this morning, Mr. Bacardi, and I haven't eaten a thing since last evening. I'm feeling weak and was on my way to lunch." Mr. Bacardi scrutinized Craig's face for any signs of deceit. Craig looked directly into his eyes without flinching. He continued, "I don't take drugs and I haven't had a drop of liquor since that last incident. Believe me, Mr. Bacardi, it's the honest truth. I'm just a little weak from not eating."

Craig sounded so convincing and believable that Mr. Bacardi abruptly stopped his questioning and began slowly thumbing through his discipline file. "Craig, your attendance has been a disgrace. Did you parents receive the letter we sent home during the vacation period? We haven't heard from them yet."

Craig cringed but wisely decided to tell the truth. "I intercepted it, Mr. Bacardi, and they never saw it." His forthright and honest answer caught Mr. Bacardi off-guard, and he looked a little surprised for a moment. He straightened his tie and continued.

"You realize that by doing that you have just compounded the problem and made it tougher on you, Craig?"

"Yes, I realize it, Mr. Bacardi," Craig replied submissively. He hung his head and waited for further reprimands.

"Listen, before we get into this matter, go get yourself some lunch before you pass out. You look terrible. Now get going." Mr. Bacardi took him completely by surprise. He looked up at the assistant principal and saw a faint smile on his face. Craig looked gratefully at him and quietly exited the office. Mr. Bacardi had suddenly taken a liking to him because of his candid manner. As Craig was leaving the office, Mr. Bacardi called to him. Craig stopped and turned around. He beckoned for Craig to come closer and in a strange whisper said, "You'd better tell them before I have to, okay? Understand?" Craig got the message and nodded appreciatively. "Now get going."

Craig's whole opinion of Mr. Bacardi had changed as he walked briskly toward the cafeteria. *If you're honest with the guy, he gives you a break. Honesty is the best policy*, he thought.

He abruptly stopped in his tracks and was almost knocked over by some kids racing for the cafeteria. The rest of the day went well for Craig in spite of the constant chatter and gossip about the trial and murder. He began to feel better and gobbled down his tuna fish sandwich. The color returned to his face, and he even talked to a few of the kids he knew. Vinny passed by, and Craig greeted him. "Well, I'll be damned—you're talking again," Vinny chided. "What the hell was wrong with you?" Craig shrugged it off jokingly and asked Vinny how many bananas he had for lunch today. He mimicked an ape scratching his underarms. Vinny shot a friendly punch to his arm and excused himself to get on the milk line.

The bus ride home was as hectic as ever as the anxiety level of the students was raised to almost a fever pitch. Centerville hadn't experienced this much excitement since the explosion in the cosmetic factory some four years ago. Murder was something you heard about on TV, and that took place in the city, but in your own hometown? Centerville was now on the six o'clock news, and it was sort of eerie to its residents to hear about Centerville and see familiar film clips of the town and local community. Film crews from the major networks and famous newscasters were seen throughout the town and county seat. Each day of the trial provided interesting and exciting news to the entire area, and the coverage was complete and comprehensive. "Some kid told me they were filming the back of Calderwood Elementary School today," Roland said to Vinny.

Craig heard the comment and leaned over to get more information. "Where'd you hear this?" Craig inquired.

"Joey Finn's mother brought his lunch to school today, and she told him about it." Roland was a good news gatherer, and his information was usually accurate. Craig sat back and remained quiet for the rest of the trip home. With all the excitement surrounding him, he still felt a certain sereneness that he hadn't felt in a long time. It was as though a large, heavy stone had been removed from his shoulders, and he felt a strange lightness enveloping his body.

The bus came to a grinding halt, and Craig stood up and rushed to the front. A few other kids had beat him to the front, and he turned momentarily to bid his farewell to Vinny and Roland. With a nod, Vinny offered a feeble wave as Craig bounded off the bus and began the slow jog to his house. Mrs. J was standing at the front door as Craig breathlessly arrived, "Hi, Mom!"

The elation in Craig's voice shocked her for an instant. She wasn't used to such an enthusiastic greeting. "You must have had a good day in school today, Craig," Mrs. J said suspiciously. "Or are you trying to soften me for some bad news?" She smiled wryly at her son and turned away. "Are you hungry?"

"Naw, thanks, Mom. I ate a good lunch," Craig replied appreciatively. "I gotta lotta homework and I think I'll get started on it."

Craig headed for his room and quietly closed the door. He thumbed through his CD collection, selected one of his favorite, and turned up the volume. Mrs. J couldn't understand how anyone could do homework with loud music blasting. She shook her head in disbelief as she tended to preparations for dinner.

Craig had no intention of doing homework. Instead, he carefully removed a sheet of loose-leaf paper from his notebook, sat down at his desk, and began writing.

Dear Mom and Dad ...

CHAPTER TWENTY-ONE
The Stone Removed

Craig was up before the alarm sounded and pushed the alarm button to the off position. There was a certain tranquil feeling that enveloped his young body as he lay quietly on his bed. Before going to bed the night before, Craig had phoned Jerry, who had agreed to pick up him at 8:00 a.m., about the same time his bus arrived for school. The urgency in Craig's voice unnerved Jerry, and he reluctantly agreed to take the day off and pick him up at his home. He had no idea why Craig was so emphatic about being picked up, but something told him that the youngster needed him desperately, and he responded. Mr. Gabor was a little annoyed when Jerry called him and asked for the day off. It meant the owner would have to tend to the horses himself. Jerry rarely took days off, and Mr. Gabor finally agreed after mumbling some incoherent words about the quality of today's hired help. Jerry apologized and assured him he would report to work the following day.

"Eggs are on, Craig." Mrs. J's voice startled Craig and he jumped out of bed and headed for the bathroom.

"Be right there, Mom."

The morning newspaper had been left carelessly on the bathroom counter by Mr. J, who had already left for work. Craig splashed some cold water on his face and glanced at the open newspaper.

Girl Says Stohler Suspects Were With Her

MONROE – Henry Barr's former girlfriend, her voice cracking, testified yesterday that Barr and his friends were with her on the night of the Stohler murder. Valerie LoBianco, 15, of Sagamore, said she was picked up early in the evening by Barr and the two friends and brought to Barr's garage where they finished off some beer they had been drinking.

"They picked me up about 8:30 p.m. and said they were half-gone and how would I like to help them finish off some beer they had left. We drove to Henry's (Barr) house and we went into his garage where we drank some beer." John Cassette, Barr's attorney, asked her how long they remained in the garage. "We stayed until about midnight, when I told Henry I had to get home. He drove me home and the other boys stayed in his garage." Under cross-examination from prosecutor Charles Bola, Valerie nodded feebly when responding to his questions, "Do you know what perjury is?" When Judge Fleming asked for a verbal response to the question, Miss LoBianco, in a barely audible reply, answered, "Yes."

The Norfolk County Coroner put Stohler's death at approximately 10:00 p.m. Her testimony established that the three boys were with her in Barr's garage between 8:00 p.m. and midnight.

During cross-examination by Bola, Valerie said she and Henry began to date when she was 13. She said that after reports began to circulate through the neighborhood that Barr, Calandria and Howser had been questioned about the Stohler murder, her parents insisted she stop seeing Henry.

"Craig—Craig Andrew, your eggs are getting cold." Mrs. J's urgent declaration caused him to drop the newspaper.

He quickly ran his brush through his hair and headed for the kitchen. "Morning, Mom."

"Did you fall asleep in the bathroom?" Mrs. J asked jokingly. Craig kissed her on the cheek and sat down to his lukewarm eggs. Mrs. J had also made his favorite, Canadian bacon. Although he wasn't hungry, Craig didn't want to offend her and began slowly consuming his breakfast. He reflected on the article he had just read, and his face contorted slightly. Mrs. J picked it up immediately.

"What's the matter this morning, son? You have a worried look on your face."

"Oh nothing Mom, nothing. Just thinking about the books I need for school today."

"You can't fool you mother, son. Thinking about books doesn't cause the apprehensive look you have on your handsome face. Stop worrying and enjoy your youth. You'll have plenty of time for worrying when you're an adult." Mrs. J began to go into her lecture on youth and adulthood as Craig hurriedly finished his breakfast.

He gulped down his milk and excused himself. "Gotta get going, Mom." He grabbed his notebook, pecked his mother on the cheek, and scurried toward the front door. Once outside, he looked back to see if she was watching from the door and began running full speed to the next block.

Jerry was waiting for him, and Craig jumped into the truck. "Hi, Jer," he exclaimed.

Jerry looked perplexed. "Where to Junky?"

"Monroe," Craig said emphatically.

"Monroe!" Jerry repeated, astonished.

"Please, Jerry, no questions. Just take me to Monroe."

The pleading tone in Craig's voice ended any further arguments from Jerry, and he drove out onto Route 52A heading for Monroe. There was complete silence during the first few miles.

Meanwhile, Mrs. J had found the neatly printed letter on Craig's desk as she was making his bed. She picked it up and began reading. As she read, a sudden weakness forced her to sit heavily on his bed.

Dear Mom and Dad,

I'm on my way to Monroe County Courthouse with my friend, Jerry. I have to do what I'm doing so please don't be upset. I witnessed the murder of Peter Stohler and never told you about it. I am going to inquire about testifying as a witness. I'll call you from the courthouse. Everything is going to be all right.

Your loving son

Mrs. J slowly crumpled the letter in her hand and lay back on the bed. She dropped the letter on the floor and clutched her hands in prayer.

When they arrived in Monroe, Craig finally spoke, "Do you know where the county court house is, Jerry?"

Jerry looked knowingly at his little friend and replied, "We'll find it." Jerry stopped and asked a passing pedestrian for directions. Craig was lost in thought as Jerry made a series of turns, and finally pulled up to a white Gothic building, parked and turned off the ignition.

Turning to Craig, Jerry asked calmly, "Want me to go with you, kid?" Craig nodded affirmatively and appreciatively, and they walked arm in arm toward the entrance of the impressive building. Still holding each other, they approached a clerk in the large rotunda. Craig turned toward Jerry and hugged him tightly. Jerry patted his back with gentle strokes.

Craig turned toward the clerk and, in a surprisingly courageous tone, announced, "My name is Craig Andrew Juncosa. I witnessed the murder of Peter Stohler. I would like to speak to Prosecutor Charles Bola as soon as possible."

Jerry's face was beaming as the clerk nervously picked up the phone and dialed Bola's office. Jerry clutched Craig's neck and pulled him toward him. Craig looked up at his big friend and smiled. "You're strangling me, you big lug."

EPILOGUE

The headline of the Norfolk News on January 20 read: *Guilty Verdict in Stohler Slaying, Surprise Eye-Witness Testimony Leads to Conviction of Three, Fourth Suspect Indicted.*

Craig boarded his school bus for the first time since the trial had ended. Only his blue eyes revealed the apprehension he felt as he stepped past the driver and headed for the back of the bus. There was a bewildering silence as he took the first step, and then a thunderous roar shook the bus. Craig froze in his tracks, totally perplexed.

Then a slow chant began to emerge in cadence from the crowded bus, increasing in speed and intensity. "Rah, rah, Juncosa! Rah, rah, Juncosa! Rah, rah, Juncosa!" As the bus pulled away, the cheers continued.

Craig was blown away from their response. All his weeks of painful indecision and obsessing and now he is greeted with thunderous cheers of approval from his peers. *There is still something very good about this world*, thought Craig.

Laura Donohue was sitting next to a window. The seat next to her was strangely empty. She stood up, reached out, and grabbed Craig's hand. He was in a state of shock as she pulled him toward the seat. He lurched forward and fell into it. Still clutching his hand, she pulled him toward her.

Craig turned and looked into her smiling eyes. In a seductive and sultry tone Laura whispered in his ear, "I haven't seen a movie in a long time and there's one I'd just love to see playing at the Centerville Cinemas."

A single, unsuppressed tear formed on his eyelid, and he hastily wiped it away before it slipped down his cheek. Leaning over, he quietly responded in his huskiest voice, "Pick you up at six."

Made in United States
Orlando, FL
30 November 2023

39813398R00165